ALLINGHAM: CANYON DIABLO

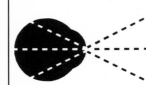

This Large Print Book carries the
Seal of Approval of N.A.V.H.

ALLINGHAM: CANYON DIABLO

JOHN C. HORST

THORNDIKE PRESS

A part of Gale, Cengage Learning

GALE
CENGAGE Learning·

Farmington Hills, Mich • San Francisco • New York • Waterville, Maine
Meriden, Conn • Mason, Ohio • Chicago

GALE
CENGAGE Learning·

LIBRARY OF CONGRESS CATALOGING-IN-PUBLICATION DATA

Horst, John C.
    Allingham : Canyon Diablo / by John C. Horst.
        pages cm. — (Thorndike Press Large Print Western)
    ISBN 978-1-4104-7491-9 (hardcover) — ISBN 1-4104-7491-7 (hardcover)
    1. Frontier and pioneer life—Arizona—Fiction. 2. Arizona—History—To 1912—Fiction. 3. Western stories. 4. Large type books. I. Title.
PS3608.O7724A45 2014
813'.6—dc23   2014036346

Published in 2014 by arrangement with John C. Horst

Printed in Mexico
1 2 3 4 5 6 7 18 17 16 15 14

For Patrick Smithwick

There will be a time when you believe everything is finished.
That will be the beginning.
— Louis L'Amour

CONTENTS

CHAPTER I:
HELL'S KITCHEN 1882

The Sicilian ran through the tenements that he did not know. Three big Irishmen were after him; almost on him. He'd soon run out of places to go and then they'd have him. He was nimble, though, and soon had them at bay like a treed cat against many big and vicious hounds, the flash of the knife, expertly wielded, in his hand. He was impressed as the big coppers laughed. They would break every bone in his face and he knew it.

Women screamed and babies screamed and the broken-down dirty floor of the building creaked under the weight of half a ton of Irishmen and the diminutive Italian assassin. Soon blood mixed with sweat and dirt on the raw floorboards. The only sounds grunts of rage and pain and the rips of slicing, plunging and tearing of skin, fat, muscle sinew by the razor sharp blade. All three Irishmen now draining blood, the Italian jumping about like a wild little monkey. He'd learned his craft well and the Irishmen were on the receiving end of a lesson on how things were done in the bad places of Palermo.

Then a shot as Sergeant Allingham's revolver barked flame. Another day in the Five Points district of Manhattan had come to a close.

Stosh Gorski read a newspaper at the foot of his sergeant's bed. His Irishmen, his comrades in arms, lined up, shoulder to shoulder, threatening to spill out of the narrow beds. They smoked as they listened to their sergeant breathe with one lung. He finally woke and looked down at the Pole and then along the brightly painted white wall at the men in the stark hospital beds beside him. He sat up and felt the pain.

"You're in a state."

Allingham made no reply. He never replied in regard to such things.

"Goddamned dagos, always with the knives. Why always with the knives? At least you Irishmen use yer fists. Hardly ever use knives."

Allingham answered with difficulty. "I'm not an Irishman."

"Yeah, yeah."

Gorski went back to the newspaper. "This goddamned place is getting to be like the Wild West. Listen to this here." Gorski loved the West. The Pole had been in America only ten years and he was always pining to move on, maybe west. He didn't want to be in New York, but he knew — everyone knew — he'd never make it further than Newark.

The Irishmen paid attention to him. Stosh always found good things to read in the papers. He had everyone's attention and, shaking the paper smooth, began to read. "Listen to this one; 'Canyon Diablo, Arizona. This town devours lawmen. Located just south of Flagstaff, the town of Canyon Diablo has existed for fewer than six months. The settlement of around one thousand has been through eight lawmen, all retired by gunplay.' "

He stopped and looked at his sergeant, grinning at the memory of the Italian shot through the head. He continued reading: "The shortest career for one lawman was six hours. He was sworn in at four in the afternoon and was dead by ten that night. The longest one, a consumptive former preacher and confederate soldier, lasted ten days."

The Irishmen grinned and passed a bottle. They needed no morphine for their pain.

They looked at Allingham sheepishly, glad for the sergeant's quick thinking the night before.

Allingham closed his eyes and remembered the battle. Sometimes his men were as dumb as they were big. They liked to fight and didn't take blades or small Italians seriously; this time it nearly cost them, could have very well been a fatal mistake for them all had he not intervened.

It was the third man he'd killed since the war. That didn't bother him so much, the Sicilian needed killing, there was no doubt, and Allingham never killed men unnecessarily. That was a matter of principle.

Killing was often just going too far. Many of his copper colleagues had killed their share of men and the men who they killed almost always needed it. But the cops — the killers — they were often killing for the wrong reasons; usually rage. But Allingham had no rage. He could typically take a man under arrest with little more than a command, sometimes a slap with a sap or a punch to the jaw; he rarely had to resort to outright killing. But the Italian needed killing.

One of the Irishmen wiped his mouth as he spoke, "Ay, Stoshy, me boy, why don' you go on out to this Arizona land and straighten them out. Bet they'd pay good attention to ye." He grinned and passed the bottle back. "You'd be famous throughout the western land."

Stosh smiled. He didn't mind that they teased him. He knew as well as they that he'd never be anything but a copper in Hell's Kitchen. It was where he belonged and he liked it there. He liked the Irishmen, his coppers, and he liked the Irish, the ones who lived in the dumps no one had the right to call homes. He almost never had to fight them himself. Stosh was good with them, and they with him, as he was a tough man, but kind and fair. They knew he could give any of the rough ones a good fight but he rarely had to. He used his brains and his words more than his fists and it generally worked out best that way for everyone.

Allingham was finally alone, as he wasn't yet well enough to leave and that was strange as his big dopey Irishmen were stabbed half a dozen times each. But then, they had a lot more girth and the blade was small. He read through the newspaper Stosh left behind. He reread the Canyon Diablo story, but it didn't interest him. He had no use for the Wild West or for the frontier or for anything, really, but his job. He was a good cop and it was the only thing he knew. It was the only thing he cared about and his men were the only men he knew. He had no family; no wife or children and all his kin were dead. He had no friends or associates to speak of. Only his Irish coppers and Stosh, of course, but he was a Pole; yet he considered none of them his friends.

"Mr. Allingham?" The physician peeked around the screen as if he was worried over what he might discover.

"Sergeant Allingham."

"Ah, yes. Sergeant, of course." The physician read his chart and then regarded Allingham's wound.

"When can I go?"

"Oh, tomorrow." The man fidgeted uneasily and Allingham looked him over dismissively, as that was his way. He waited for the doctor to leave and when he loitered, the police sergeant went back to his paper, raising it as a screen between them.

"Sergeant?"

Allingham dropped the paper, staring him down. The man evidently had a point and could not get to it; yet another thing that Allingham found annoying in his fellow man. "What is it?"

"I fear that you have some other issues, eh, another . . . another condition."

"An infection?"

"No, no. None of that. Your wound is clean." He fidgeted again and could not understand why. He'd seen many sick people in his time and told them the bad news without hesitation. But the sergeant intimidated him as the sergeant was not a normal man. He was severe and not appealing in any way. He was ugly and big, ruddy, with protruding ears and narrow eyes, thick lips which hung under a protruding bulbous nose. He did not chat or try to put men at ease. He didn't waste time and energy on such things. He looked and acted unnatural, and the doctor felt as if he was now regarding some otherworldly creature: a centaur, a missing link, a beast, something other than a human being. He acted, in many ways, to the doctor's mind, like many surgeons he had known in his time.

"I've consulted with my colleagues." He continued, and remembered a question. "Sergeant, have you been feeling poorly?"

"No. Well, perhaps a little tired. A little short of breath."

Allingham looked up from his newspaper, then placing it in his lap, he glared at the irritating physician. "Is there something you have to say?"

The doctor ignored the demand, knew he

needed to get to the point and now felt a bit silly in his hesitation. He continued.

"Yes, yes, eh, well, that would make sense. Ever coughed blood?" He was hesitant to ask this question, as coughing blood was always an ominous thing.

"Consumption?" Allingham was guarded, not that the disease particularly frightened him, but rather because he'd have to stop working.

"No. No, sergeant. You have a mass . . . in the lung. We are certain. No — convinced — that it is not TB. It is a cancer."

"I see." Allingham went back to the paper then thought of a question. "What does this mean?"

"There is no treatment, no cure."

"And how long will it be then, before I die?"

The doctor shrugged. "Difficult to say."

Allingham glared at him.

"No, it's not. Give me an answer. How long before I die? How long does a person with cancer of the lung live once the mass can be detected? It is a straightforward enough question."

"Six months."

The doctor wondered if perhaps Allingham really was a surgeon. He felt compelled to check the chart to see that there was not, perhaps, some mix up. There wasn't, of course, Allingham was a copper.

"You are fit, but you have no more than months." The doctor lit a cigarette and offered the sergeant one. They smoked and Allingham suddenly regretted that he'd taken him up on the offer. He did not want the doctor there and now he'd be there until the cigarettes were smoked.

"Sergeant?"

Allingham continued to read his paper as the doctor spoke into the front page. "May I suggest a spa?"

Allingham dropped the pages, looking through the smoke at the doctor with an expression that suggested it was as stupid an idea as it sounded.

"That's for the rich. I'm a police sergeant and not crooked."

"You've got time in. I heard your men say you've been at this a long time. You will certainly have a pension. A few months in a spa . . . , they've got them out west, out in the Arizona territory."

Allingham stared at the paper. There it was, Arizona again. "It isn't so expensive as all that."

"And this will help how?"

"I'm not going to sugar-coat this for you."

He could not understand why he was being so charitable. Something about the brusque sergeant made him want to help Allingham.

"Dying from cancer of the lung is no walk through the park, sergeant. It is going to be unpleasant, to say the least, and this New York weather, this winter would be no time to die in New York. There has been good success for patients with TB in the dry land out there. Winters are milder there, downright pleasant, I've heard. It might make things easier for you, with your lung, with the cancer."

The physician sat for a moment and felt, at the least, duty-bound to talk. Allingham made it difficult, impossible, really. He always had. The doctor stood up, extending his hand. Allingham did not shake it. He continued reading the paper. He glanced up when the doctor was nearly out of the room, remembering a question. "No one else knows this?"

"Just my colleagues."

"None of the men who were here? None of my men, not the Pole?"

"No."

He waited. Allingham was finished with him. He walked out.

Allingham wandered as he considered his

predicament. He'd never thought he'd die in such a way. He never actually thought about dying. Even battling criminals it had not crossed his mind. Even back in the war he had never given it any thought. He'd been in three battles and had been wounded. He'd seen men destroyed all around him but it had never entered his mind that it would happen to him. Now, at the age of forty, after surviving all that, the war, days as a copper on the meanest streets of New York, a mass in his lung would be his undoing — and it would not go well. It would not be quick; he would languish, likely for weeks, in some miserable bed.

He thought and walked and finally arrived at his apartment house. He climbed the three flights of stairs. His wound hurt and he was shorter of breath than normal; that was intriguing. Now that he knew what it was, it was actually noticeable. When he hadn't known, it was not at all bad. He just thought he was getting old, thought that he was over forty and that was it. But now he knew; he had a cancer in the lung and it was killing him.

No one acknowledged him as he climbed the stairs. He'd lived there fifteen years, spoken to no one for more than twelve. The landlord stopped trying after the third. Allingham was a good tenant, he never missed a payment, never asked for anything, never complained. No other tenants spoke to him as he would not address or even acknowledge them. This was not due to shyness. It was simply not worth the energy expended and Allingham did nothing that was without purpose, ever.

He did nod to one tenant, a woman whom no one could ever accuse of being physically appealing in any way. But she held a certain attraction to Allingham. She was a Russian Jew and this was unusual as there were no other Jews in Allingham's neighborhood. She had no clan or family and was all alone with a child, as her husband had died within a year of moving to New York.

One day, a long time ago, Allingham bumped into her on the steps. She nodded, as did he and immediately noticed an odd thing; the woman was holding a bundle, a dead child that she'd birthed on her own, as she had no money for a midwife. She looked wild and disoriented as Allingham held out his arms.

He was used to such things. Sometimes it seemed that all he did on duty was collect little bundles, stillborns and abortions or ones who'd live an hour or two, just enough time to break the parents' hearts. He'd take

them to the morgue. He'd find them everywhere, especially around the brothels. He'd
retrieve them from trash piles or from under
a stair stoop or in an ally. He believed that
human beings, all human beings, regardless
of whether they were fully developed or not,
deserved a better final resting place. Even a
mass grave in Potter's field was better than
on a garbage heap. He knew what to do with
the child and the Russian handed it over
willingly.

It was the only act of kindness he'd ever
shown anyone in the tenement and it was
the only act of kindness the woman had ever
received, at least that she'd known, as Allingham also paid half her rent. He did
nothing for personal accolades or to bring
attention to himself, but something about
the woman holding the little corpse struck a
nerve, something about her made him
compassionate in his own quiet way and he
took care of her and her living child. No
one, except the landlord, would ever know.
Allingham even avoided contact with him,
choosing instead to go through an interme-
diary, and put everything down in writing.
He'd never speak directly to the man. He
did not want the man to look pleased or
proud or even suspicious of his actions. His
reasons for his actions were his own and he

had not tolerance or time to waste on letting the landlord give his opinion one way or the other.

Of an evening he'd listen to the woman and her child, working away making garters or assembling suspenders or brushes; the woman worked late into the evening after working all day. He'd hear them speaking and even, sometimes, laughing and he was surprised at this, as the woman should not have had much to laugh about. It was true that she lived in a tenement far beyond her means and station in life, and it was a palace compared to where the other poor Russian Jews lived, but other than that, Allingham could see no reason for her to laugh or be happy.

He thought about what would happen toward the end, when he was in the final stages of his disease, lying in bed in his empty apartment, listening to the woman and her child living and laughing when they had no reason to and this made his wound hurt; it made him want to formulate a plan. He surveyed his apartment; it was clean but dreary and he spent as little time in it as possible. He had not decorated it and the furnishings were at least fifty years old, the wallpaper selected by a woman who was ancient when she chose it. It was not cheerful. It was the opposite of cheerful and the thought of staring at the pattern as the cancer ate his body was repugnant to him. He had to make a plan. He simply could not waste away in this place.

It was early and he washed and dressed listening to the woman and her child speak through the walls of the apartment in their native tongue. He liked that as he did not want to eavesdrop. It was better, more entertaining or comforting, really, to not know what they were saying, like when listening to a pretty female voice in the theatre singing in a foreign tongue. He didn't care that the words made no sense to him; it was nice to hear and was more entertaining that way. He liked the sound of happy voices; it was a comfort to him.

Before going out he wrote a letter to an attorney he knew, a man he could trust. He composed a Will of sorts and named the woman as beneficiary. He did not want his death to result in the widow's eviction, and this was sure to happen once he could no longer pay half the rent.

He never wore his uniform except on duty. He had one interest outside of his career as a policeman, and that was to dress well. He did: always and impeccably. His clothes were always clean and of the best quality. One could say that he was even a little foppish in this respect, until one got to Allingham's face. No one could accuse him of having a foppish face. He shaved regularly and kept his hair cut and his teeth clean, but there was nothing he could do to change or improve his appearance, as he was an exceedingly ugly man.

He dined alone, at a different place each night, as he did not like to be familiar with restaurant staff. If they saw him only once every ten days there could be distance and that is what he preferred, constant distance between everyone and himself. He did not like to chat. It did not interest him. He did not care to receive or share information. In this he was an utterly solitary man.

He was also, not unlike a surgeon, very logical, clinical and calculating. He accepted the news of his impending death in this way. He knew the facts; much as he would take in the facts of a crime scene: he'd collect the evidence, interview all parties involved, then formulate a plan. The only difference now was that the death he was investigating this time was his own. He'd make sense of it. He knew he could not defeat it, but at least he'd make sense of it.

He knew that dying was inevitable and

now, knowing more or less, the precise time of his death was significant. He also knew approximately how it would go if he did nothing. He would die in the middle of a New York winter in his dreary apartment and this would be very miserable indeed.

He thought about Arizona. He really had nothing to lose. Travel and discovering new lands held no interest for him. Meeting new people meant nothing to him. He would not go for these reasons. He'd go there and die in a hospital bed in Arizona, and when he considered it that way, it seemed no better than dying in his apartment in New York, except that it would not be cold. It would likely be stiflingly hot and he hated the heat, actually preferring winter over summer in New York. It seemed a stupid idea and he wondered how the doctor had ever achieved his medical degree; the man seemed a complete imbecile for suggesting such a thing.

And then, a thought occurred to him. What if he did not die in bed, cancer consuming his body? He could, instead, die a violent death. There were half a dozen rogues he could fight to the death, not ten blocks from where he was dining at that moment. He could pick a fight with any of them and die in such a way. It would be tricky, though. How to provoke a fight and make it look good and then actually let the bad man win. He had never let a bad man win in all his time on the police force. He always got his man, albeit, not before losing a little of his own blood; but he always won, he always got his man.

He rejected this idea immediately. The very thinking of it made him weak and he coughed hard and saw the slightest hint of scarlet against the pure white linen of his neatly pressed handkerchief. He did not want to destroy a lifetime of impeccable police service. He did not want to murder bad men. It would not do and he would not do it.

He regarded his handkerchief. He was weakening already. He'd weaken and then he'd have no choice. Something would have to be done.

He considered suicide. He could shoot himself through the head. More than a few of his police colleagues had taken that route over the years. Or he could take gas. He remembered the stories from when he was young and gas had become so prevalent. Suicides by gas skyrocketed. He could gas himself, but if he did that, would he endanger the people in his apartment house? That would not do. He might kill the Jewish woman and her child, or worse, blow the entire block to smithereens. He could jump into the river. He was too good a swimmer, though. If he jumped from enough height, perhaps he'd lose consciousness and drown or break his neck on impact.

He gave himself a headache over these thoughts, as though, he was not a spiritual man, suicide was repugnant to him. He was always annoyed by suicides. They'd given up; he would not be a suicide.

He thought about Arizona again. Canyon Diablo. He could get himself shot and killed there. Perhaps he could hold out longer, last longer, in a desert place, at least according to the sawbones at the hospital.

He could be one of the lawmen gunned down and nothing would be known of it back in New York. He'd take his pension and move on. They'd be surprised at headquarters as he'd not missed a day of work in all the years he'd been there, except for the times he'd been recovering from wounds; but that didn't count, as he was still on duty, even in the hospital. He never had a sick day, never took a leave of absence or a holiday of any kind. He never gave anyone any indication that he was working toward some sort of retirement, as he never was. In all his time working, he'd never given not working any thought whatsoever, as it was the only thing that interested him. Now he'd retire and they'd all look at him as if he'd lost his mind.

They'd wonder why he would do such a thing. But then, they would not have to know. The only one who'd inquire would be the Pole. He wondered at that. The men respected him but he knew they didn't much like him. No one did and that was all right by him. It wasn't his job to be liked or be friends or be the conscience or moral guide to his men. It was his job to lead them. Happiness did not enter into it. Their happiness and his happiness were immaterial to the success of the endeavor. But the Pole; the Pole liked him and the Pole would want to know. But he'd never know. Allingham would make certain of that. The Pole would never know.

Allingham found himself at the racing stables learning to ride. He'd ridden a little over the years, but never seriously and thought that in Arizona knowing how to ride a horse would be handy.

He had a vague notion of the West, knew most of it was a lot of nonsense conjured up by the dime novels, to his mind. Most of the West was no different than the East, he knew that; same people, same deadly sins, same nonsense, only in a different longitude. But he knew transportation was primitive and riding would be a useful skill.

He rode and, as with everything Allingham pursued, he became competent in short order. He did not think much about dying when he rode; this was typical of him. Constant work was always his way. It kept him from being bored and lonely and it kept him from dwelling on negative things. A man without hobbies or pastimes or friends or an ability or interest in interacting with others had a lot of time on his hands. He was not prone to sullenness and constantly guarded against it by occupying his mind with tasks and work. It was what kept him going day after day.

In this respect, he was not unlike some of the criminals he helped to put away. Some of the worst ones were kept in solitary confinement. This was tough on a human being, as human beings are not meant to be alone, and Allingham was alone. In a city with many thousands of people, crammed together shoulder to shoulder, Allingham was very much alone. But, just as the resilient prisoners in stir learned to cope, so did Allingham in his self-imposed solitary confinement, and he filled his waking hours with work, constant work. It was the only thing he'd ever known.

He thought about writing to the Safety Committee of the town of Canyon Diablo and then changed his mind. He would not inquire ahead of time. He'd go there and present his credentials in person. If they would take him, he'd go on with his plan. If they would not, he'd stay in Arizona and see what effect it had on his health. He'd decide what to do once these things happened and did not have much of a plan beyond this. It was almost an attempt on his part to leave his future to fate, which he tried to never do. He always endeavored to control his destiny, but now that his destiny was essentially laid out before him in the respect that he now knew, with relative accuracy, the time of his demise, fate seemed a bit of a comfort to him. It was nice to be, in part, out of control of the time between the present and the moment, sometime in December or January, when he would die. Let the chips fall as they may.

This was no small feat, as Allingham was not a gambling man.

He eventually put his retirement papers in and that was, as he suspected, a significant surprise to his superiors. Knowing him, however, they did not pry. Most of the sergeants were pleased as many of them secretly, a few openly, hated Allingham for his efficiency, his coldness, his solitary lifestyle.

He could do his job with maximum efficiency, no wife or children or other things to hinder him. They hated him for that. He made them look bad and they were glad he'd soon be gone. No one would shed tears over Allingham's departure. No one would be renting a hall or throwing him a retirement party.

The superiors accepted the notification and said nothing more. The Irishmen invited him to the pub for a farewell drink, he declined. This was not something they gave much thought to since they hadn't planned anything special for him. They went to the pub after their day was done and only invited Allingham out of respect. They knew he'd turn them down so there was no great risk that he'd ruin their evening.

Allingham had no faith, belonged to no church, never spoke of religion in any context, and this made him suspicious to the Irishmen. Everyone should have a faith; even if one wasn't Catholic, it was still all right with the Irishmen, as long as some faith was acknowledged and pursued. A man without faith was an aberration and Allingham was an aberration in spades.

The Pole invited him to his home and he accepted. He did not know why, but the Pole had gotten to him over the years. There was something about Gorski, something pure about the man. He was a good man and a kind man, and he took care to be this way to Allingham. It wasn't patronizing, it wasn't that Allingham was a poor soul, a charity case. Stosh Gorski just plain liked people, and he liked Allingham, could get beyond Allingham's little peccadillos. He could appreciate the man, be a friend.

Stosh Gorski's wife knew enough about Allingham to not be put off by his glowering demeanor and odd ways. The evening went well, at least as well as it could, and they sat to supper. Allingham ate silently and then, without warning, stood and began clearing the table. No one stopped him. They did not see it as an insult and knew it was Allingham's way. He did these things to avoid the banter and nonsensical conversation that was certain to follow and they allowed him this small indulgence. The sooner they could get through this, the better.

With the table cleared the Pole got drinks out as his wife wandered into the kitchen. She had dishes to clean and did not want to intrude. She wanted to give her husband some time with his odd friend and they both, husband and wife, suspected that something was seriously wrong with Allingham.

Stosh sat and smoked and watched Allingham fiddle with his watch. It was a habitual action he did when he was especially bored and the Pole knew that he'd not be there much longer. "So, retirement it is."

"Yes."

"Any particular plans?"

"No."

"I've always thought I'd go back to the homeland. See the old people one more time. Maybe you could go back to Ireland."

"I'm not Irish."

The Pole nodded, as if he was just remembering that Allingham was not an Irishman.

"Where is your homeland, Allingham?"

"New York."

The Pole nodded and grinned slightly. In a land full of immigrants who knew their history and were not capable and, subsequently, ashamed to hide it, Allingham stood out, as one genuinely ignorant of his heritage. It was more likely that he did not care. "Allingham." He stubbed his cigarette out. "If there's anything I can do. Anything at all . . ."

Allingham stood up. "It's time I was getting on." He looked at the Pole, nodded his usual terse nod, and was gone.

CHAPTER II:
GOING WEST

Every bump between the rails, every click-clack pounded through Allingham's brain: click-clack, can-cer, click-clack, can-cer. He thought a lot about dying. He felt fine, and as he moved further west his breathing was improving significantly. He did not cough except in the early mornings and after a cigarette, but there was now no blood. He wondered how a dying man could feel so well.

He spent his time reading and avoiding conversation. This was not difficult, as he'd paid extra for first class and was mostly alone. His habit of answering with one syllable responses helped put an end to banter. He never asked anyone about their lives, why they were going west, what they'd done, what they hoped to do. He asked no one any such questions because he did not care to know any of the answers; did not care to know about them and he did not care to put anyone at ease. It was not so much that he was a cruel or uncaring man, he was the opposite, but he cared for very particular things and the lives of strangers was not counted among those things.

He made it to Flagstaff and found a good room. He was careful with his money and never splurged on anything except clothing, but now he was at the finest hotel in town. It was still rough and Spartan, primitive by New York standards, but it was a decent place and this made him feel a little out of sorts, but then again, he thought, what was the point of being thrifty now?

In two days he'd be before the Canyon Diablo Safety Committee, applying and interviewing for the job of sheriff of the settlement. He did go so far as to have his dossier sent over to the head, a Mr. Halsted, not so much to present it as an application, but to let them know his credentials ahead of time.

He hoped it would decrease the time it would take to get through the process as he found this to be tedious as well. He was more than qualified and, even if he were not, the committee would not likely have to fire him. He'd be retired, as had all the others, by gunplay, likely within a week.

Allingham hated red tape, hated all the

gyrations and machinations of bureaucracy, seemingly put in place to hire an excessive number of people to complete a simple task. And now he'd have to sit among a bunch of people and tell them what they already knew. He'd be the next lawman, the next enforcer in Canyon Diablo.

After settling into his room, he took the stagecoach to the little town. He sat across from a stunning woman dressed appropriately for the wealthy. This he thought odd, as there was nothing, according to what he'd learned about the place, which would remotely attract such a woman to the settlement of Canyon Diablo.

Next to her sat an austere and dark Indian wearing a turban the color of saffron, with long moustaches and beard. He was dressed well, armed well, and with impressive posture; back straight, shoulders back and always, always vigilantly watching his surroundings.

Allingham liked Sikhs. He'd known a few in his long years of police service. He had never arrested a Sikh, never had any Sikh cause trouble of any kind. He liked their faith, which seemed much more straightforward than his own — at least the religion that he'd known growing up — the religion that he'd immediately lost on the battlefields of the great rebellion. Allingham, unlike many men in conflict, was driven away from, rather than closer to his faith.

He was not handy with the fairer sex. He liked women well enough, had one brief love affair once and ruined it, but that was nearly twenty years ago. However, it did not stop him from looking and he snatched glances at the beauty when he could. He was careful in this. He had no interest in speaking to his traveling companions and did not want to suggest that he would.

He was, additionally, not certain of the relationship between the woman and the Sikh. The man was significantly older than the lady and of another race. They could certainly not be a couple. But then again perhaps they were. Allingham had heard that many strange people were attracted to the West. He considered the possibility that perhaps the woman and the man were together in other than a business way. It was abundantly evident to him that they were not blood relations. She eventually smiled at him as there was no one else in the coach but the three of them. She'd spent most of her life with the Sikh, so there was nothing really to compel her to chat with him. She looked out the window and enjoyed the air, as it was not particularly dusty on the road this day. The windows could be left open.

She regarded Allingham, carefully looking him over. He was dressed well, looked fine and not a little out of place with his New York clothes and small derby. He did not look like someone who would fit in the wild places of Arizona, and she worried over that a bit.

He looked tough enough, though, and Rebecca Halsted knew tough men, knew what made a man tough and what did not. This one was tough. He had a tough, ugly and battle-scarred face, but his clothes did not match that. She worried about what the lawless men would do to him at the settlement and decided to engage this strange man in conversation.

"You are new to the land, sir?"

He looked up, into her beautiful blue eyes, and was suddenly befuddled, nearly speechless. He did not want to be abrupt with this one. He could not fathom why, in a million years, she'd want to converse with him. He caught himself.

"Yes." He looked at his lap, wanting to give more than a one syllable answer, yet he was grossly out of practice. "I am."

She reached out to shake his hand and he thought this odd as well. He took it and felt the lightness, the femininity, the charm in the gentle touch.

"I'm Rebecca Halsted." She looked to her companion. "This is Mr. Singh."

Allingham nodded, returning his gaze to his lap. He felt better about her, at least she had the protection she would need in the terrible place. He could not help but wonder why she and the Sikh were heading there. The woman apparently wondered the same about Allingham.

"What brings you to Canyon Diablo, Mister . . . ?"

"Allingham." He began to correct himself, "Serg . . ." then remembered. He was no longer a sergeant . . . "Allingham."

He looked away and then remembered that her question was not a rhetorical one. "I'm the new policeman there."

"Oh?" She smiled coyly, as she knew him now. So, this was the famous Allingham. Her father had shared his dossier with her and she'd been intrigued, even planned to pick out a mount for him once she met him in the flesh, as she knew that he'd not likely be much of a horseman, living all his life in the big city back east.

Now, she put a face with the name and the remarkable career of the man she'd read about, the man who'd wanted the job of lawman in Canyon Diablo. She remembered that she was initially intrigued by him, at least the man on paper. She did not think he'd be so ugly, though. But this was not something that concerned Rebecca Halsted much. She was not swayed by the physical attributes of men. She liked men with character and guts, men like her father and Mr. Singh, and perhaps this Allingham chap.

"Well, after the old codgers from Flagstaff appoint me, that is." He appeared bored, even dismissive at the prospect. He'd not paid attention or made the connection between the name of the pretty woman and the man who'd be heading the group responsible for hiring him. He continued in his superior tone. "I'm evidently to go before some Safety Committee to decide if I am suitable to protect their business interests in the settlement." He looked out at the desert passing them by. He yawned at the open window. "A lot of humbug, if you ask me." He did not know why he said that. Maybe he was showing off a little to the lady and her companion.

The comment was not lost on Mr. Singh, as he turned his attention to Allingham, a look of disappointment on his face. Warrior saints did not tend to speak badly of their fellow man and he did not like to hear it from another.

Rebecca Halsted touched her protector's sleeve, as she'd been with Mr. Singh all her life and could intuit his thoughts. She gave Allingham a little sideways grin. "I see."

Allingham fascinated her and she looked him over again more carefully. He returned her gaze from under his hooded brow, looking anywhere but into her eyes. That intrigued her as well. He was afraid of her, she could tell, and this was not a man who, according to his record, was much afraid of anything.

They parted ways after disembarking at the Canyon Diablo livery stable. As Allingham looked the place over, some of the miscreants wasted no time and soon a few sauntered up to him, looking him up and down, taking his measure to see how easy he'd be.

New arrivals offered the prospect of wealth or booty and they were quick to descend upon such individuals, hopeful of an easy mark. Allingham was not an easy mark, however. He looked upon them as an alpha wolf would on a mangy pack. They turned away and moved on. They did not know that he was the new law; they would find out soon enough.

He made it to the northernmost point of

the town and was able to take it all in by standing in the middle of the dusty street. It would easily fit into lower Manhattan's Five Points with room to spare. How could so many murders occur in such a small and sparsely populated place? It was mind boggling.

It was a typical end-of-the-line settlement, but as Allingham was not familiar with the railroad or railroad things, he was not familiar with the set up. But it wasn't all that different from what he'd known in his life. It was the same kind of situation he'd seen in the war: dirty thieving camp followers and sutlers, cheats and confidence men who preyed on the young men in the army.

Many of the soldiers during war — at least until Roosevelt, the philanthropist from New York, made it possible for their pay to be sent home — would be penniless within the day of their payouts which sometimes amounted to as much as four months' wages, all gone to the parasites who offered little of value in return.

He hated them back in the day and he hated them now. And the brothels! The whores were a menace. They kept the men from their work during the war, kept them distracted. Many were soon diseased and unable to fight. Too many would be sent home before they could fire a shot and then they'd take the diseases back to their homes and spread them to their wives. It was terrible and ugly and Allingham remembered it well. Canyon Diablo made him remember it well, as it was typical of such settlements. The poor railroad workers, just like the soldiers during the war, were trapped. Many had not been paid for several months. They could not leave and they could not work. They were stuck in this Godforsaken desert with little to do but get drunk, gamble, waste their remaining money on whores and catch diseases. These were the lucky ones. The unlucky ones got dead.

It was a dirty place; dirty from the dust of the desert, and the horrible inhabitants. Every building looked old, disheveled, poorly built; obviously thrown together without care by those either grossly incompetent or not proud enough to do a decent job in the construction.

That was the problem with the place. It was populated by too many men who had neither pride nor enough self-respect to do anything right or decent or good. Everything was done in a half-hearted, careless, and lazy fashion and this carelessness and laziness permeated the very air they all breathed. Sloth and greed and ugliness had descended upon the settlement like a great rotting funeral shroud, a festering blanket, smothering them all, poisoning them to the core of their being, rotting their minds and souls. It was a thoroughly corrupt place.

Allingham marched down the center of the street as men milled about. He never walked or sauntered or jogged anywhere. He marched, head erect, arms swinging slightly from side to side. He looked as if he were some deranged soldier who'd lost his platoon, gone so far ahead that his men were no longer in sight, a solitary soldier in an army of one. Now and then he'd move his upper body, as if his head had been fused at the neck, look left then right, waiting to discover an assassin or to repel an attack.

The place stunk of many bad things: sewage and urine and horse manure, human excrement and decay, and the settlement was not even a year old. There was no consideration for sanitation and trash piled up here and there, adding rotting food and the moldering remains of animal carcasses to the mix. Rats scurried about, even in broad daylight, as no one molested them.

Further down the street, the brothels could be found, one on each side, then three gambling houses, another three saloons and a few lunch counters. Many were little more than tents on wooden floors. Some didn't even have wooden floors.

Shooting could be heard off in a distance, down an alleyway, then music, then the shrill cackling of a woman, like a witch or some other horrible creature from a nightmare. Allingham, in his own perverse way, was a little pleased with it all. He was convinced now that he'd made a good choice, that he could easily get himself killed here. It would only be a matter of time.

He turned a corner and nearly ran into two misfits standing on each side of a squatting man who was, defecating in the middle of the street. This was a bit much even for Allingham, who'd walked up on his share of humans behaving badly in his time. He stopped abruptly and took in the situation.

The three eyed Allingham with contempt. One grinned idiotically at the look of disgust on Allingham's face.

"Ain't never seen a man takin' a crap before?"

"Not in public."

Allingham decided to go to work early. He pointed to the previously squatting man, who was by now finished and pulling up his trousers.

"You, there." He spoke in his calmest

monotone, the one he'd honed for many years; a voice that all had learned to take seriously or suffer the consequences.

"Pick that up." He pointed at the turd between the man's feet, which elicited peals of laughter from the little gang.

They approached and Allingham prepared himself. He'd dealt with worse in his nearly twenty years in the Kitchen. These men would soon learn.

"How 'bout we serve it up for your dinner, Mister?" The largest man glared and stood too close. Allingham obliged him and with no further provocation, sapped the man soundly with his leather jack, the constant companion since his first days as a constable. The man's legs buckled and he dropped next to the pile of excrement. He did not move again. The others backed up, hands on their six shooters, cursing the new dude, but they did not pull their guns.

"Now, you, there. I'm going to say it only one more time. Pick that up."

"But it's, it's a turd!" The man looked at Allingham in disbelief.

"I know well enough what it is; I just saw it come out of your backside. Pick it up. Now!"

The men looked on, confused. Finally the defecator complied looking forlornly at the excrement in his hand, as if he'd not dealt with such material before.

"Now, throw it away."

"Where?"

Allingham looked about. No place was more or less filthy than any other. He himself was at a loss. "I don't know. Somewhere no one can step in it."

The man did and they started to walk away. Allingham stopped them. "Cover it with dirt. It's going to stink." They kicked at it, lazily, looking at the new lawman contemptuously.

Allingham pointed at the two again and then at their companion lying on the ground. "Take him with you. Don't leave him lying in the street, someone'll surely run him over."

They poked and prodded and pulled their companion away.

Allingham continued on. Perhaps he wouldn't get killed here. The men were too stupid and cowardly to kill him. He'd have a lot of work to do to get knocked off before the winter arrived.

He made it to his future office, not more than a stone hut, really, with a shed roof and two rooms, one for the jailor and one for his guests. It sat at the end of town, furthest from the brothels and saloons, just across the way from the livery stable.

Inside he found a fat, sallow man sleeping in a broken down bed. A dog lay at the man's feet, giving a lazy wag at Allingham. The man stirred, slowly sitting up, he rubbed the sleep from his eyes.

Allingham looked him over, then at the surroundings. The place was well ordered and clean. The jailor looked like hell, an odd coloration and Allingham first suspected him a drunkard, but there were no bottles about, and Allingham had never seen a drunk yet who'd not surrounded his bed with empty bottles. He sniffed the air accusingly.

"Who are you?"

"No one of consequence, sir." He rubbed his head and reached down to pat the dog. "Name's Hobbs. Who, may I ask, are you?"

Allingham ignored him and looked the place over. It was too small, only two rooms with one bed and a stove. There was only one holding cell and that took up the entirety of the other room. The two rooms were separated by a heavy wood door.

"We'll need more room than this."

The man looked sideways and grinned. "So, you are the new law?"

"For now."

Allingham looked at the dog, then back at the man. "What is your job here?"

"Oh, it varies: jailor, undertaker, clerk, cook, janitor. Whatever's required at the moment."

"We'll need more buildings." He regarded the adobe covered stone walls. It was a good building. It would not burn and it was cool. "More like this construction. Can you arrange it?"

"Oh, sure. There's some Indians and Chinamen can use the work. They'll do it and do a proper job of it; but we'll need money."

Allingham ignored him. He turned and began to walk out and then thought of something. He looked at the man and his dog again.

"What's wrong with you?" He nodded at the man's overall appearance, his complexion. He needed no further prodding.

"Liver's shot, sugar in my blood, joints are worn to a nubbin', heart's going." He grinned, "Oh, and I get the wind colic somethin' fierce whenever I eat anything cooked by a Mexican." He rubbed his chin and then thought of something else. "Not a drunkard, if that's what you want to know. Not a drunkard."

Allingham walked out.

■ ■ ■ ■

By late afternoon he was standing at the livery stable waiting for the stagecoach to Flagstaff, back in the company of the pretty lady and the Sikh. They'd apparently had a productive day, whatever that entailed, by the demeanor of the lady and the satisfied countenance of the Indian. Allingham did not inquire.

As Allingham followed the two into the coach, a bullet passed his protruding left ear, followed by the crack of a shot. The Sikh looked down the street, but Allingham knew what had happened. He'd deal with the defecating man next day. He sat down and said nothing throughout the journey back.

He was busy until late into the night, spending the evening, past midnight, drafting ordinances. These he'd take to the printer next day. He felt well, his breathing was good and he coughed no blood and this again puzzled him. How could a dying man feel so well? Maybe there was something to this business about the Arizona climate.

His thoughts turned to the pretty woman. She was a curiosity; must have been a temperance worker or some other such nonsense. He'd known his share in his time. Salvation Army ladies, temperance ladies, suffrage ladies, nuns, nurses, missionaries, he'd known them all, along with many of the wealthy who would meddle in his affairs and in the affairs and duties of his men.

He never held it against them. They wanted to help, wanted to do something about the deplorable conditions of the poor areas in the city. They respected the lawmen, knew they were at the forefront, trying to maintain order and keep the worst of humanity at bay.

He knew that it was his job as a lawman to not just investigate crime and stop the savages from being savages, but to maintain order; help the little ones, the foundlings and the women who'd been abandoned, the old, the decrepit, the downtrodden. It was a policeman's job to help them all. Anyone who did not understand that was not a constable for very long.

The pretty lady was likely one of them, the ones he'd known in New York, driven by an obligation as one of the fortunate ones to help the downtrodden. This was likely why she was in Canyon Diablo that day. Perhaps she had an orphanage or had been working with a Flagstaff physician helping the sick or the poor. He'd find out soon enough, and the thought of that pleased him.

He'd like to work with her. He'd like to please her a little. It would make the whole enterprise that much more enjoyable, but he really didn't understand why. He knew, as he peered at his ugly reflection in the mirror while he undressed and prepared for bed, that she was out of the question — by a mile.

He got into bed and suddenly felt very much alone and a bit melancholy. Why was he there? Now that he was, there were a hundred things he wanted to do to make the terrible settlement better. Why? What difference would it make? He'd be dead in six months — or sooner. If sooner, everything he'd have done would likely be for naught, undone in a week. That was the way with the law in the most corrupt places.

In New York, at least where he worked, when there was a blizzard and the constables could not patrol properly, it would revert to a Sodom and Gomorrah in a matter of hours. It would go back to its worst state, and this is what would happen to Canyon Diablo once he was dead. He knew it and wondered what the point of it all was. On top of that, if he cared too much, he'd want to see the end result of his work. This was counter to his goal of having himself murdered before winter. He'd end up too careful, too vigilant, and being so would not result in his death.

He thought about why the place consumed lawmen. Every one of them before him had used force and intimidation and tried to shoot his way out of every situation and that was why they were all dead. They were not scientific in their approach and this is what Allingham brought to the table.

He knew how to handle bad men and knew how to civilize a place. He'd helped do it in the city — at least as well as one could civilize Hell's Kitchen — and he'd do it here.

It was all very exciting, like being handed the keys to a little kingdom; a terribly diseased, wrecked kingdom and being told to make something of it. He'd have free rein, he knew that. He'd be logical and methodical and not cost the money-hungry ones too much. That is all they cared about really, anyway, to his mind. As long as he'd stop the train and coach robberies and keep the railroad goods safe, he'd be their hero — as long as he didn't cost them too dearly — and he wouldn't.

But all this planning and scheming was in

no way a recipe for getting himself killed. It was the plan of a man who intended to be around for a while and this vexed him and kept him awake until nearly sunrise.

He finally did sleep for an hour just before the sun rose. It was a deep and restful hour but not enough and he was still tired when he rose to have his breakfast and plan some more. By the time the printer opened, he had fifty ordinances written. They covered everything from spitting, (and defecating) in public to discharging firearms, fighting, public drunkenness, lewd behavior, robbery, theft, disorderly conduct . . . so many things that would not be permitted, and when the infractions occurred, he and his men would be on them, fining them, putting them to work, forcing the really bad ones to move on.

That was the key. The money from the fines and the fees he'd charge the brothels and saloons and any other place where the law was burdened or required would pay his wages and for the improvements he planned to implement. The troublesome businesses would be taxed and fined and the money would be put to good use.

He'd make it so unpleasant for the bad element that they'd move on. They'd leave and be the problem of some other village or town, or maybe they'd move out of Arizona altogether. He didn't care where they went, just as long as they went away. The ones willing to behave could stay; the ones who would not would have to move on, either out of the region, or to prison, or to the gallows, Allingham didn't much care.

He'd take control of the physical garbage as well. There'd be a sanitary system with trash pickup and laws against littering. He'd get rid of the stench and the vermin. There'd be clean water and clean streets.

He felt good now, despite a lack of sleep and by two in the afternoon was actually looking forward to sitting before the Committee of Safety in the courthouse in downtown Flagstaff.

He was a little surprised to be greeted by the pretty lady and the Sikh and further embarrassed to learn that the woman's father was the head of the committee. Allingham did that often. He was a man of few words and this was primarily because the few words he spoke usually came out dreadfully.

He insulted people without intending to. It was like a gift; a terrible and hopeless gift for rude, terse and inappropriate verbal confrontation. That was Allingham. And now he'd done it to the pretty lady and the Sikh. The Indian regarded him, disappointment in his eyes, and a gentle bearing that did not match the ruthless quality of his noble warrior clan.

The pretty lady's father shook Allingham by the hand, leading him to a chair in the middle of the room. Old men, the pretty lady and the Sikh sat in an arch, nearly surrounding him. The meeting quickly came to order and Allingham sat in the bright room, backlit by sunlight streaming through dusty windows, accentuating his pasty skin, his protruding ears glowing pink like two fleshy flags framing his ugly mug. He sat straight in his chair, his starched shirt and high celluloid collar trussing him up as if he were tied into a straightjacket. He looked beyond them all, waiting, as if on trial.

"Mister, ah, Sergeant Allingham." The pretty woman's father addressed him as he read, for the third time, the lawman's dossier. "I must say that yours is a most impressive record. We feel very fortunate to have you as a candidate."

He suppressed an urge to sneer. *Candidate.* The concept was, to Allingham, preposterous, as the term candidate implied some competition for the job. But no other fools were queuing up for this assignment. Allingham was it. The one and only *candidate.* The pretty woman interjected, capturing the sergeant's attention. She stared at him with those beautiful eyes. She could not help but punish him a little for his arrogance. "Why are you here, Sergeant?"

He stiffened and she could immediately tell, could see the lie working its way over his tongue and through his teeth. And he knew it, too. As if by telepathy, she was telling him, *don't play with me, don't tell me an idiotic story that not even a child would believe. Just don't do it.*

But he did, he went ahead and told the ridiculous lie. "I wanted to move." He looked down at his lap, then at the floor, then at her father; everywhere but into the pretty young lady's eyes.

Her father sensed it, putting up a cautionary hand, he smiled at his daughter. She was like her mother, God rest her soul. "Now, Rebecca. We are certain that the sergeant's motives are pure. They are also his own. It is not our business to pry into things that don't concern us or the performance of his duties. Sergeant Allingham has the highest recommendations from the New York City Police Department, and even a personal letter from the governor and police commissioner."

"I understand, Father." She spoke plainly enough, clearly enough, but not to her father. She looked at Allingham and gave him a just discernible smile. He was off the hook for now, but not for good. She'd be resuming her torture again, and soon, he could count on it.

"I'd like to know what motivates a man such as he to leave a career, leave his work and home when he is at the top of his game, to come out here to our humble Arizona territory, to come out here and," she looked on at Mr. Singh with an ironic smile, "how are we so blessed?"

Allingham waited stiffly for the torture to end. His blood was up and he was sweating. Sweat ran down his back and off his brow. He dared not wipe it. He did not want to show Rebecca Halsted that she was affecting him.

He had never advanced beyond sergeant in his illustrious career for just this reason, as he could not play the political games. He could not put up with this kind of interrogation. He'd just as soon tell the young woman to go to hell, but he couldn't. He looked up, back at those eyes.

He was a superior police officer, the best in his profession and he did not feel the need to explain himself or sell himself or otherwise entertain the ridiculous questions of some do-gooder, regardless of how pretty and refined.

Her father continued as he could not bear the discomfort of the man in the chair. He changed the subject. "Sergeant Allingham, we understand that you've made a visit to Canyon Diablo. What's your assessment of the place?"

"It's a cesspool."

The men of the committee laughed politely. The new lawman did not mince words. Halsted continued. "As you may know, the land is actually part of the reservation and, as such, under federal jurisdiction. We've made some inquiries; you'd receive an appointment as a US Marshal and be paid by the federal government. You'd have more authority that way, and we'll be here to support you, but you will have the freedom to do what you need to keep the peace . . ."

One elderly gent spoke up, "And stay alive."

He was not joking about this and Allingham was pleasantly surprised by the look in the old gent's eye, the look in the eyes of everyone on the committee.

He'd underestimated them. They were not

selfish rich men looking out for their business interests. They loved the land, wanted to make something of it, and this nonsense in Canyon Diablo had to come to an end. They took this seriously and this is why Allingham was before them, being interviewed and interrogated even though he might not live the week out. It was that important to them.

He walked from the courthouse to his hotel room with his new commission. He was a US Marshal with the authority to do as he saw fit. He was given the freedom to enact what ordinances he wanted and was offered a significant budget, which he refused. He'd get the funds easily enough, but not from the citizens of Flagstaff. The Canyon Diablo businesses would fund it. They'd behave or pay, and Allingham was certain they'd pay a lot of fines before they learned to behave properly.

He had a good dinner alone, avoiding an invitation from Halsted and his daughter to dine at their home. He hated dining with people. He preferred to dine alone. And in addition to this, he did not want to be interrogated by the pretty lady again. She was intriguing and he could tell that she knew when he was lying. She'd also not stand for his cryptic and evasive responses to her questions.

She'd pry everything out of him and he did not want that or to rudely refuse to answer her questions. He did not want them to know his ultimate goal. He had no intention of letting them know of his suicidal endeavor. Inventing a plausible excuse was not in his nature and it was not their business, really, anyway. He'd rather avoid her altogether than bear the discomfort of a smart and beautiful woman prying information out of him.

Yet, he was pleased to receive attention from her. What did she really care about him? She shouldn't. Her father had things in hand as they related to his professional duties. The woman should have no personal interest in him, it was preposterous. No one, especially a well-to-do and pretty lady had ever taken an interest in him. There was nothing, physical, intellectual or emotional that would make him attractive to her. Yet, she was, and this confounded him very much.

Afterward, he took a stroll through the part of town near the hotel, breathing in the clean air, heavy with the odor of freshly cut timber. This is what brought the Halsteds to Arizona, as they were timber merchants, and Robert Halsted and Mr. Singh were good business men, partners in the endeavor and they'd added significantly to their fortunes in Arizona.

Rail cars were full of it. The town reeked of it. It was an altogether pleasant odor and on top of this, Allingham was struck by the empty vastness of the land. Even in a town, it felt, to Allingham, empty. In New York, this amount of real estate would hold tens of thousands, along with their odors and garbage and noise. Here there was solitude. Here he experienced an emotion that he'd never felt before. He was enjoying himself a little, and this was no insignificant thing, as Allingham never, ever enjoyed himself or had fun of any kind.

He rode a horse for the first time since the racetrack in New York and found this pleasant as well. The animal was a good one, especially chosen the day before by Rebecca Halsted, as the woman was a capable rider and wanted to do something for the curt, ugly policeman. It was not lost on Allingham. Confounding, but not lost on him.

She had taken her time and found him a good horse. She took his measure and chose an animal that would fit him, handle his weight and be comfortable to ride. It was a little humbling to him.

The mount she chose was much like himself, although Allingham, as a man ignorant of the equestrian arts did not immediately see or understand it. The gelding was tall at the withers with stout legs and a strong back, head long with a roman nose and ears set close together, sagging a bit to the side. But, again, like his rider, the animal had intelligent eyes and an alertness about him that belied his rough coat and straggly tail. The long slope to his shoulder indicated a smooth gait with the ability to go for long distances, if need be.

He rode his new horse on to Canyon Diablo with saddle bags full of ordinances: a new ten gauge, six shooter and Winchester completing his outfit.

By noon he was tying up to the post outside the jail. The jailor, Hobbs, was busily working, directing a small army of Chinese and Indians and Negroes. There was no shortage of labor in the camp and many wanted the additional income. They'd have the buildings up in no time.

Hobbs regarded his new boss and smiled, then looked down the way at the stakes marking the location for the future barracks and Allingham's own house. "They'll have everything finished in a week."

Allingham was pleased and of course did not show it. Hobbs looked better to him; healthier. He was in the sun and his skin color did not look nearly so ghastly. But there was something else different. He looked better because he was engaged in some real work, something that was tangible. He was no longer sitting around, waiting for the next bad thing to happen. This was progress, and it made Hobbs feel well.

There was something about this new man that gave Hobbs hope. He did not like the way the town lived now. He didn't like to see the dead men in the streets every day or the filth or the brothels or the poor offspring of the whores, wandering about.

He was a good and decent man stuck in a bad and corrupt place, and now this new man, was going to make it right, or die trying. Hobbs hoped that it would be the former. He did not want to see this one cut down.

Allingham handed Hobbs the pile of ordinances, instructing him to post them in all the businesses and public places of the town. Everyone would have time to digest the information, while Allingham hired deputies.

He looked Hobbs over as the man grinned at the many new laws, then up at Allingham. He whistled through his teeth. "Not with an army of police could you enforce these."

"Bet me."

"All right. You're on. One dollar says you can't. I'll give you 'til Christmas."

Allingham gave a terse look, almost a smile. "Don't need that long, I'll do it in half that time." He watched the workmen constructing his new digs. By late afternoon they had the foundation laid and piles of stone collected from the desert, enough to complete the project. Lumber for the roofs and floors and window sashes and doors would be coming from Flagstaff in another day. "I need you to hire us a jailor and get the word out that we're hiring three deputies. Three dollars a day and room and board. We need a cook, too. For us and for our prisoners."

Hobbs calculated in his mind and suddenly had a thought. "But I'm the jailor, Marshal."

"No you're not. You're my secretary. You're also the Public Works manager and in charge of payroll and fines and prisoner management and whatever else I can think up for you to do."

Hobbs looked on, pleased. His color was better, almost pink, changed from the ashen grey. His mind raced. So many things, so many wonderful things to do.

His reverie was interrupted by three men on horseback. Allingham recognized the first one as the defecating man. They sat and looked down arrogantly at the new works project. Allingham regarded them. He waited for them to take it all in. They'd find out soon enough, but he wanted them to see what he was up to. When he surmised that enough time had elapsed for their limited intellect to comprehend, he called out to the defecating man.

"You there. Get down from your horse. You're under arrest."

The men grinned at each other. The one who'd been knocked senseless the day before did not laugh so much. He rubbed his head and thought about what they would do to Allingham.

"I don't think so." He then thought about it. "For what?"

"Discharging a firearm in the town." He nodded and Hobbs peeled off three copies of the ordinances. He handed one to each mounted man.

"Can any of you read?"

"Yeah."

"Then I suggest you read these and pass them on to your pals. The fines are dear and you do not want to have to pay them."

The defecating man looked up from the ordinance. "Mister, are you stupid, or crazy, or drunk?"

Allingham ignored him.

"I ain't payin' any goddamned fine."

"Well, that is not a problem. You have choices."

"What choices?" The man with the sore head spoke up. The dude from the East intrigued him.

"Five days of labor for minor infractions, ten for more severe. Your boss there will have to serve only five, if he doesn't pay the fine."

"And no appeal? Mister, this is the United States of America, you can't go and just fine or lock up people or make 'em do labor all on your own."

"No, it's not."

"Not what?"

"The United States of America. Arizona is a territory and I can very well do these things. You will have a third option. If you want to appeal, you'll be transported to the Federal court in Phoenix."

"Awe, this is bullshit."

"No, it's not."

The defecating man looked on at his companions in disbelief. "Goddamned Phoenix is almost a hundred fifty miles away. Why not Flagstaff? They got a court up there."

Allingham folded his arms, eyes fixed on the defecating man, deciding how he'd get him off his horse. "Now, you can pay the ten dollars or work five days or go on down to Phoenix and await trial. They've got a thirty day backlog from what I understand. You'll be jailed until then, unless you can make bail."

He waited, but was losing patience. He was not used to so much banter, but this was important and they needed to be educated, and he needed them to tell all their reprobate friends.

By now the Indian and Chinese and Negro laborers had stopped working. There was drama and they were enjoying the show. These workmen, the majority of them, were just trying to get by, trying to hold out until the rail work could resume. They were decent men and hated the scum that had moved in and taken over their little town. They were, in a way, the victims of the decadence of the town. This new marshal looked the part, talked the talk, now they'd see if he was the genuine article.

"If you men will remember from yesterday," Allingham eyed and then nodded at the man he'd knocked out, "I don't like to repeat myself. Now, you," he pointed to the defecating man, "get down from your horse and go on into the jail."

"Go to hell." The defecating man went for his gun and Allingham his, while closing the distance between himself and the mounted man. This unnerved all of them. What man ran toward a shootout? When he was a foot away, he pressed the muzzle of his pistol to the defecating man's mount and pulled the trigger. The animal dropped, spilling his rider onto the dirty street.

The man got his bearings, looking about for his six shooter, now a good distance away. The others backed up; they did not want their horses killed as well.

"You son of a bitch, you shot my horse!" The defecating man went for his gun and Allingham, as he'd done the day before to his companion, sapped the man soundly, this time with the butt of his gun. The man was down, senseless, a knot growing larger by the moment through his greasy hair.

In short order, the man was jailed, his horse broken down by the workers. They'd eat good for a few days. Hobbs beamed at Allingham who sat, writing notes and formulating a plan.

"Never seen a man do that before." Hobbs looked away as he busied himself with some work. He was learning that his new boss was not fond of idle chatter. He regarded the ugly policeman.

Hobbs had been around a long time, around tough men and bad men, but he'd never met one like Allingham. Most of the lawmen he'd known were just as comfortable on the other side. Most weren't worth the shot and powder to put them away. But this one was different. Pure and incorruptible, from what Hobbs could see. He was of one purpose, and that was to be a lawman. He didn't joke or act friendly or do anything that did not further the task at hand. He was intriguing and Hobbs hoped to learn more about him, at least, some day.

"Well, I'd better get busy." He stood up and put his ordinances in a pile, tucking them under an arm. Allingham stopped him.

"Do you carry a gun?"

"No."

"Can you handle one?"

"Oh, sure."

Allingham rummaged through a carpet bag. "Here." He rummaged again and pulled out a receipt. "Sign." Hobbs complied. Allingham was by the book, always.

"Use it if you need it. Don't let anyone get behind you. Don't let anyone touch you or get within a foot of you. If you see an infraction, come get me. Don't enforce any of these yourself."

Hobbs grinned. He was in the war now and Allingham was making certain he knew it.

Chapter III:
Deputies

Allingham sat on his horse and peered over the edge of the deep cut into Canyon Diablo. So, this was the thing that would change his life forever. He thought on that. Actually, it was the thing that was supposed to end his life forever.

Only the day before he had a good chance of being gunned down. The men were mostly stupid and cowardly, but there were three of them. Certainly one could have gotten a killing shot, if he'd let them. Why didn't he? He was not so suicidal as he might have hoped and now this whole enterprise seemed ridiculous. He took in a deep breath and it felt good, felt fine. He hadn't coughed, hadn't spit up blood. Why would a dying man feel so well? It made no sense.

But he was enjoying himself. He liked this place, liked the challenge. He liked the good men and the way they responded to him.

75

Hobbs and the Indians, the Chinese and Negroes, even the old men of the Safety Committee and the Sikh and the pretty lady from Flagstaff, they all wanted the lawlessness to end.

Even back east, the poor, the petty thieves and prostitutes stuck in Hell's Kitchen didn't want the evil to prevail. They all wanted and needed the police in their own way. No normal people want to live that way. They might have talked tough and pretended to hate the lawmen, but they needed them. They were glad when the law was around to keep the really lawless ones under control.

A rider approached and eventually made it alongside. He nodded to Allingham as he peered over the edge. He removed his hat to wipe his brow, revealing a head of curly hair, the kind most women like on a man. "I'll be go to hell." He looked at Allingham and smiled as he put his hat back over his curly hair. "Bet there's a fellar up there in Chicago puckerin' pretty bad."

Allingham ignored him, then had a thought. The man was intriguing. "What do you mean?"

"The dope up in Chicago who built the bridge too short." He removed his hat once again and absentmindedly wiped his brow.

"That's what's the hold up, you know."

"No."

"Yep. That's it. Some dope made the bridge too short, had it shipped all the way down, then all the way back up to make it longer. That's why everyone's sittin' on their asses. They're waitin' for a new bridge to be built, and the railroad company doesn't have enough money to pay them for it."

Allingham was amused and this was a stretch as nothing much amused him. A comedy of errors. This is what made Canyon Diablo the hellhole; a math miscalculation. Who'd a thought?

"Heard you're hiring deputy marshals." The man had a half grin on his face. Allingham would learn that he always looked this way, as if everything was either ridiculous or amusing to him.

Allingham looked him over. He was not quite thirty, so too young for any significant wars. He sounded like an easterner but looked like a cowboy. He wore a mismatched sack suit, not poor, but not well made either. He had an old black garrison belt, likely from the war and a six shooter, butt forward at his left hip, and a big knife on the right. This was the utilitarian outfit of a cowboy, not the garb of a gunfighter or lawman.

He wore chaps and his hat was more like what the Mexicans wore, with a wide brim and was once tan, but now a mix of many colors from sweat and dirt and dust. He had a habit of removing it to wipe his brow, almost a nervous tic of sorts. He had no hair on his face. His collarless shirt was buttoned to the neck and he wore no tie. He sported a scarf instead and this hung down low, as was the custom.

Allingham thought he'd do and reached into his vest pocket. He pulled out a little book and handed it to the man. "You can read?"

"I can." The man grinned and leafed through the police manual. He was tickled that it was from New York. It seemed thoroughly out of place in the desert.

Allingham turned his horse back toward the trail leading back to town. "Nine tomorrow morning, know what's in the book." He was gone.

Paddy and Mike O'Shaughnessy sat, taking up most of the room in the jail. They were twins. Actually, they were giant twin Irishmen and could not be told apart, except that Mike wore a hat that was black and Paddy one that was grey.

Hobbs greeted Allingham like a proud

parent, as if he'd somehow, in the hours that his boss had been away, birthed the two and raised them up for the very task at hand. "Got two deputy marshals for you."

Allingham surveyed the little jail, as if he were looking over a sea of applicants. He ignored his secretary's banter.

He turned his attention to the men, looking them over suspiciously. They reminded him of *his* Irishmen from New York. He didn't bother to ask if they could read, as he'd never yet met an illiterate Irishman. "Either of you men ever done police work?" He knew the answer to the question, but asked it nonetheless.

"Yes, Captain." Paddy spoke first. "My brother and me did policing up in Chicago for many years."

Allingham snorted. He'd heard only bad things out of Chicago. He looked the men over accusingly. "There will be no graft here." He looked each in the eye. They did not flinch. "Or drunkenness, or cavorting with whores, or gaming."

Paddy squirmed in his chair and Allingham thought the man was getting up to leave. He was not. He was simply picking his trousers from the crack of his behind. He looked at Allingham seriously.

Mike spoke up. "We engage in none of

that, Captain. We like our drink but it has no hold over us. We take no bribes. And the whores, well, they're whores, it's not our way."

He handed them procedurals. They'd sit before him, along with the cowboy, the next day.

Allingham regarded Hobbs. He liked the man. Hobbs was a good judge of character and was getting everything in order. He was a good secretary. He made no mention of a jailor again, and suspected that Hobbs had not looked for one.

Hobbs announced his other newest addition to the force.

"Found us a cook, Captain." Hobbs liked the sound of captain better than marshal. It sounded better when the Irishman addressed Allingham in this way and Hobbs decided he'd call the man Captain as well. Allingham didn't correct him. As if on cue, a portly Mexicana sauntered in. She had coffee and biscuits for them.

"Hola, Señor." She smiled and Allingham regarded her with a barely discernible nod. He looked the food over and it was good. He waited for her to leave and watched Hobbs watch the woman's backside as she sidled out.

"I thought anything made by a Mexican

gave you wind."

"Well," he ate a biscuit and talked as he chewed. "Rosario promised not to go too native on us. She knows what makes a man fart and she promised not to make such things." He thought on it a bit. Rosario was not quite his age but she was pretty and as a young woman stunningly beautiful. And Hobbs liked women. It was evident that he was getting more than victuals from the pretty Mexican cook.

Allingham was pleased. Of course, he would never let Hobbs or, for that matter, anyone else know it. But he was pleased with the progress they'd made in such a short time.

"What do we do with him?" Hobbs tipped his head in the general direction of the prisoner who could be seen through the open doorway. "He refuses to pay the fine and I can't get him to work."

Allingham called out. "Every day you don't work is added to your time in jail. And you get fed only after working."

The man looked through the bars with bleary eyes. He was hungry. "Awe, that's a load of bullshit."

"No, it's not."

The man muttered and stomped like a child. He cursed Allingham using an impressive staccato of swear words that Allingham had, of course, been called many times before. He waited for the man's rage to burn out. It didn't. Instead, the prisoner picked up a chamber pot, half full from the previous night and threatened to throw its contents at the lawmen.

Allingham closed the door separating them, then called through it. "If you make a mess in there, you'll clean it up. Don't make things worse for yourself."

The prisoner quieted down.

Hobbs smiled at his boss. "Never thought of that."

Allingham grunted. "Food is a great motivator."

In another two days they were ready. The Irishmen would work at night and this pleased them well enough, as they liked to be busy, and nights were always busy in Canyon Diablo. And besides this, their significant girth made the heat of the day nearly unbearable for them. They slept in their cool adobe barracks while Allingham and his new assistant, Francis, would patrol during the day.

The young man with the curly hair was from a small town in Pennsylvania and had been in Arizona for only a couple of years.

He had no law experience but could read well enough and could recite, verbatim, anything asked of him from the police procedural. He was calm and fearless and had a way with people. He reminded Allingham a little of Stosh Gorski in this respect, and it's likely why Allingham took him on so quickly.

They were ready for business and Allingham thought it best, the first day, to walk through town together, starting at the worst end, where the brothels and most dangerous gaming houses could be found. Everyone knew about them by this time, as word traveled quickly, the streets littered with Allingham's ordinances; more than a few had been used to clean up after nature's call. But Allingham's original goal had been achieved, all had been duly warned.

The business owners, at least the ones who ran the dodgy places, were in for yet another surprise, however, and Allingham decided to start at French Annie's brothel. He'd heard that she was the most outspoken, the most violent, and the one with the worst temper. She'd help him spread the word sure enough.

French Annie was on them immediately. A true she-wolf, she knew how to run things, knew how to manage a situation. But so did Allingham. He soon had her under control. Her little squad of whores was dismissed and the lawmen fanned out, Francis taking up a position at the far end of the parlor where French Annie would greet her guests and hold court of an evening. The Irishmen guarded the door, doing their best to avoid distraction, as they liked women and the whores did little to hide their feminine offerings. Some lingered and loitered, and watched the big coppers with the look they knew was irresistible to most men.

"How about a few drinks for you and your men, Sheriff?"

"It's Marshal. No."

She lit a cigarette and blew smoke in Allingham's face. He plucked it from her lips and crushed it on the carpeted floor between them as he handed her a copy of the ordinances, all the while staring her in the eye.

Annie had been pretty twenty years ago. Now she was not. She had an incomplete set of teeth and was plagued with bad skin, scaly and red with blotches. No one bedded down with her and this is how she became a madam. It's also how she got the word French added to her name. She could no longer make money on her own back, so she had to make it on the backs of others or by engaging in services that did not feature coming in contact with her damaged skin. It was a tough way to survive but it was the only way Annie knew.

"We will be collecting your safety fee every day, unless you want to pay ahead by the week or by the month. You may pay any of us and will receive a receipt. The fee is five dollars per day." He waited. Annie did not disappoint him. Her face turned a bellicose red as her rage grew.

"A safety fee?" She fairly shrieked.

"Yes, that's right. It's a fee all businesses will be charged from now on. The money used to fund policing and sanitation efforts in the town. In addition," he pointed to the ordinances, "extra fees will be charged for any infractions to the business owner where the infractions occur. If we are called for any other issues or problems, an extra fee will apply. Cash only."

"This is bullshit!"

"No, it's not."

"It's illegal. You can't do this."

"No, it's not, and yes, I can."

He turned to walk out, stopping short as one of the prostitute's children ran in, nearly knocking Francis down. Allingham stopped her and looked the girl over, tilting her head up to the light with a finger placed under her chin, he said, "She's been beaten."

He looked up at French Annie and then back at the child. "How old are you?"

They both answered in unison, Annie calling her seventeen and the child declaring she was twenty.

"Nonsense. She's not more than twelve."

"Yes, she is."

"When were you born, child?"

"April."

"No, what year?"

French Annie called out. "1866."

"That would make her sixteen."

The child liked the little game. She smiled coyly and spoke up. "1872."

"That would make you ten."

He reached out and grabbed her by the shoulder, pushing her in front of him. "Out, out."

He looked back at French Annie. "No children in here from now on. Get them out."

She was on him, shouting and spraying spittle at the back of his head, showering his protruding red ears.

"You bastard. You'll not get away with this. This place eats lawmen for lunch. You'll be dead by Saturday!"

He ignored her and this made her angrier. "You goddamned Yankee scum think you can come out here with your fancy Eastern and New York ways and tell us what to do. You can't, you ugly bastard. You ugly goddamned pig-faced, big-eared jackass. You are the ugliest son of a bitch I've ever seen."

He turned and held out his hand. "I'll collect the first payment now."

She looked him in the eye and for reasons not even she could understand, pulled sweaty bills from between her breasts, handing them over without further complaint. He wrote out a receipt and walked out.

Francis sauntered past, smiling his little sideways grin. He tipped his hat as he walked out. "See you tomorrow, ma'am."

They moved in a troop, the Irishmen bringing up the rear, Francis walking abreast of Allingham. The little girl ran up to Francis, smiling broadly at him. "What's your name?"

"Francis."

She pointed at Allingham. "What's his name?"

"He's the Captain. You just call him Captain." He pointed back at the Irishmen. "That's Mike and the other is Paddy.

They're twins, ya know."

"I can see that." She looked at him in a way that a little girl should not be familiar with when it came to looking at a man. "I ain't seen you in the house."

"No, no. Don't do that sorta thing." Francis looked away, embarrassed. He could feel his face redden.

"I do." She grinned.

"Well, ya oughtn't. It ain't right. Why, you're just a little girl." Francis looked at her with a pained expression. "Who clobbered ya, anyway?"

"Oh, no one." She skipped along and followed the men and Francis looked on and enjoyed the child acting like a child for a change. "What's your name?"

"Janie."

He tipped his hat. "Well, Miss Janie, where's yer ma and pa?"

"Hah. I ain't gotta pa. Ma's a whore, but she died last spring. Now I'm on my own."

Francis thought on it as he walked and watched the child. He should have made inquiries but he didn't. He should have asked permission of the captain, or at least Hobbs, but didn't.

He let Allingham and the Irishmen march on, and pulled Janie aside. He'd catch up to them eventually. "You come on with me,

Miss Janie." She smiled when he called her that, "You ain't allowed in the brothel any longer, there's an ordinance against that."

"What's a ordinance?"

"A law, put out by the Captain. No children in the brothels." He smiled and looked toward the captain with obvious respect. "So, that's that. What the Captain says, goes."

"I ain't a child." She grinned the ugly knowing grin again. "In another year, they're gonna pay me. They say, with my looks, I'll be richer than 'em all."

Francis looked at her as he removed his hat and wiped his brow. He was speechless.

He led little Janie into the barracks and called out. "Mamacita, got a helper for ya."

Rosario turned, wiping her hands on her apron. She looked the girl over and smiled.

"This here's Miss Rosario. Miss Rosario, this here's Miss Janie. She'll help, she's going to be our new jailor."

Rosario called the child over, pulling a lock of hair from the little one's eyes. "No jailor, that is not a job for a pretty little girl. She will help in la cocina. Come, child."

Francis turned to rejoin the men. He had work to do and he was thoroughly enjoying the captain's performance. He didn't want to miss a thing. He called out over his shoulder. "We boys are goin' to be hungry, Mamacita. You and Janie make up a big feast." He smiled as he walked out.

"He's grand." Little Janie watched him as he moved down the street. "How old is he?"

Rosario looked on at Francis. "Oh, I don't know, child. He's a man and that is all you need to worry about. He's a man." She looked after Francis. "A very good man."

By evening they had nearly every one of the shady business owners looking for an assassin. Allingham only went after the brothels, saloons and gambling houses. This would be a sin tax and he'd not bother legitimate businesses with it. Lunch counters, dry goods stores, any place that provided good commerce or service was not charged.

In these places he made it clear that they would be fined only if the law were called. They'd have to police themselves or pay for the policing services by the marshals. That was the key and it was met with little resistance by the decent people of the settlement. It would be a good incentive for them to keep their shops free of the no good bums who descended on the town. Pretty soon, the miscreants would find no welcome anywhere and, hopefully, that would be inducement enough for them to move on. Even a bad man cannot survive long without the services of a lunch counter.

As they made their way back to the jail and barracks, five men stood in a row blocking their paths. They wasted little time and pulled their six shooters as the lawmen approached. This was too much for Allingham and he fairly sprinted, leaving his little force behind wondering what to do. They could not return fire if needed, for fear of hitting their boss.

The men were equally put off and stood like a bunch of schoolboys waiting to be chastised. Who ran toward a gun battle? No one shot at him. No one did anything. They stood there, stunned, not knowing what to do next.

Allingham picked the most confident looking one and stopped, mere inches away. The man tried to hide his gun, as if he suddenly thought the whole endeavor a foolhardy one.

"Hand me your gun. You're under arrest."

"For what?"

"Assault."

The man complied and, by now, Francis and the Irishmen were taking the rest in hand. Francis, with his little sideways grin, laughed at one of the men glaring at him.

Francis grinned more widely. "What are you lookin' at, ass?"

"A dude with a stupid grin." The bad man was bold and Francis laughed. He considered thumping the man but didn't. Instead he escorted him to jail.

That evening they celebrated in the barracks. Hobbs watched Rosario move about. He, as did she, had a certain glow, a certain glint in their eyes and this was not lost on Allingham who sat, stone faced, in a corner watching the group form a band.

Francis was talking incessantly as was his wont. He told funny stories and Rosario laughed at him and the Irishmen smiled. He'd tell a joke and at the end he'd blurt out, "I'll be go to hell."

One of the Irishmen, Paddy, looked on and challenged the young deputy. "What does this mean, Francis, 'I'll be go to hell'?"

"Yes, Francis," Mike chimed in. "Is it, "I'll be, comma, go to hell? Or should it be I'll be gone to hell?"

"Don't know, boys." He ran his hand through his curly hair. "Tell the truth, my old uncle from up in Coatsville used to say it. Don't know what it means, it just means what it means, I guess. I'll be go to hell."

Allingham looked on. It was a good bunch of folks. They all got along. They were decent people and no one tried to outdo the other or brag or show off. They complemented each other well and they'd do a good job. He was pleased.

He watched little Janie sitting on the floor, Hobbs's dog in her lap. He barely recognized her until the light hit her and he remembered the wounds on her face. She looked different now. Gone was the crass and chintzy dress, as Rosario had her clothed like a native Mexican girl. Janie loved the new garment Rosario called a rebozo. The child liked it as it was bright red and had fringe on the ends. She wore it, as Rosario had shown her, draped over her little shoulders. She looked natural, like a little girl ought to look, sitting among decent folks, happy, with a dog in her lap.

He watched Francis hold court and that pleased him as well.

The young man was a father figure to the little retired whore, and the lad patted Janie on the head as she fussed over the dog. He smiled down at the child. "You know what they say, Janie. When dogs love a person, means the person's got a good heart. Dogs know better than people, can spot a good person better than any human ever could."

Francis smoked and looked at the Irishmen and then his watch. "I like dogs. My ma, she always liked cats. Can't train 'em, you know. Cats, that is." Francis had them now, as they all leaned forward waiting to hear a good yarn. "I had a uncle, used to keep cats, he had one liked to eat snakes."

Rosario gave a grimace. She did not care one way or another about snakes, but a cat eating snakes seemed revolting. "Oh, Francis."

"True, all true, at least what my uncle said. He had one little cat, she used to eat snakes, then one day, she et a snake, and then she got all crazy. She clawed at her belly, meowed out loud, ran from one end of the house to the other, couldn't settle down. It was the damnedest thing and went on for days and days, and then, one night, this was in winter, she was lying there, in front of the fire and my uncle was readin' the good book. You know, the Montgomery Ward catalog, and all of a sudden, that doggone cat stuck its tongue out, and dang if it wasn't pink, like a cat's, with the sandpaper finish on it, but it looked for all the world like a doggone snake's tail."

Little Janie looked up and smiled. "No."

"Yep, yep, and that tail tongue come out and curled around that cat's nose like a odd lookin' question mark."

The Irishmen looked at each other, grinning, as Francis continued.

"Then, that old cat, she let out a cry that would raise the dead, raised the hair right up on my old uncle's neck and guess what she did next?"

"What, Francis, what?"

"She squatted down on the hearth, right in front of the fireplace, squattin' and a shakin' just like a dog shittin' peach stones, and guess what?"

"What, what?"

"A damn snake's head popped right outta her hind parts and took a look around."

"No!"

"Yep, yep, true story. That cat et a live snake and that snake was stretched out all the way from that cat's mouth to her ass, and still alive. No kiddin'."

Mike grinned, "And what koind of snake was this, Francis?"

"Well, a rat snake, of course. That cat, I think, got itself mixed up with the name."

He smoked and watched the effect his story had on his audience. Francis was pleased. "That's what he said, God rest his soul, that's what my poor old late uncle said."

Paddy swallowed the last of his beer. He

was ready for the night's work. "So, this uncle, Francis, what happened to him, this famous cat man, what ere came of him?"

"Oh, they found him hangin' from a rafter. He hanged himself in the barn, wearing my aunt's dress." He looked serious then. "But that don' mean he was crazy, that don' mean the cat story's not true. I believe, sure enough, believe every word's true." He smiled.

He put them all in a good mood and this was how it was with Allingham's people. His people were always better than the other squads of policemen in New York. Allingham had a way with his men and this was not even known to him. His coldness and lack of communication, coupled with his decisive and fearless leadership made his men proud of him, made his men respect him and want to do for him, even if they didn't like him all that much. They never wanted to let their taciturn boss down.

But it was also Allingham's skill at choosing men. He was a good judge of men, knew which men fit together, and he'd chosen this bunch. He may have been hard and terse and a poor communicator, but Allingham was also fair.

He was no martinet, and he did not make the men do stupid or unnecessary things, just because he could. He believed a man should be left alone to do a job, and if he was given the proper tools and training, and if the man's mind was right, if he was a decent and moral fellow, he'd do good service.

A man such as that did not need coddling. Did not need to be praised like he was a little child and Allingham would never do such a thing, and it all worked. He had the best men in the police in New York and he had the best men now.

And already the town was quieter. It wasn't as if they'd cleaned it up already, to the contrary. Six men were in jail, tomorrow they'd be digging privies under the watchful eye of Hobbs and his Chinese foreman. But the rest were on guard. They were talking about it. Allingham had their attention. They were behaving much like bad school boys would behave the first day with a new and unknown headmaster. They needed to know what he was about; needed to feel him out.

Hobbs was listening to the banter in the barracks, but he also had an ear to the town. He smiled and looked on at Rosario completing the after dinner tasks. At this rate, the place would be a decent town in a month. He was certain he'd lose his dollar, and didn't mind a bit.

Francis had been doing his best all evening to keep up with the Irishmen. But, being Irish and each with easily a hundred pounds on him, he was soon drunk.

Allingham did not mind as the young fellow was even more pleasant inebriated. He laughed a lot. He made people happy wherever he went and the round Rosario and little Janie were quite taken with him. His day was done and he had no further duties to perform. It was no sin for him to be in his cups a little, or even a lot.

"Captain, how's it we're going to keep the children out of the whore houses?" He belched and then thought better of using the term. "Ah, bordellos." He nodded an apology toward Rosario as he was a gentleman and respectful to ladies. He looked at little Janie who'd fallen asleep next to the dog.

"Ordinance twenty-three."

"Yeah, I know the ordinance well enough, Captain, but how do we keep 'em out? Can't lock up little children."

Allingham was finished for the night. He was tired as it had been a long and productive day. He stood up and looked Francis in the eye. "Soon enough I'll show you." He went to bed.

Francis walked Rosario and little Janie home, as Rosario lived in the desert just outside of town and refused to be moved. She liked her little shack and wanted nothing more. The place was dry and kept the dirt and dust and sun off her. It was all she needed and Francis looked it over and smiled.

There was a new bed in the hovel. It was an odd sight, out of place, as it was a bed with a brass frame and was store bought in Flagstaff and looked incongruous in the rough digs. It had been a recent gift from Hobbs, and Francis, though he was often a little thick regarding such observations, could figure out well enough what was on Hobbs's mind. It was a very nice bed.

Rosario quickly prepared a bed on the floor for little Janie and the child was soon asleep, dog tightly pressed against her back. Hobbs, it seemed, had lost his four-legged companion, but he didn't mind. He'd looked at Janie as they left the barracks, animal in tow, and wondered at her tortured life. He was pleased the dog could be of some comfort to her. He'd find another soon enough as he always had dogs. They seemed to find him.

Francis had sobered up in the fresh air and the walk had cleared his brain. He kissed Rosario on the cheek and patted little Janie on top of the head. The child did not stir. He thought of something.

"Mamacita, you got a shootin' iron?"

The Mexicana reached down and picked up a ten gauge lying next to her bed. It had the barrels cut down. "Sí." She held it up for Francis to see. He belched and smiled. Old Rosario didn't need protecting. "And a six shooter and a knife." She grinned. Francis deduced that Rosario knew how to use them and would if anyone crossing her path needed killing.

Francis was alone in the barracks as his Irish companions were on patrol, and Hobbs off someplace other than bed, battling the curse of insomnia which plagued him more as he aged. He slept fitfully and dreamed strange dreams as he was not used to drinking so much beer.

He dreamed of the beautiful daughter of the railroad's head surveyor and civil engineer, a kind man from Virginia who had treated Francis well from his first day in Canyon Diablo. His daughter was the most beautiful woman in the settlement. He thought of her often at night. He imagined

100

bedding her and he hoped to do so soon. Suddenly, the dream was too real. He felt movement in his bed, hands, real flesh and blood hands moving over him. He jumped up and looked about.

"Girl! I'll be go to hell!" He jumped further yet, away from his bed, and lit a lamp, the dim yellow light reflecting the child's form, Janie standing in the shadows with not a stitch of clothing on, the pagan dress and rebozo given to her by Rosario in a heap at her feet. She looked at him again with the corruption in her eyes.

Francis averted his gaze as he threw her a blanket.

"Jesus, child. What are you on about?"

She smiled coyly. "I like you, Francis. Come on." She dropped the blanket.

"No, no, no!" He was angry now and ashamed at his primordial reaction to the caress. "That is not right, Janie. That just ain't right."

She looked lost, naked and vulnerable and not a little confused, as her offerings had never been refused in the brothel. These new men were a strange lot indeed. They weren't like any she'd ever known.

She began to cry. "You hate me!"

Francis lit a cigarette and smoked as he pulled his suspenders onto his sinewy shoulders. He lit another lamp and the room was bright. The dog was asleep again, by the door, as it had followed the child back from Rosario's. At least little Janie had had some protection walking from the hovel to the barracks.

He poured her a cup of water. She drank and cried and her nose ran. She wiped it with his blanket as she sat on the edge of his bed.

"I don't hate you at all, child. Just the opposite." He reached out to comfort her, then thought better of it. He maintained his distance instead. "That's why I'd never have a thing to do with you in that way."

This made no sense to the girl, as sensual pleasure had been the only substitute, all her life, for love. She'd never known a mother's love. She cried harder and looked on at Francis who now worried a little over his snotty blanket.

"I don't understand." She coughed. "This don't make no sense."

He sat down beside her and smoked and thought on it. This was a difficult problem, and Francis was not equipped to help confused little girls. It was not something he thought much about, as he had no sisters, only brothers, and little contact with the opposite sex.

"Janie." He looked into her pretty brown eyes. "That carryin' on. With men and such. That ain't natural. What they do down there in the house, where you were, that ain't right. That kinda carryin' on, that's for people who love each other, grown up people, between a husband and a wife. It ain't the right thing, Janie."

She stopped crying and he handed her one of his handkerchiefs. She blew her nose and finally began to calm down. She stood up, dropping the blanket and began dressing without giving it another thought. She was scandalous, to Francis's mind, as she seemed to have no sense of modesty. He wondered if she'd ever not be corrupt.

"They all, up there," she pointed toward the brothels, "say that the more men a gal gets, means the more she's liked."

"Well, liked and loved ain't the same thing, girl. Hell, I like lots of folks, don' mean I'm goin' to do, you know, *that* with 'em."

She was exhausted and needed sleep. They both needed sleep. He got her to lie down then pointed to his bed and called the dog over, who dutifully flopped down beside the child. Francis covered them both and kissed her on the forehead. He turned out the lamps.

"Go on and get some sleep, Miss Janie."

"Francis?"

"Yes, child?"

"You got nice curls."

He spent the rest of the night in the jail's office, listening to criminals snore.

Rosario awoke to find the little girl's bed empty. She got up and had a pee and started cooking for the day. She had many prisoners and the men and now the little girl to feed. She was pleased to be busy as she liked to work. She'd worked as long ago as from the time she could walk and talk and this had gone on for more than five decades.

She'd done much harder work at times in her life and now the new job at the jail was welcome. Her last husband had been dead ten years and all her children were dead as well. She'd lived in the same hovel for more than a dozen years, keeping goats and trading up in Flagstaff for the things she could not make or grow or forage for herself. It was a hard life, but it was life. She lived well enough and was happy.

The settlement had sprung up like a deadly mushroom in her backyard and it provided her with money as she did washing and cooking and these services were sorely required by the many inhabitants of the little town.

She met Hobbs right away. He was a good man and very clever and friendly and they were intimate after knowing each other only a short time.

Rosario knew this to be a mortal sin as she was a pious Catholic, and not a loose woman, but she was beyond the childbearing age and because of this, she surmised, it could not be so much a sin as it could not result in bastard babies. Besides this, she knew well enough that Hobbs did not cavort with prostitutes, so it was unlikely he would be diseased and pass anything onto her.

She liked making love and he was there, willing, and convenient, not unhandsome, and kind. She liked when he made love to her. She liked making love and it had been a long time since she'd had a man.

Redshirt was the last man she'd had since her husband, and the old Navajo chief had not been around for a while. He was married, and that did bother Rosario a bit. At least Hobbs was unattached, free. She did not like the idea of taking another woman's man, but Redshirt was big medicine in the region, and Rosario had become smitten a little by his power and prestige. He was a good man too, but Hobbs was better in two respects. He was available and unattached.

She remembered the first day the gringo from New York came into Canyon Diablo. Hobbs was pleased and excited and he asked Rosario to be the cook and when she didn't hesitate and said yes he was fairly giddy.

"This one's a good one, my dear." He pinched her cheek and gave her a hug. "This one's going to make it right."

And she liked Allingham immediately. He was odd and ugly and not at all friendly, but he was also not cruel and he did not look on her the way some gringos did, as if she were something less than human. There was something very dignified about Allingham, and this she valued more than a man who used a lot of sugary words.

She had food cooking and as she finished her morning's preparations, thought about her new little charge. The poor thing was thoroughly corrupt and she worried that she'd not ever break the bonds the brothel had on her. She figured that the child was back with the whores and couldn't blame her for that. It was the only life the poor creature had known. Such habits were difficult to break, and living among decent folks, it seemed, would be boring to her, she'd not be used to sitting around a fire with good people of an evening, resting

106

from a hard day's work, or talking about pleasant and mundane things.

She thought about the Irishmen. She loved them the most. Though Francis was a dear, the Irishmen, they were Catholics like her and they could relate to her better than any of the gringos. And above all, she liked the way they were gigantic and gentle and she liked the way they were devoted to each other. They were good brothers and kind and respectful to her.

She'd sit with them in the morning as they'd eat and prepare for bed. Hobbs would be gone on some errand and Francis would be off patrolling with Allingham and she'd have the two giants to herself. Sometimes she'd just listen to them talk as she worked on things for the evening meal. She loved the funny brogue and sometimes she could not understand a word they were saying, but at the same time could understand it all. It didn't matter anyway. It was good to see them interact, hear them talk. One was busy scheming all the time, and the other, she could tell, was there to humor him, support him, following him to the very gates of hell if that was what was required.

She set everything in a dogcart Hobbs had procured from the railroad and hitched her favorite goat to it. He was an old one and very docile and Hobbs had a way with animals. He'd had dogs all his life and was good at training them and quickly taught the goat as well. This made Rosario's life easier as she liked to do most of her cooking at home, even though the new barracks had a proper iron cook stove. Old habits die hard and Rosario liked what she was used to.

She was in before the Irishmen and was glad as she wanted to be ready when they'd finished their night's work. They were always hungry and Rosario would put several bottles of beer in her clay pot to cool them. The lads loved cold beer with breakfast and wondered at her cleverness. It had been a long time since they had a cool beer.

She could see the diminutive form, hunkered down with the dog in Francis's bed and was pleased and relieved to learn that the child had not gone back to the whores. She was also delighted at the realization that Francis had been chivalrous enough to give up his bed, had not stayed in the same building as the child. She wondered where he might have gone when he wandered in, stretching and yawning and bleary-eyed.

"Good morning, ma'am." He kissed her

cheek as he had with his own mother all his young life and made Rosario very happy.

He stretched again and looked tired and smiled as Rosario handed him a coffee.

"Where did you sleep, mi hijo?"

"In the jail. I'll be go to hell, them boys can snore. Don't know how Hobbsie ever stood it."

"Did she give you much trouble?"

"No, Mamacita. She's a good little thing. She's just confused, needs a lotta love, needs the love of a good mamma, bless her soul. That's all."

She stopped Francis as he always seemed to be moving. She grabbed him and gave him a hug. "You are a good, good boy, Francis, a good, good boy."

CHAPTER IV:
ROSARIO

Hobbs crawled into bed and woke her. She remembered that she was annoyed with him and scooted back abruptly, her ample frame enough to tumble him out of bed and onto the dirt floor.

"Damn, woman! Why'd you do that?"

She continued to face the wall of the hovel, away from him. She spoke into her pillow. "You know well enough. Go sleep with the dog."

He got up and winced. His bowels were waging a regular little war with him. Rosario continued. "And go outside to pass wind. It smells like a gut pile in here, you filthy man."

"I'm . . . I'm sorry." He waited and the knife-like stab of the gas bubble moved on. At least now he was in less pain. He waited and watched her. He'd only aggravated her twice since they'd been together. Something had really set her off and Hobbs was confused as he never tried to make her unhappy. He wondered at his latest infraction, but was not the kind of man to let things simmer and fester. He needed to resolve this quickly, his bowels could not take much more.

"Darling, I'm sorry."

"For what?"

"For whatever I did to set you off. I'm sorry."

She turned and looked him over. She did love him but he needed to behave.

"How can you be sorry for something that you have done when you don't even know what it is that you've done wrong?"

"Well, I'm sorry for setting you off. I don't mean to." He darted for the door. He relieved the pressure outside and had started to re-enter the dwelling when Rosario held up her hand.

"Wait for it to leave your clothes."

He did and shook his pants to move the gases along. He looked on at his dear love. "I'm sorry, I won't do it again."

"You are such a fool, Hobbsie. You don't even know what you did wrong. How will you not do it again? You cannot make such a promise. It is a silly and empty promise. You are such a fool."

"Well, then, tell me. Tell me what I've

done wrong." He needed a peppermint, did not have one, and settled for a cigar. She was up now and sat at the side of the bed. She was pretty in the candlelight.

"You said some things to the Irish boys and you gave a little grin and you looked at me. That is not the right thing and I did not like this. We, what we do, is our business and I am not someone you may tell about. I am not some conquista, some whore you bounce on and brag to your men about."

She was angry but not so much so that she was through with him. He blanched and that was a good sign. Hobbs was embarrassed and had meant no harm. He understood the impropriety of his acts, nonetheless, even if what Rosario saw was misinterpreted. He would never brag to the men about her. He could not even remember the incident, could not make the connection, but what Rosario saw was real to her, and that was enough. He had to make it right.

"I . . . I do humbly apologize, Rosario. I, I never had such thoughts. Never had I intended to convey anything disrespectful on your behalf. I, please, do accept my apology."

She got up and poured him some chicken

broth. "This will calm your stomach, Hobb-sie."

He ate and knew that he was forgiven. She moved around the room picking things up and setting them down again. He was smitten, even thought that perhaps he loved her, and this was a stretch as he'd been without a wife for nearly thirty years.

"I am a Catholic, you know this, Hobbsie, and I know you are not. You are a Jew and it might be okay with your God to be with a woman when you are not married, but it is not such a way with a Catholic. It is called a mortal sin and I must live with it."

"I'm sorry, Rosario. I am, I never, I've never taken such affairs lightly. I know, I always thought, that, well, it was more than just being a comfort to each other. It meant, means more to me than that."

She worked on the morning meal and sat quietly for a while. She was not really so nervous about the mortal sin. She could no longer bear children, she knew she was beyond that, and had, over the years begun to take a lot of what the church proclaimed with a grain of salt. It did not bother her so much, but she wanted things straightened out with Hobbs.

Hobbs continued. "You know, Rosario, it is not looked upon favorably with us Jews, either. Jews don't like cavorting and carrying on. The religious folks, I mean, the rabbis do not like it any more than do the padres."

He put the soup bowl down and did not feel as gassy now. "But we, Rosario, we're no spring chickens." He walked over and took her hand, led her to the bed and they sat down together. He pushed a lock of hair from her eyes and kissed her temple. "I just, I don't know. I don't think your God or my God, I guess He's the same God, would begrudge folks like us a little happiness. You make me happy, Rosario. I like being with you, I like waking up in the morning with you. I hope I make you happy, am some comfort to you as well. I just, I don't know that such a thing could be a sin in God's eye. Especially a mortal sin. That sounds so, so severe."

She smiled and thought she could detect the slightest hint of moisture glistening in his eye. "You are a good man, Hobbsie."

She kissed him and rolled back onto the bed, pulling him in with her. "You just make sure you behave from now on. You make sure you behave."

They awoke well before sunrise as neither slept more than three hours at a time. He looked and could see she was awake. She was praying and he waited for her to finish. He kissed her gently on the cheek.

"Sleep well?"

She nodded.

"Still happy with me?"

She nodded.

He pushed his head down onto her breast and held her tightly. "I'm glad."

Rosario smiled. "You are glad for this work, Hobbsie?"

"I am, Rosario. He's a good one, this Allingham. The men are good. Old Francis, what a lad, and the Irishmen. They're all good men. They're going to make it right."

He saw a sadness come over her and sensed it in her demeanor. He looked into her eyes. "What is it, darling?"

"I'm worried. I'm worried, Hobbsie. I, all my life, it is, it seems God's little trick. As soon as things are going good, He brings something bad down on our heads. It is this feeling. I feel that something bad will happen to the men. Something bad will happen and this will all go away."

Hobbs knew. They were lawmen, in the worst town in the territory. It was likely, inevitable, that some, perhaps all of them would not last the year. He'd buried enough of them in the past. Seems all he did was bury lawmen. But he needed to think other thoughts and wanted to encourage Rosario.

He smiled and said, "With two dogs they killed the lion."

She looked at him a little surprised. Hobbs never spoke in such a way. "What does this mean?"

"An old saying. There is strength in numbers, darling. We have many good men. The other lawmen acted alone, acted bravely but stupidly. They fought the bad men with guts and lead, but they did not fight with brains and strength of men. We have all of that with our little crew. Our little police force." He smiled but seemed sad to Rosario. "I think we will win. I think we will make the town right and everything will work out as planned. All of our boys will survive, they must, they have to." He sounded like a man who was trying to convince himself of something that made no sense at all.

"Well, I hope you are right. You pray to your God, Hobbsie, and I will pray to mine. Those boys must survive. I cannot bear another broken heart. I don't think I can bear to lose even one of them."

She watched out through the open door as the sliver of light worked its way over the horizon. The Irishmen would be home soon. They'd be hungry and Rosario would be

ready for them. She looked back at Hobbs
dozing in the bed. She let him sleep.

CHAPTER V:
REBECCA HALSTED

Rebecca Halsted prepared for her monthly journey to Canyon Diablo. She checked on Mr. Singh who was finishing some correspondence at his desk. He looked up at her and smiled warmly.

"Ready, Mr. Singh?"

"One moment, Kaur."

He had been with her from the time she could remember. Most young girls such as she had a nanny; Rebecca Halsted had a Sikh warrior and would have it no other way.

The Sikh had come into their lives more than twenty years before when Rebecca's father was sent to India. The two soldiers became fast friends and constant companions. When Rebecca's mother and Mr. Singh's family were taken in the mutiny, it was a natural transition for him to move on with the Halsteds. There was no longer anything in India to keep him. He was alone in the world.

The two army officers had formed an unbreakable bond, the kind that is forged in battle, becoming lifelong friends, devoted to raising the only child left to them.

They'd moved back to England and then eventually on to the territory of Arizona. The place was wild and Halsted wanted his daughter protected, and Singh, the best man for such a job was her constant companion. She had had two fathers all her life and Mr. Singh had taught her many things.

By late afternoon they were in Canyon Diablo and it was remarkable in its change. She'd heard stories about the odd new marshal but was nonetheless impressed. Everything looked different: cleaner, neater, quieter, and it had only been a few weeks since his arrival.

Mr. Singh was likewise impressed and hopeful as, according to his faith, he had an abiding respect for all of human kind. Canyon Diablo made him sad as it embodied the worst of the human condition. Perhaps now things would change for the better. By all appearances, at least, it was heading in that direction.

They stopped at the jail and were greeted by Rosario and Hobbs, who welcomed them to the new barracks. Hobbs had known of the pretty woman but had not yet met her. He was pleased to have a celebrity in his midst.

"Well, Mr. Hobbs, I see you and the marshal have made some progress."

He brightened. "Oh, not me, ma'am. The Captain's your man. He's the one to make things right, and of course, the men."

The words were a comfort to Mr. Singh. The ugly policeman was not perfect, but he was obviously effective and at least of the same purpose. He would make things right. The fact that Hobbs was respectful regarding his new boss was encouraging. Perhaps Allingham was not such a monster after all.

They watched Francis bring in some prisoners. The men had been digging privies and were as exhausted as they were filthy from the hard work, as they'd constructed many outhouses in the past days. They were orderly and well treated. Francis looked on the visitors with his broad smile. He removed his hat and bowed to the lady. He turned his attention to Mr. Singh and stared at his turban, nodding and then extending his hand.

"Where're you from, Mister?"

"India." Mr. Singh nodded and smiled at Francis as he shook his hand. He liked the young lawman right away.

"I'm Francis. Deputy marshal."

"Hira Singh."

"Glad to know ya, Mr. Hira Singh." He looked at Mr. Singh's pretty companion. "And who is this, Mr. Singh?"

"Rebecca Halsted. She is the daughter of your employer, sir."

They arrived at their destination and found the children well. It was early and many of the prostitutes were there, caring for and playing with their babies, as business did not pick up until after sundown.

This was Rebecca's attempt at helping the doomed town. The babies were constantly coming, it seemed, and many of the prostitutes would otherwise be forced to have them grow up in the brothels.

Rebecca hoped to break the vicious cycle and created the safe haven for them to keep their children, a protected place for the little ones to live. She had an open door policy and never questioned or lectured or tried to invoke her own morality or faith on the wayward women.

None of them needed lecturing. They knew they lived a squalid life. No one had to tell them it was wrong. In this, they were grateful to their patron for her generosity of spirit as well as her open purse.

They were always attentive and many took an extra interest in Mr. Singh who treated them with more respect than most of them had known from a man in their sad lives. He was also handsome and exotic. He was a fine looking man.

He would call them Kaur, princess, even if it did not fit, as the term was reserved among the Sikhs for only honorable women. But that was Singh's way. He was an exceedingly tolerant and kind man. The soiled doves appreciated it, even if the translation was unknown to them. A couple of them finally felt bold enough to ask the kindly Indian. "Ah, it means princess, and has been the way we address women, since more than four hundred years. The Guru said, 'You are my beloved princesses, my daughters, and you must be respected. How can this world be without you? Without women this world cannot be. Women are humans and all humans deserve equal rights. You are an individual, you are a princess, and you can keep Kaur as your last name.' "

The women giggled as the only princess they had known was the fancy whore from down in Louisiana that French Annie and One-Eyed Sal constantly fought over. They were certain that Mr. Singh did not mean that kind of princess.

They loved the kind Indian man with his clear crisp English, his calm and soothing voice. Some even cried and thought that India, the land of the Sikh, must be a paradise for women. When they told Mr. Singh this he nodded his head cynically and sighed. "If only that were true; if only that were true."

That evening, as Allingham's crew had their meal Francis regaled them with the story of the special visitors.

"She's a beauty." He grinned and scooped beans onto a plate, which Rosario now seemed to be serving at every meal, much to Hobbs's dismay. The old jailor muttered at the Mexican cook as she glared at him from time to time. The old boy was back in the dog house again.

Allingham ignored him and thought of the lady. She was indeed a beauty.

"And that fellow with the turban, that Arab, he's a nice sort."

"Not an Arab, a Sikh." Allingham spoke into his plate and wondered what effect the meal would have on Hobbs. He was grateful to have his own room.

"Same difference, all wear them turbans." Francis shrugged as he pushed his plate away. He poured beer for himself and the

Irishmen who were getting ready for their night on patrol.

"No, it's not." Allingham looked at the young lad. Sometimes he wondered at the young deputy's ignorance. He felt talkative this night. "Could not be any more different."

"Really? How so, Captain?" Francis did not like to be ignorant or considered a fool. He wanted to learn some things from the captain, from all of them, as they seemed to know so much more than he. Francis, by his own admission, was a bumpkin.

"Sikhs are from India. Arabs are from Arabia. They both wear turbans but that's where it ends. Sikhs live by the code of the saint-soldier. Always controlling internal vices and constantly immersed in virtues. They are the best of human kind."

"Well, I'll be go to hell." Francis stroked his chin and looked at the Irishmen. "Saint-soldiers?"

Allingham looked on as he ate. "That man could cut all our throats faster than you could pull your six shooter." He stood up and brushed the crumbs from his lap. "So you'd better show the lady due respect."

Francis watched him walk out the door.

"Saint-soldier. I'll be go to hell."

Rebecca was animated that evening as they dined. Her father smiled at Mr. Singh as he watched his daughter speak enthusiastically of the settlement. He was pleased and guarded. She was so much like her mother it constantly astounded him, and Mr. Singh's influence had not been lost on her. Rebecca was an indefatigable philanthropist, and now she had renewed energy by what she'd seen of Allingham's successes.

"Father, you must come down and see what they've done. It is remarkable! Isn't it, Mr. Singh?"

"It is, Kaur."

"So, this man, Allingham. Englishman?"

"I don't know, Father. He's an American. I don't know what his family was before that. You know the Americans. They're, well, they're Americans."

He knew not to tease his daughter about men. They'd formed a truce over the years. Halsted thought his daughter should be married by now, but no one ever seemed to fulfil her expectations. It was a bit of a disappointment to the Englishman, as he'd known at least half a dozen acceptable candidates, but Rebecca never saw anything in them. Now that they were in the wilds of Arizona, the prospects were even more bleak.

"He's not married." Robert Halsted spoke at the table.

"No, Father, he's not." She could tell where he was going. He was always calculating. He wanted Rebecca married. Not to get rid of her; to the contrary, he wanted grandchildren before he was too old to enjoy and spoil them. He wanted them very badly.

"Not surprising." He looked on at Mr. Singh with a half-smile. "Terse fellow and, frankly, one of the ugliest men I've ever seen."

"Father!" She smiled. She knew her father was not malicious, but he often said what other people thought. "That's not kind. He, he's not so much rude as he's, well, awkward, I believe. He's been with the brutes for so long, I don't know that he knows how to make idle or polite conversation, and he can't help, certainly, how he looks."

"Rebecca, he's a lawman. He's not . . ."

"Not what?" She liked to spar with him, and neither became angry when engaged in such arguments.

Mr. Singh excused himself. He did not agree with Robert Halsted on these issues.

Rebecca was a grown woman and independent-minded and wise beyond her young years. It was evident to them all that she was interested, perhaps even a little smitten, with the ugly lawman. But that was her business and Mr. Singh did not want to discuss it further.

Halsted spoke to the back of the Sikh's turban as the Indian walked out. "He . . . frankly, Rebecca, I don't know that he has much, well, *range,* my child. He doesn't seem to know or have any interest in anything beyond police work. Dreadfully dull subject."

"I know, Father. I know you've always expected my life to turn a certain way. I should marry a man like you or Mr. Singh, I know that. That is your greatest blessing and curse on me." She stood up and walked around the table and kissed him on top of his bald head. "You two have set the bar too high, Father. It is hard enough for a woman to find a man as good as her father. I have two wonderful fathers. There is no one in the world, no man yet born, who can hold a candle to both of you."

She cut a cigar for him and held a match as he drew on it. "This Allingham, I don't know, Father. He is confounding. He is the most confounding man I've ever known."

■ ■ ■ ■

Mr. Singh sat down beside his partner as the man stared pensively into the fire. Halsted acknowledged him and went back to his reverie. He needed to talk.

"Do you remember that chap, Bankes?"

"The sergeant. Oh, yes." Mr. Singh poked the fire and sat back down. He sipped his coffee.

"I was thinking of him. Remember, we put him up for the VC and he was the first one to be awarded it posthumously?"

"I remember." Mr. Singh did not like to talk of the mutiny, but his friend would sometimes bring it up, especially when he was worried over something. And now he was worried over Rebecca.

"He was a mean and crusty old devil, wasn't he?"

Mr. Singh remembered the man only too well. He'd been in the army since the age of ten. He had loved it, but was the worst martinet either had ever known, especially for a sergeant. Being autocratic was generally a trait reserved for officers. Sergeants could be tough, but they were rarely sadistic.

"He gave my men a bad time."

"Remember how he died?"

Of course Mr. Singh remembered every detail, as he had witnessed it. The rebels had cut him to pieces and he bled out before they could mount a rescue. He knew that Halsted knew it, as well, and also that it was a rhetorical question. Singh was his sounding board.

"He died saving the men he tortured most. Remember how terrible he was to my Sikhs?"

"Yes." Halsted poured another scotch and sipped it as he stared into the fire.

Mr. Singh continued. "I remember when he was near death, when he knew he was going to die. It was then that he became most alive. He even called me sir. He never called me sir. He would only call me captain." Mr. Singh smiled. "He could not bear to call an Indian sir."

"This Allingham chap. What do you make of him?"

"I don't know. He is rude, but not unintelligent." He understood why Halsted had brought up the sergeant from their army days. "There is something decent about him, though. He seems lost. He seems to be in some crisis or funk, something unnatural. He seems to be here for some particular purpose, but," Mr. Singh shrugged, "what that is, I do not know."

"I don't like it."

The Indian poked the fire again and sat back down. He thought of Rebecca and was confused as well by her interest in the lawman. Mr. Singh had spent his entire life pursuing humility. Vanity was a vice to avoid always, and in this pursuit he'd done well, and these qualities he'd tried to pass on to Rebecca. He was convinced that it was why she'd been so choosy about men. Now she seemed to be choosing one that was the opposite of what she'd known and lived by, at least in this one respect. He was heartened by the fact that the policeman's physical traits had not dissuaded Rebecca. She was a beauty, and only other beauties had ever been presented to her. Handsome young men who'd perfectly complement her in a portrait frame. No, Rebecca was not superficial. She'd not worried over the physical attributes of her suitors in all the time she'd had any, and that was going on more than a decade.

Allingham seemed to hold nothing in the way of a virtue or quality that should be found appealing to Rebecca Halsted. He wondered at that. She was a treasure and he trusted Rebecca's instincts regarding men. She'd had so many suitors, and there'd been a few good ones over the years. Singh, like

Halsted, could not understand what the policeman could offer.

Allingham the man. He *was* lost. He was intelligent and all-consumed — as was the British sergeant those many years ago — with his work; with carrying out the tasks at hand. There was some appeal, some nobility, in that, but beyond that, he could not see anything remotely captivating or even mildly interesting about Allingham.

Granted, Allingham was certainly a fair man, unlike the soldier. They'd known that well enough from the stories and the demeanor of his men. Francis, for example, was not cruel to the prisoners, and that was largely a credit to Francis, but it was also due to Allingham. Because of his leadership, how he treated his men, how he trained them, the fact that he led by example, was all Allingham. The same held true for the Irishmen. They were good men, but they were superior lawmen, and that was due to Allingham's leadership, no doubt.

Even the Mexican cook was not a nameless servant. She was part of the crew that Allingham had put together. In the little time he'd spent among them, he could tell. It was not unlike his own company in the army. Both he and Halsted were superior officers with superior men. It all came down to being a good leader, and Allingham was clearly a good one.

"Robert." He waited for his old friend's attention. "There is something we do not know about this Allingham, but his business is his own. He is doing good work in the settlement and he is a moral man. I believe we must let Rebecca pursue what she wants. She is a grown woman and a smart woman. She will know the way."

Robert Halsted looked up from his drink. What Mr. Singh was suggesting was really no different than anything else they'd ever done regarding Rebecca. They gave her full control of her life. "A policeman." He shook his head slowly. "A bloody policeman."

The Sikh smiled. "Robert, you did not expect to find a prince or, at the least, a duke, out here for Rebecca. Not out here in the wilderness."

"No, no." They'd both been plagued by the notion, for as long as they'd been in Arizona. She should have been tucked away in a first-class boarding school when she was young, mixing with people more akin to her own station in life. She should have been associating with the wealthy aristocracy of New England, or at least with the nouveau riche.

Even in America there were people who could match them in culture and station. Robert Halsted had no reservations about Rebecca finding an American. He liked the Americans. It was why he'd come to America. There had been a number of them. Granted, not recently, but when she was at her most appealing as a young debutante, a woman primed for marriage. But none had caught her eye or, more importantly, her heart. She could never find a man to equal her fathers.

They had taken her around to the best schools, and she would have none of it, insisting instead on remaining with them even when the living was rough. They knew it would eventually come to this. It was all backward and now Rebecca was getting older; far beyond the expected age to marry.

But Allingham was a worse prospect than Robert Halsted could ever imagine. He'd resigned himself to the idea of Rebecca marrying an older man, as that seemed to be all there was left to her. Certainly younger men no longer interested her. She was too much for them, in her maturity, intellect and worldliness to make a successful marriage. But Allingham? He had nothing, to the Englishman's mind, to offer his daughter.

He was most definitely not worldly, at

least beyond the world of the gutter, or engaging, or handsome, and he was not much younger than Halsted and the Sikh.

He didn't mind so much that Allingham had no money, the concept of marrying into wealth had stopped bothering him years ago, and he was expecting to bestow a significant dowry on his daughter. It was the primary reason he worked so hard. It was a damned vexing problem.

"You don't suppose it's still possible to ship her off somewhere? Italy or France or even back to England?" He grinned sheepishly at Mr. Singh as he already knew the answer.

Mr. Singh smiled. "I am not a gambling man, Robert, but if I were, I would not make such a wager."

CHAPTER VI:
ONE-EYED SAL

One-Eyed Sal was the other madam in Canyon Diablo and the source of constant anxiety for French Annie. She ran the nice whorehouse. She was always pleasant, never raised her voice, and her girls acted in kind.

Sal really had two eyes, but one was lazy and seemed to move about with a will of its own. In her early years, when she was appealing, she'd often wear an eye patch, as some of her customers were put off by the eye during the act. These were the few men who actually regarded their whores as human beings, and would like to look them in the eye. The Mexicans called her camaleón as the lazy eye reminded them of the creature from Africa. Sal received Allingham in her normal calm, quiet way. She'd give the lawman no trouble. Fact was, she welcomed the changes he'd made, as did some of the gaming house owners and at least one saloon keeper. They were tired of the constant shootings and fighting and violence. Every time a man was murdered, commerce would drop off; the idiots would be distracted and have to take a look at the carnage and brag and boast about it. And when there was a sizable gun battle, it could ruin business for an entire night.

They were fine with the new marshal if it meant they could make money, and five dollars a day was a bargain. They'd have to pay a bouncer nearly that much and the money was going to the overall improvement of the town, as neither Allingham nor his men were pocketing any of the proceeds. It was evident that they were not corrupt and no one, not even madams and miscreants, wanted to live with the odor of waste and decay, human or otherwise. Everyone agreed that even the fly and rat population had diminished since the arrival of the new marshal.

Sal had no problem with the ban on children in the brothels, either. She encouraged them to go to Rebecca Halsted's safe house. It was better, really, for commerce as the whores were less distracted by their crying children. No, she had no problem with Allingham.

But Sal was no angel. And on a clear day at

noon, Allingham and Francis were given ample evidence of the reserved madam's true nature. They could hear the fight from a block away and soon stood over the two wild women, Sal bleeding and Annie mostly unclothed. Hanks of each woman's hair abounded on the street around them and they were both thoroughly, like two powdered pastries, coated in dust.

They were fighting over the same old issue: the Princess. The special prostitute was a constant source of anxiety between the two madams. She was the prettiest whore in the territory. She wasn't young: thirtyish, even, perhaps a little older, with hair that grew well below her backside and skin the color of porcelain.

The Princess was smarter and shrewder than the madams and no one knew anything about her, where she hailed from or even her real name. Her accent, most likely affected, suggested the south, perhaps Louisiana, but the Princess never told anyone anything about herself. She'd play the madams against each other and they derived no income from her at all, as she kept everything she made for herself. Additionally, the Princess required a hot bath twice a day, her own room with a clean change of sheets every morning and a full time servant, all paid for by the house. Her toady doted on her constantly, as he'd been with her for many years.

He was known as The Ape as he looked very much like such a primate, with a small-ish head and large brow that hooded beady, undersized brown eyes. No one liked him as he was constantly complaining about the service his princess was receiving. He was haughty and terse and superior, and every-one disliked him. But he was under the protection of the Princess, and subse-quently, under the protection of whichever madam had claim to the special whore at the time.

Nothing was ever good enough for his princess; the bath water too hot or too cold, the sheets too stiff or not clean enough. Er-rant hairs in things seemed to set him off most, and he'd become downright violent at anyone's teasing. He loved his princess and was completely devoted to her. She returned his affections as one would a faith-ful canine.

The Princess added to her appeal as she was also sterile, the happy result of a botched abortion at the age of sixteen, so she would not trouble either madam with yet another unwanted pregnancy or be out of commission during her confinement.

Alas, despite all the expense for the royal treatment, she was a great draw, as the customers dreamed of bedding the famous Princess. They would invariably grow tired of queuing up for her and most would settle for one of the less desirable harlots. This was the Princess's greatest attribute; she was slow and methodical, servicing only a limited number of men each night. There were always plenty of customers left over for the other girls who were ready and waiting as second prize.

This day's battle was over One-Eyed Sal's latest recruitment tactic: she offered to actually pay the Princess to work in her bordello, much to the consternation of French Annie. It was scandalous. Who paid whores? The whores always, always paid the madams. The slavery, disguised as indentured servitude, had worked for eons. There was no call to change it now.

Francis jogged up, ready to place himself between them, until Allingham put up a cautionary hand. It was one of the first rules in policing; never get between ruffians fighting, even if the ruffians were women.

The marshal watched for a few moments, letting them wear themselves out, and finally called out, as a Master of Hounds would at the commencement of a hunt to control his pack. The women stopped, still holding onto each other, hair, clothes, fingers and arms intertwined. They gazed vacantly at Allingham, like a pair of Pavlovian dogs.

He cast his eyes over the crowd. This was what disgusted him most about humanity. The spectators had that same demented fascination that one sees at a dog or cock fight, entranced, gorged on the violence and depravity. Whenever he saw the mob in its puerile glee, he imagined what it must have been like in Rome, in the days of the Caesars and gladiators, very little among the baser sort, ever changed. They were leering and cheering, and now thoroughly annoyed with him, as he was ruining their fun. "You may continue to fight, but I want to warn you, fines are mounting. You are both up to thirty five dollars apiece. Keep fighting if you want to pay more."

He turned and walked away. The women stopped. They looked at each other and then at the marshal's back as he strolled away. For the first time in her life, French Annie was speechless.

Francis regarded his new boss as they strolled away. He had a lot to learn and the man was an amazing fount of knowledge, even if he shared little and spoke less.

"Captain, can't seem to keep the children from the brothels. Can't seem to get a handle on it." He smiled his normal smile, looking at a pretty woman carrying a parcel; he tipped his hat and wished her a good day. Allingham had not noticed her.

Allingham thought on it. He'd been distracted and hadn't bothered to tell his men of his plan. The whores' children were on his mind, though. Of all the illegal enterprises conjured up by man, Allingham found prostitution the most loathsome. He'd fought in the great Civil War to free blacks, yet women it seemed, could continue to be enslaved. It made no sense to him, and he did his best back in New York to push them off his beat whenever possible.

Allingham liked women, loved them, really. It was not the fault of a woman that he was alone. He simply lacked the capacity for intimacy and no longer thought much of it. In his twenties he tried to find a wife and have a family and he'd done a fair job at persuading a woman to say yes, but as with all such endeavors involving human interaction, Allingham managed to muck it up. The engagement was broken and after that, Allingham just kind of gave up. He did this with anything that he could not control, and he could not control, or woo or capture the heart of a woman, so he simply stopped trying.

But he never had animosity toward women. He liked them, lusted for them from time to time, but he'd never been able to square it in his mind that women and sex should be traded like a commodity, like a piece of meat hanging in a shop window to be carved up and sold piecemeal. It was thoroughly repugnant to him. He would never satisfy his basic urges in a brothel, and thought men who did weak and of the worst character.

He hated everything about the brothels, but most especially the madams and pimps. He hated them for their predatory practices, their malice, and inhumanity. He'd seen plenty of what madams and pimps would do to whores to keep them in line, from the beatings and murders to the introduction of addiction: alcohol, laudanum, opium. He had nothing but contempt for them.

"I'll have it managed in a week. Don't trouble yourself over it. Just keep fining the madams."

"Yes, Captain."

Francis was a good complement to Allingham, a polar opposite, except that he, like Allingham, was tough. He could handle himself and he was fearless, but otherwise the two could have not been more differently made.

Francis was handsome and young, always pleasant, curious and courteous. He dressed plainly and always had a kind word. He was an uneducated man, but that was more due to his youth than lack of care. He'd not had much opportunity for learning, though his mind was sharp and he could read and write well. Study never interested him but now, going into his third decade, with his new boss showing him how very little he himself knew about life and the world around him, Francis had a renewed interest in learning new things.

"Those madams are a pair of wildcats, eh, Captain?" Francis was learning when to pry or at least attempt to pull things from the captain.

"Hmm."

"You didn't go in and pull 'em apart, I see."

Allingham gave the young man a sideways look. Reaching up with his hand he pulled his rubbery lips back, revealing a gap between his teeth. "My first year as a copper. Two Irishmen, bigger than ours, and I stepped between them." He pointed an index finger skyward. "First and last time."

Francis grinned as he nodded. "I see, Captain, I see."

They all ate dinner together, before the Irishmen were to go on duty. Francis smiled down at his plate. For three days now there had been no beans. Rosario moved about, fussing over the men and humming. When she'd pass Hobbs she touched him lightly on the shoulder. Francis thought about teasing them and then decided against it. He'd never before seen a menu change based upon lovers' moods.

Little Janie was better, too, as Francis had spent his evenings teaching her to read and write. He found a slate and chalk and now she could easily spell her name and identify the most rudimentary words. She knew the alphabet by heart.

His next trip to Flagstaff he'd get her a primer and some children's books. He was very proud of his little charge and she no longer looked on him with corruption in her eyes. He was hopeful.

A dapper man stood in the open doorway and removed his hat. He was French Annie's partner and owned a gaming house next door to the madam's bordello. He was a tall man, dressed beyond his station in life and in this way he stood out as much as did Allingham.

He was foppish, more like a riverboat gambler than a desert rat, with his Chinese silk vest, scarlet red, adorned with little gold dragons throughout. He sported a planter's hat of beaver fur and black pinstripe trousers and matching long frockcoat. He wore a six shooter and it was silver colored with pearl grips. He reeked of some manner of hair treatment.

"Captain Allingham?"

"Marshal Allingham. We are dining." Allingham did not look up from his meal.

"I see, sir, and I am sorry for the intrusion."

"Then don't." Allingham wiped his great lips with a napkin. He did not stand up.

"Don't what?"

"Intrude." He pointed with his fork to Hobbs.

"Make an appointment with my secretary." The man, sufficiently humiliated stood awkwardly, not certain what to do. Allingham had made his point. He was finished eating anyway and decided to give the man an audience now. He'd likely not have the answers he was looking for, and it was just as well to not delay the inevitable. He'd disappoint the intruder now.

Everyone was present; the Irishmen prepared to go on patrol, Hobbs eating, Francis preparing his evening tutoring of Janie, and Rosario, moving about, constantly working. It would be good for them to see Allingham perform a little. He waited for the man to turn away, go back to his gambling house. He called out to him.

"What do you want?"

He stood hunched over, hat in both hands, obsequiousness personified. "Oh, thank you, sir." He walked inside a little too quickly, knocking against a table. Rosario offered him a cup of coffee and he took it, releasing the hat with one hand.

He regarded little Janie who gave him a sideways grin. She knew him well and had refused to have relations with him which vexed him, and now she was out of the question altogether. A lost conquest.

He moved his gaze on to Francis who, for a change, was not smiling, but rather looking at the gambler as if he were deciding whether or not to gut him. He loathed such men, probably as much, perhaps even more so, than did Allingham. He saw the corruption in the gambler's eyes as he ogled little Janie. What sort of son of a bitch would bed a twelve year old?

The gambler blanched. He caught his

breath, steadying himself against the table. He looked at Allingham as if just recalling the reason for his visit. He was angry with himself. His lustful thoughts were an unnecessary distraction, he was convinced that he'd shown his hand and certain Allingham could read his mind. He knew absolutely that the curly-haired young deputy could. He averted his eyes, trying his best to focus on his hat's brim and the business at hand.

"I, I just wanted to talk a little about your plans, what we, the folks down at the far end of town, have in mind to help you out." He produced a cigar and slobbered all over it before clenching it between his teeth. He offered one to Allingham who refused. Francis stood up and plucked it from the gambler's grasp before he could return it to his pocket.

Young Francis liked cigars, but never wasted money buying them. He smelled it and clipped the end with his big knife, letting the gambler light it for him, enjoying the dancing flame held between them in the gambler's wildly trembling hand.

Francis, snakelike, struck at the effeminate hand, engulfing it with his own tough and sinewy one, holding it still to light the cigar. He slowly squeezed as he energetically puffed on the cigar, making sure the exhalations from his effort were directed into the gambler's eyes before releasing his hold. He sat back down next to Janie.

The gambler recovered and spoke through a suppressed sneeze. "But there's a matter of some delicacy." He waited for some reaction from Allingham. He got none and continued. "This business today, with Annie and Sal. It's got to stop. It simply has got to stop."

Allingham ignored him. Then thought better of it. The gambler was wearing on his patience. "Do you have some sort of complaint or point to make?"

The gambler struggled to find his words. He was used to controlling the conversation, controlling the situation. He was so rattled that he lost track of the point he needed to make about Annie and Sal.

"We've, well, to be frank, Marshal, we are all very appreciative of what you've done. Murders are down by half . . ."

"Seventy-five percent."

"Yes, of course, of course. But there's a matter of all these pesky ordinances, and fines, and the forced labor. It's, it's, well, how do I say this, Marshal, it's a bit much for the folks around here." Feeling bolder, more confident now that the words were flowing, as the gambler featured himself an orator, even aspiring to someday enter politics as he had all the qualifications in the way of greed and conspiratorial thinking, he continued with mock conviction, "This is a free society, here in the West. We understand and appreciate why things must be more restrictive in such a place as New York. There being too many people there — *and* all the foreigners, and we all know how badly they behave." He looked at the Irishmen and felt the sweat run down his back. "But out here, it is sort of . . . how do the French say it, liaise faire?" He grinned and Allingham sat, stone-faced. The gambler continued. "A sort of live and let live mentality."

"Oh?"

"Yes, well, if a man wants to act in a certain way, well, you know, these men, they are used to freedom. They work hard. This is a hard land, they want to blow off some steam. They want to have a little fun, and well, frankly, sir . . ."

"Do you mean by to live and let live to allow men to act like savages, shoot and cut each other up, rob, cheat, steal, relieve themselves in the streets, act the fool and make it intolerable for the rest of society to go about its business? Do you mean by to live and let live to have women treated like pack animals and abused and inoculated with diseases? To have little children constantly subjected to depravity? Is that what you mean?"

"Oh, well, sir, you'll have to agree, those are some rare and isolated examples. It's just, well, Marshal, ever since you came here, well, business is off. The men don't want to come into town any longer and spend money. They don't seem to find much entertainment these days. It has, frankly, put quite a kink in our collective ropes."

Allingham was finished. "Nothing we have done is out of the ordinary. Nothing we have done has been unreasonable, it is . . ."

"Un-American!" The gambler straightened his back and jutted forth his square jaw; he was feeling bold. He immediately regretted cutting the marshal off.

"Un-American?"

"Yes, that's, that's what I said. You, you Yankee carpet baggers, coming here and imposing your will. Imposing a bunch of government regulations and restricting the free will of the people. It's, it's un-American."

"Get out." Allingham pointed toward the door. The gambler smiled. He tried to recover but was going to get nowhere with verbal persuasion and knew it. He removed his hat from the table, revealing a wad of bills. "Oh, look at that."

Allingham frowned dismissively. "It's not ours." He cast his eyes about the room.

"Well, just some new-found wealth, then. No harm tucking that into your vest pocket, Marshal." He grinned at Allingham and then at the rest of his staff.

"Hobbs, give the gentleman a receipt for this." He handed over the wad of bills to his secretary. "We'll put it toward the foundling's fund." He addressed the gambler. "And by the way, please tell the madams that all children less than sixteen will be removed to Flagstaff tomorrow. Any child caught in the company of a prostitute, or in any of the brothels, will be removed to our foundling's home."

The man stood, agog, as did the staff. None of them had been prepared for this and Francis could not contain himself, blurting out an "I'll be go to hell."

"But they're not foundlings! The whores take care of their children. Miss Halsted has a place for them to go. You can't take a child from its mother. It cannot be done!"

Allingham looked at little Janie. The gambler read his mind.

"We aren't. We're moving them to a proper

home in Flagstaff. The mothers are welcome to join them. There is room for all."

Francis stood up, grinning. He grabbed the dude by the neck, turning him around to face the door. "I think we've talked enough for one day, mister. It's time you went on back to your hole in the ground. Get crawlin'."

The gambler stood, red-faced. He was furious. "You bastards. You'll not get away with this. I'll contact the governor. I'll contact, I'll contact . . ." He couldn't finish his sentence. Like his partner, French Annie, Allingham had rendered him speechless. As he struggled, Allingham remembered something else.

"Oh, and by the way. We'll be delivering a trader's application to you tomorrow. Have it completed by the end of the week."

"A what?"

"A trader's application; for your trader's license. It helps us determine who is doing business in our town. Name, date and place of birth, all the particulars so that we know that we don't have any fugitives in our midst."

The gambler stormed away.

Hobbs grinned. "What's a trader's application, Captain?"

"Don't know yet. I just made it up."

■ ■ ■ ■

The madam smoked and watched the man pack through the haze in the room. "So, you're yellow."

The gambler didn't look up as he stuffed another silk vest into the gaudy carpet bag. Periodically, he rubbed his sore hand. "No, not yellow, just like my neck the length it is." He looked about for any items he might have missed. He looked at the old prostitute intently. "There's plenty more places to open a gambling house. Don't need this shit now."

"And what of our plans?" She had always hated him, but now her hatred was turning to rage. "You said . . ."

"I said a lot of things. One of my many vices; I say a lot of things. Some might say I'm full of hot air." He looked her in the eye. Why he made her the offer he'd never know. He himself wasn't a bad looking man and with enough money, he'd been able to bed down with younger women. This one held no appeal to him now.

"That bridge won't be finished for another six months and this place'll be good for another six after. There's plenty opportunity, just be patient. This bastard won't last much longer. Can't."

"Oh, I'm not so sure of that." He grinned as he lit a cigar. "He's . . . he's different, this one. He can't be bought, he's fearless, and he's got some good men. Can't figure it out. Never met a man yet who didn't have some weakness; this one doesn't seem to have a one."

One-Eyed Sal looked on a little surprised. There seemed to be an attitude of reverence in his eyes. He noticed her watching him and had a thought. "You'd better beat it out of here before Annie sees us together." His eyes darted about, as if he'd catch her peeking out at the pair of them from behind the door.

"She knows about us. Annie knows everything; little bitch." She suddenly appeared hurt. She hadn't expected much to come of this liaison, but now that he was leaving, she became a little sad. "Where will you go?" She honestly wanted to know.

"California. Not sure where yet, but California. Sick of this dust and dry damned land. Somewhere by the sea."

This made her feel worse. She'd been there. She loved the sea. She thought about her own situation. "I could go along with you."

"No, you couldn't." He sounded cruel and

knew it and then thought better of it. It was not healthy to get Sal riled. "It's just, Sal," he reached up and touched the cheek below the wandering eye. He patted her gently. "I've got a lot hangin' over me, Sal. That marshal, I can't give him my information. I got to stay low or they'll have me back in Fort Smith and, like I said, I like my neck this length." He grinned uneasily. "A man like that, even if I leave, I'll bet he'd either come after me or set the other law dogs on me. Can't have it, Sal, can't have it." He fiddled with a cravat. "I gotta travel light, gotta travel alone. Sorry, Sal."

He returned to his packing and was satisfied that he'd finished. He looked around the makeshift room. It was a dump and he'd be glad to be shed of it. "You ought to move on, too." He meant this. He was a snake and a bad man, but not completely evil. He had some regard for Sal. He liked her more than he did Annie even though he'd bedded Annie a lot more. Sal was special.

She ignored him and finished her smoke. She thought about what he'd said. At least she wasn't wanted anywhere for a hanging offence.

"Well, I'll give him another week. If he's not dead by then, I'll see what I can do to make it happen."

He patted Sal's hand with the one Francis had not manhandled. When she wasn't puffing on a smoke and talking of knocking off US Marshals, she looked for all the world like someone's mother and this is how she appeared to the gambler now.

CHAPTER VII:
THE PRINCESS AND
THE CUTTHROAT

Eli Crump walked his mule into the settlement of Canyon Diablo on a late afternoon, fairly giddy with the prospect of spending his fortune. He'd been working hard, alone in the desert, for more than ninety days with nothing but a mule for company.

He went to the saloon first, got drunk enough to feel good but not so much as to be useless. He asked where the Princess was working and was directed to One-Eyed Sal's.

It was early enough in the day that the queuing for the lovely whore had not yet started, as the Princess did not do commerce before five in the evening. She rested until then, as she worked until three every morning, took a bath, then slept until one, took another bath, ate, and counted her money.

Eli broke her routine by getting past her minion, The Ape, and called out to the woman fresh from her bathing regimen.

She cut him off. Eli was the most despicable man any of the whores had ever known. He stunk even after bathing, which in itself was remarkable and rare, as they'd encountered their fair share of gamey men. But the Chinese girls down at the bathhouse always got them clean.

Something about Eli made him reek of dead fish all the time, and that was only his body odor. His breath was worse as he still retained teeth that were as black as tar, which only slightly masked the stench emanating from his stomach. Every exhalation smelled of a gut pile rotting too long in the sun. He smelled like a tanning factory in July, and nothing could get the taint out of the whores' noses after one of his visits. He was a thoroughly repulsive man.

"Now, Princess, wait, just wait. Just hold on a minute." He quickly pulled out a nugget of gold the size of a walnut. The sight of it raised one of the Princess's eyebrows.

"Where'd you get that?" She stood up as she combed her hair, dropping the towel to the dirty floor. Eli nearly fell over. The Princess had a habit of doing such things. It was one of her cruel jokes. She used her beauty as a torture device, as effectively as a riding crop or cat-o-nine tails on her willing victims.

"Oh, here and there." He was pleased as he gazed at her, half-drunk with lust. He swallowed hard and tried to control his shaking. He'd gotten her attention. She was interested, had actually spoken words that did not feature profanity or epithets.

"What do you want for it?"

"One night."

She breathed deeply through her mouth, as he was stinking up her room already. She swallowed hard as the idea of him on her made her want to gag.

"One hour."

"Two."

"Don't push your luck. One hour." She held out her hand and he dropped the nugget into her outstretched palm. She looked it over, hefted it and knew it was rich, knew it was more than she made in months. "Plus, you have to get a bath and do *something, anything,* about that rotting mouth."

He clamped lips over scum-covered teeth and looked on at the beauty standing before him. She gave him a little show, cocking a leg provocatively high on the edge of the bed. She watched him turn to jelly as she languidly climbed onto her bed and reclined on the freshly laundered sheets. The Princess rarely wore clothes and now she lay, outstretched, her long hair, like Lady Godiva's, strategically placed so that it covered her more intimate parts. The show was over for now.

"Deal." He spit in his hand and held it out for the Princess to shake, to seal the bargain.

"You've *got* to be kidding." She waved him off dismissively. "Go, go away, before I change my mind. Scrub, scrub like your life depended on it. Hire as many Chinese girls as you can. Get yourself as clean as possible and come back at five."

He turned away, looking doubtfully over his shoulder as his great nugget disappeared into the strongbox next to the Princess's bed, the key around her neck securing the lock. At least Eli had paid in full; she could not change her mind.

Like a pair of nervous newlyweds, they separately prepared for the evening, or at least, the hour of bliss. The Princess sent The Ape out for things to burn: oils, candles, anything to mask the stench. She used most of a bottle of perfume, liberally dousing her sheets. She dumped the remainder on a posy, readied at the head of the bed. She considered stuffing cotton up her

160

nose then thought better of it. A good dose of laudanum at the appointed hour would, hopefully, dull her senses so that she might very well remember little of the encounter. She could only hope. At least she'd only have one customer this night. She'd treat herself to the rest of the evening off. She'd bathe as soon as the prospector was gone.

She had her lackey pull the curtains to darken the room. Only candlelight illuminated the place and this she thought would help, as she would be unable to see too much of Eli during the act. He was as off-putting to look at as he was to smell.

He made his way to the baths and hired three Chinese girls to work him over. They scrubbed and scrubbed with lye soap, changing the bathwater three times. The girls would sniff him periodically, checking their progress, nodding doubtfully and starting again. He was a revolting bastard, indeed, and even the poor Chinese girls had difficulty controlling their gag reflex. They'd had dirty men to clean by the dozens but Eli was the worst any had ever seen.

Turning their attention to his mouth, they created a concoction of coal oil, alcohol and spearmint which he gargled and spat and gargled again. They scrubbed his teeth with soap and powdered sand until his gums fairly bled. Three teeth came out as a result of the effort. These he spat resolutely into an empty whiskey glass, feeling the gaps and rotting effluent now freed by the dead molars with his tongue.

By five he was as clean as possible, wearing a new shirt, trousers, and underwear. Even his beard was clean with the matted hair, knots and food remnants combed away. The hair on his head was combed and even trimmed a little. He waited outside the Princess's door until her man called him in.

Finally, at a half past five, he was there, in her little lair, her bordello of happiness and his heart beat so strongly, even painfully, in his chest that it radiated up his neck and past his ears until he could easily count his pulse banging away at his eardrums. She was breathtaking, and now she reclined, like Bathsheba, her long tresses moved aside, revealing all her womanly charms.

She was so clean, as she lay, legs splayed, feet bare, the soles pink as a baby's. Even her feet, toenails and fingernails were clean. She smelled heavenly.

She smiled a decadent smile at old Eli; she seemed to be enjoying this a little. He was mesmerized; she could do anything to him at this point. She could make him end his own life if she had it in her to do so; but she didn't. He was a pretty good prospector and if she could endure an hour with him, she could get him to come back with chunk after chunk of the yellow gold. She'd be rich after half a dozen sessions.

"Pour us a drink, Eli."

With shaking hands, he poured. She'd never before called him by his Christian name. He handed her a glass, tossing his own down in one gulp.

"Easy, there, Eli. It's good wine, but it's my own recipe, it has something extra in it and I, we, don't want you nodding off before getting down to business, do we?" Her lips curled into a wicked grin.

He smiled and the wine and laudanum cocktail had an immediate effect, as Eli was not a drinking man. He'd spend months alone with no spirits and his body had grown unaccustomed to it. The new drink added to the amount he'd consumed in the saloon, those effects not yet wearing off, he was fairly dopy after the first glass. The Princess had a thought. If she'd get him drunk enough, perhaps she'd not have to do anything but lie on her bed and speak to him as if he were a human being. He could sleep through his hour.

But the Princess was not so lucky as Eli, with a sudden burst of energy, resolutely stood over her, lowering the suspenders. He was ready and then, just as suddenly, stopped, as nature had come calling at a most inopportune time. He looked around for a chamber pot.

The stench soon hit her. Stuffing the posy under her nose, she breathed in deeply.

Turning her head, side to side, she spoke with authority. "Not in here, Eli. She pointed past him toward the bedroom door. Go on down to the jakes out back."

The Princess gulped wine as she waited for him to return.

"Jesus Christ! I'll be go to hell!" Francis looked on at the room as Allingham conducted his investigation. They'd been called by The Ape, as the assistant knew well what happened to murdered whores. He loved his Princess too much to have her unceremoniously dumped in the desert.

Allingham turned to the hulking man, blubbering inconsolably.

"When did you find her?"

"Half hour ago."

They sent him to cry in the parlor and returned their attention to the Princess's room.

Allingham suddenly reeled. Becoming overwhelmed was an unknown emotion to him. He'd seen many ghastly things in his time and the Princess's condition was terrible, but not, by far, the worst.

It reminded him of his own situation. He'd be a corpse in a bed like this soon, if he didn't do something about it. He did not want to waste away and die in bed, but somehow could not keep from beating his opponents every time one could potentially kill him. His plan was a failure. He couldn't let anyone kill him now.

He recovered and went about his detective work, turning his attention to the task at hand. Not thinking about dying seemed the only course of action for him these days.

He breathed deeply and coughed, tasting the metallic tang on his tongue; a physical, tactile reminder. He swallowed it, along with his feeling of impending doom.

He looked back to the doorway, now crammed with curious whores. They were excited over the incident and One-Eyed Sal was soon among them, awaiting Allingham's orders.

"Get out." He pointed to the doorway and then at the whores. When they retreated, he closed the door behind them.

"Ain't never seen anything like this,

Captain." Francis was pale, but steady and Allingham was pleased by his reaction and resolve. The young man was shaken but not addled to distraction.

Allingham turned his attention to the Princess, lying on her back, staring up at the rough boards of her bedroom's ceiling. Even in death she was beautiful and now that she was exposed for all to see, Francis felt a little ashamed of his carnal thoughts.

"Let's cover her up, Captain." Francis wanted the distraction to end.

Allingham held up a hand. "Not yet." He looked at Francis. "Move nothing." He did not see a beautiful woman before him; he saw a crime site and he was investigating. He'd seen plenty in his time and each was nothing more than a puzzle to be worked out. He liked a good murder. He could not help himself; he liked to figure them out and catch the murderer.

"It was that Eli done it, don't you think, Captain?"

"No."

"Why not?"

Francis was intrigued. He wanted to learn from the captain who marched past him and down to the baths. Francis followed.

Eli had left his old clothes, even his gun belt and six shooter, and Allingham surveyed them carefully. He pulled Eli's big knife from its sheath; it was clean. It was also dull and Allingham grunted just discernibly.

"Come on." He turned his back to Francis and marched away.

"Where to, Captain?"

"We've got to find that prospector."

Some men directed them to Death Cave, Eli's base camp. Francis knew the place well as the Navajos showed it to him some time ago. It was haunted according to those who believed in such things. The Navajos were proud of it. Many generations ago their ancestors had caught a band of Apache marauders who used the place to hide after hitting their villages.

The Apaches were crafty and soon realized the cave was well hidden and large enough to contain them and all their horses. They would attack the Navajos and then ride down into the canyon and into the cave. Every trace of them would disappear and, for a long time, the Navajos thought it some manner of sorcery. Until one day, a few of their war party heard voices and saw smoke slipping from between thin crevices at the top of the mountain. The Apaches were trapped. The Navajos killed more than forty by burning them alive. Even their horses were destroyed.

It was a fitting place to follow up on a man who'd been involved in the near decapitation of a whore. It made the hair stand up on the back of Francis's neck.

By early morning they found the place and Eli's mule stood outside of the cave still wearing its rack and wandering about unhobbled and untethered. This in itself was a strange sight as Eli was known to fuss over his mule. The animal was his constant companion, yet he'd left her unattended and uncared for.

Francis called into the cave and waited. He ventured farther in, gun drawn as, despite his boss's declaration, he wasn't so certain Eli had not cut the whore's throat. He was ready for the worst. Instead, he found Eli crouched and naked, rocking on his haunches before a roaring camp fire.

Eli ignored them as he stared into the flame, babbling and crying like a child.

"Hey there, Eli, what's new?" Francis squatted across from him as he tucked his six shooter away. It was evident that Eli was no threat to either of them.

Allingham continued to investigate, looking about for clues, finding nothing more than a well ordered camp. Eli had set up housekeeping for an extended stay. Everything had its place as Eli was a house-proud or, at least, a cave-proud, hermit.

"All done, all done." The deranged prospector kept repeating over and over.

"What's all done, Eli? Tell us, old friend, what's all done?"

Allingham interjected in his authoritative tone.

"When did you figure out she was dead, Eli?"

The prospector looked up wildly, as Allingham's question seemed to pull him from his trance. "I didn't kill her, I didn't kill her. I didn't! I loved her. And, and she was lovin' me. She was so beautiful. Clean she was, the cleanest gal I've ever seen, cleaner than a newborn babe. She didn't say bad things when I was on her. She didn't even tell me to hurry up. She let me have my time, take my time. She was so, so beautiful."

He raised his hands, staring into them wildly. He looked as if he was seeing something terrifying as he held them out to Francis and Allingham. They'd been washed clean. Eli's entire body had been washed clean. "Look, look, bloody, bloody, bloody, can't get them clean! Can't get them clean!"

"I know you didn't kill her, Eli." Allingham looked at Francis and then continued. "Do you like being with dead women, Eli?"

The prospector looked up as if Allingham had accused him of fornicating with his own mother. "No! No!" He began to shake and cried into his hands. "My God, my God, what have I done?"

Allingham continued to investigate. Nothing gave him any further evidence. He was satisfied and called Francis to follow him out.

He was preparing to mount up. Francis looked at him, obviously confused. "We ain't taking him in, Captain?"

"No law against being intimate with a corpse, Francis." He looked back at the cave. "Poor devil is done in." And as if it had been a signal, a shot could be heard from within the cave. Francis raced back inside.

He emerged in short order, pale and incredulous. He looked into Allingham's eyes. "Son of a bitch shot himself through the head, Captain. Shot himself right through the goddamned head."

As they rode, Francis confessed his confusion. "All right, what the hell's happening? I don't understand a goddamned thing that's goin' on."

We've got to get the murderer now, Francis."

"And Eli wasn't; yer sure of that?"

"Yes, I'm sure of it. Eli didn't kill her. Eli's only crime was that he fornicated with the Princess after she was dead. But he's no necrophile."

"No what?"

"Necrophile. Someone who has relations with a corpse, or corpses. I thought Eli was one, but he wasn't."

"I'll be go to hell." Francis thought on it and grinned, but he was not amused. "People have relations with dead people. Jesus Christ, Captain. Jesus Christ! Never heard of such a thing."

"Yes, I needed to be sure. Thought I might find corpses in his cave, but there were none. Sometimes necrophiles will keep corpses, collect them, but Eli didn't even have the remains of animals in his cave. He did not have interest in the dead."

"I'll be go to hell."

"Eli just had bad timing, and he was drunk or doped, or both. But he apparently left the woman's room, then came back in after the Princess was murdered. He did the deed and that's why she was so good to him. She was dead, so she couldn't tell him to hurry up or how bad he stunk or otherwise give him hell. She was so kind to him because she was dead."

"How'd you know he didn't kill her, Captain?"

"Her throat was cut with a razor." Allingham rode on, next to Francis. He stared ahead, speaking in a monotone, much as he would if he were testifying in court. "Eli had no use for a razor, he had a beard, and his knife was too dull to produce that kind of a wound. He didn't pick up a razor from the room as he didn't have it on him, and he would have likely left it behind, as he did his gun, belt and knife at the laundry. He was also left-handed and the murderer used his right hand to slash her throat. He cut the Princess from left to right, likely standing over her, facing her, as the bed was pushed against the wall. No one could have come up behind her and cut her throat from behind the head of the bed. A left-handed person would have to contort himself to do that. A left-handed person would have cut her right to left."

"I'll be go to hell. How you know all that, Captain?"

"The wound started from her right. The blood spray from the blade splattered in a pattern on the bed and then on the wall. And there was a wound to her face. She'd been punched in the face, on the left cheek. That was what stunned her. The person hitting her was more likely right-handed, and he was wearing a ring with a sharp edge. It left a little impression on her skin. That's how I know it was a wound from a fist, a right-handed fist."

Allingham looked at Francis, not a little disappointed. "Didn't you see any of that, Francis?"

"No, Captain, sorry. I was lookin' at her tits." He was embarrassed and Allingham grinned a little at the young man's candor.

"And the wound, the cleanness of the wound. It was from a narrow blade, a razor. Eli's knife was big and dull, as I said. And Eli's gun belt was set up for a man who uses his left hand. And, as far as his fornicating; she was dead when he did it. If you would have taken your eyes off her tits for a moment you'd a noticed she was smeared with blood; on her privates, on her torso, that was Eli during the act. It was dark in there and he probably didn't notice due to his inebriated state. He got bloody during the act and spread the blood around. And her wound. It was so deep it was fatal almost instantly, and the fact that she'd been knocked senseless from the punch. Did you see how much blood was around her neck, on the pillow and on the bed? If she hadn't died right away, she'd a moved around, left blood all around, but she just laid there and bled out."

Francis thought on it. "I'll be go to hell. Bouncin' up and down on a corpse. Can't believe that, Captain."

"Yes. And he figured it out himself later. That's why he killed himself. He couldn't bear to think of having relations with a corpse. So, I know he didn't do any of it on purpose. Just at the wrong place at the wrong time."

They rode on and Francis had another confusing thought. He could not understand why they'd ridden all the way out to Eli if he wasn't the killer. "What's next, Captain?"

"We get the assistant. He knows something of it. That's also how I know Eli didn't do it. The strongbox was still there; not forced, but open and empty and the Princess still had the key around her neck, covered in blood. It had not been removed, pulled from around her neck to unlock the box and then replaced. Someone with his own key took it, Francis. It was her assistant, and I wanted to leave, give him enough time to get his affairs in order. I sent word to Hobbs, before we rode out here to find Eli, to arrest him. Mike and Paddy just as likely have him in jail right now. He'll have been caught with all the evidence we need. He was either getting ready to light out of there directly or planning to go up to Flagstaff for the train, I'll bet my paycheck on it."

They rode on and Francis became quiet. He'd never heard of such things and half thought on the idea that Allingham was making it all up. He thought about New York. People fornicating with corpses. It must be a corrupt doggone place. He wondered at Allingham's detective work. How did he know all that? How could he? It was as if he'd been in the room with them when it all happened, yet Francis knew that was not the case. He and the captain were eating dinner when the murder happened.

That was Allingham. Francis was once again amazed at his boss. Any other lawman would have gone with a posse and strung poor old Eli up; hanged him for nothing more than having a ride on a corpse. And that monkey-faced bastard would have gotten away with it, off scott free with all the whore's treasures. Old Allingham was an amazing copper indeed.

He looked at his boss. "Well, one thing's for sure, Captain."

"What's that?"

"She was one pretty whore."

Allingham looked on down the road. "Especially around the tits."

The Ape sat in the cell staring at his lap as Allingham surveyed the items in the lackey's carpet bag. Eli's gold nugget was there and money from the strongbox.

"We even found this, Captain." Hobbs held up a straight razor and Allingham gave it a good look.

"You there," he called over to the Princess's distraught servant. "Why'd you kill her?"

"I didn't! I didn't!" He began to cry and through his sobs he proclaimed his love for her. "I swear to you, I didn't! I swear!"

"So, you didn't kill her, yet you vamoosed with her money and all your worldly possessions, and even had the murder weapon on you."

He stood up, grasped the bars and pushed his ugly monkey face toward Allingham. "I loved her."

"Yes, but something snapped, didn't it? Something. Like Eli. She wouldn't bed you but she'd bed old Eli, the most repulsive man in the land, but she'd never give you one. You got angry about it and killed her.

Didn't you?"

"No, no. That's not true. That's a lie. I never, I never wanted her in that way. I never, I, she was, she was more to me than that. She was . . ." He cried again and then looked up at Allingham. He looked around at the other occupants of the cell. "I'm telling you, you got the wrong man. The murderer is still out there. The murderer is getting away with it." He coughed and cried all the harder. "Please, please, you've got to keep at it, Marshal. You've got to find the right man."

Allingham walked up to him, looking him in the eye. "You're it, and you're going to swing for it." He nodded to Francis. "Get him up to Flagstaff, they'll take it from there."

That evening, Francis regaled his little family with stories of men fornicating with corpses. Told the official name for it. Rosario cringed and refused to believe such a thing could really happen.

He went on to tell them all about the captain and how he figured everything out; laid out the whole murder, just as if he'd been a fly on the wall watching it unfold. Francis grinned. "That old boy, he's going to get his neck stretched good and proper.

177

You sure did get your man, Captain."

"No, I didn't."

They all looked up from their plates and waited for Allingham to explain.

"He didn't commit the murder, either."

"Then why'd we get him up to Flagstaff, Captain?"

"Because I don't know who killed the Princess yet, but we had an audience this afternoon. Once our prisoners get out, they'll blab and tell everyone that we think it's the assistant. That should put the real murderer at ease. He," Allingham wiped his mouth with a napkin, "or she will stay around, maybe even brag about it."

"She?" Francis was intrigued. He never imagined a woman as a suspect.

"Certainly." Allingham looked at the lad as if he were stupid. "I've seen women do just as horrible, actually worse, in my time." He looked at Rosario and decided not to elaborate.

Mike spoke up, "And how do ye know, Captain, that it wasn't The Ape?"

"Mostly because of him. I did think it was him at first, but when I probed, he didn't change his story. He didn't break down and confess, and his razor was dirty, but dirty of old soap, not blood. Anyone who'd clean all the blood from his razor would have gotten soap residue off of it, and a lot of soap scum remained, especially at the hinge." Allingham then held up a plain silver ring. "And this."

They stretched their necks to see what it was about. Allingham continued. "The Princess was missing a ring and I figured it would be found on The Ape; which it was."

"Well, a murderer would take a ring, sure enough." Hobbs blew his answer across the steaming rim of his coffee cup.

"But not a plain, nearly worthless, silver band like this. This is a sentimental item. This is something kept as a keepsake. The Ape was smart enough not to have anything incriminating on him, if he were the murderer, but he kept this. This was something a man in love would take to remember her by."

Francis grinned. "I'll be go to hell, how'd you know she was missin' a ring?"

Allingham rolled his eyes. "Francis, you did actually see the corpse, didn't you?"

"Yes, Captain." He shuffled self-consciously.

"A ring leaves a dent when it's been worn a long time. There was a dent, and the spot the ring once occupied was clean of blood. Her hand got bloody, but not where the ring protected it. He took it from her hand when he left. He took the money and Eli's chunk of gold and this plain ring. But the Princess had valuable jewelry, and he left all that jewelry behind. And then there was the ring the murderer wore when he hit the Princess. It had a sharp edge. The Ape didn't have such a ring. He wore a ring on his right hand, a ring that matched the one worn by the Princess. It was smooth; it would not have left such a mark. No, it wasn't him."

Francis looked on. The captain was one smart bastard. "I'll be go to hell."

CHAPTER VIII:
FLAGSTAFF

The whores sat about of an evening as they had finished their work for the day. Many looked around wondering if they were going to awaken from this dream. Their insides would shake and their bellies tighten as the sun went down every evening. It had gone on for so long, the beginning of the hellish nights, that they were fairly conditioned to dread the dark.

Now they did not have to dread it. They were all clean as they were able to wash after their workday was done and then they'd have a good supper and then they'd stay clean all night and everything smelled fresh and good from the laundry and no stinking men came in to lie on them, grunt and bounce up and down and blow their horrible whiskey and tobacco and rotten-toothed breath all over them. They'd not have to smell their stench: unwashed bodies and filthy backsides and stinking feet.

No one was threatening them or cursing them or blaming them because their customers couldn't perform, and no one was firing guns. Their babies were clean and well fed and happy and the girls with the various diseases were seen by the local doctor who did the best he could for them. For most, there was no cure and they knew it and just had to wait to go mad or die, and this was a good place to do it. If one had to go mad and die, the refuge was the best possible location for it.

Little Janie was now with them and they were glad for it. She was the youngest whore in Canyon Diablo and they knew that wasn't right. No one should really have to be a whore at all, but for a child to be a whore was the worst thing imaginable. Now she was safe and she was happy and talked incessantly about the deputy named Francis with the beautiful curly hair who she declared would be her husband one day.

No one wanted to tell her the truth and break her heart. Instead they'd just humor her. They'd listen to her prattle on about what a handsome man he was. She'd whisper that she'd seen him in his underwear and that he'd seen her naked but he was a good man and didn't try anything with her. He had looked away and given her a blanket to cover her body. She said that it broke her heart but then he explained it to her and now she understood that the acts they'd done at the brothels wasn't really love at all. Francis had taught her that and that made her love him even more because she was certain she'd win him over and one day she'd be his wife.

The nuns continued to help her with her words and now she could read. She'd spend the evenings reading to the other girls and they'd encourage her. The ones who were literate would politely correct her when she had trouble with a word or sentence. They took her place at the laundry so that she could spend the day reading to the children, and was becoming a proper little teacher. And the nuns were good to them. They nurtured them and did not lecture or cajole them about what they'd done. The nuns offered everything they could to make the healing begin; to stop the vicious cycle and give the girls some stability and a new start in life.

In a very short time, the nuns didn't need to come around for days at a time. The girls were shown what to do. They were smart girls and they soon took control and ran the laundry. They kept the children well and made certain no one stayed up too late or was tempted to go back to the whoring life.

They had no leader. They were full up with madams or pimps and did not need a leader. They ruled by consensus and all agreed that there'd be no smoking or drinking or taking laudanum or even playing cards. They would not even play Pope Joan or Old Maid or whist. They all wanted to divorce themselves from the vestiges of the whoring life and cards were just another reminder. The men liked to play cards in the brothels as much as they liked to in the gambling houses.

Instead, the girls worked on refined things like needlepoint and knitting and reading. They were working on something for Miss Halsted, as she was so good to them. They owed her, to their minds, for their new start. They were, additionally, taking up a collection and were voting on what gift to buy her.

This was the source of many a late night conversation. Some wanted to buy her a dress, but did not have the ability to determine what would be appropriate to such a refined lady. Others wanted to buy her perfume or a comb and brush set. They squabbled and argued about it often, but always in a good-natured way.

They were settling in and becoming respectable. Many of the town's folk, particularly the men, would bring laundry in, and they had contracts with no fewer than three of the lumber companies, even the railroad men were giving them good commerce.

Some of the young, eligible men of the town started poking around, not because the girls were former whores, but because they were girls, and many of them young and pretty and would likely make a good wife. As there were more men than women in Arizona these days, the girls soon discovered that they possessed a commodity that was not only rare, but desirable. There was a future in all this, and the ones not completely turned against men and such carryings on, found the new suitors a welcome added benefit.

Some of the girls had already found love in the form of their sisters-in-arms, and these set up housekeeping together. The nuns were kept in the dark regarding this, as the girls did not want them meddling nor did they desire to upset the sisters. Some things were better just not said. What the nuns did not know would not hurt them.

Little by little, their numbers swelled. Whores from all over the territory learned of the safe house, the safe haven in Flagstaff. Even whores with no children, and old whores who could no longer bear children were coming around. No one was ever turned away.

None of this was lost on Allingham, who made regular inspections. He was pleased with the results, and the girls were respectful and pleasant to him, but always on a business footing. None of them were ever very warm or outgoing with Allingham. He was too intimidating, and they had, just like everyone else who knew the man, difficulty reading and understanding him.

His actions were always appropriate. He never ogled or lusted after them and this perplexed them, as they'd known so few men who did not. They were convinced that he was acting on orders from the lady. None could ever imagine that Allingham had thought up any of this himself.

But he showed up regularly, respectful in his own businesslike way, and this they welcomed, as they knew he was watching over them and protecting them.

It was one of his greater triumphs and Allingham had the satisfaction of not only changing the conditions of Canyon Diablo, but also of the nearby towns and settlements. In a short while, places like Winslow and Holbrook, even down as far as Prescott were being impacted by his new policy on prostitution. Allingham was happy for that. He felt the twinge again, the gnawing pain in the pit of his gut, the realization that he was somehow, perversely happy at doing so much good and if he were only allowed to live longer, could do even greater things. He'd never felt this emotion in his life. He knew, of course, that what he did back in New York was good and right, but he never felt like he'd had such an impact on society. But out here it was different; it was tiny, in terms of human population, and attracted such extremes; especially the most nefarious of human kind.

There were also too many unattached men. Men needed women to calm them, civilize them, make them behave, just as a child needs the calming influence of a strong mother. These men needed women and Allingham was taking away the candy; the candy of prostitution and behaving badly, of letting them run amok and act the fool, as men turned to lawlessness when the temptations were too great. The land of Arizona needed men, grown up, responsible men, not self-indulgent scoundrels, and it seemed that's all they'd gotten for too long.

All the other states and territories were civilized and respectable by now. Their lawman had pushed the flotsam of humanity out to Arizona, and Allingham was here to rectify the situation. He'd do his best to bring civility and order to the place. He'd make it possible for them to grow up and act like decent men.

Chapter IX:
Francis

Francis was now in the habit of patrolling on his own, as Allingham was often occupied with other duties and projects. The young man liked being on his own. He liked interacting with the people, both good and bad. By now he'd thumped a fair number of the bad men, killed three, and they all pretty much knew, despite his pleasant demeanor and constant smile, that Francis was not a man to be trifled with.

He stopped short as a man vomited a great fountain across his path. Francis looked at the man dubiously and then glanced at the sun overhead. It was late morning and, to Francis's mind, not the normal time for drunks to spew their guts out. He looked the fellow over as the drunk wiped his mouth with a filthy shirt sleeve.

"Goddamn, mister, you're a mess."

Bewildered and a little annoyed, he belched in the deputy marshal's face.

"Look at the mess you've made, mister." Francis pointed at the vomitus on the ground. "Goddamn, I've seen little children with better self-control. What the hell's wrong with you?" Francis was not angry, but he meant what he was saying. He didn't like to see another human being in such a state.

The poor devil looked as if he might cry as Francis dug around a vest pocket for his tobacco pouch. He twisted a smoke and handed it to the man; he twisted another for himself. "When'd you eat last, mister?"

He regarded the detritus on the ground, as if it might give him the answer to his question.

"Don't know. Yesterday maybe. Think so. Can't remember." He hesitated, concentrated and then looked at Francis. "Not much hungry these days."

"Come on with me. I'm gonna arrest you, get you something to eat." He led him by the shoulder, like a kindly old school master; this looked odd, as Francis was at least thirty years younger than the drunk, who complied without argument. The old vagrant was thoroughly played out.

"Goddamn, son. Man who drinks like you and don't eat; he's gonna die."

The man looked Francis dead in the eye

and said, "When?"

Francis helped the derelict through the door and regarded his jailor. "Hobbsie, gotta new prisoner for ya."

The drunk stumbled back into the cell and flopped down. He began stinking up the place and Hobbs opened a window and the door. "What's the charge?"

Francis grabbed a chair and sat back as Rosario wandered in. He greeted her with a bob of his head. There were still no beans on the menu and Francis was pleased. He loved his new family and didn't want them squabbling. "Buenos días, querida madre."

She smiled and reached over, pinching Francis on the cheek. He was the only one to try addressing Rosario in her native tongue and it was not lost on the old cook.

"You are a sweet good boy!" She ambled past Hobbs and was humming. No beans and humming meant Hobbs was also being a sweet good boy.

"Oh, I don't know, Hobbsie, littering, vagrancy, assault by retching." Francis checked his boots. They'd not gotten splattered. "Nope, cancel that, no assault." He looked at Hobbs and smiled. "Hobbsie, he just needs a little rest, needs a meal."

He watched Rosario as she poured him a cup of coffee. As he drank it he said, "He'll work it off, poor old sot."

As ordered by Allingham, Rosario dutifully opened a bottle of beer for their new prisoner and prepared him a small meal. Francis pointed at her with his coffee cup. "Never in a million years a thought of that. Captain's a smart man. Like a doctor he is." And Hobbs agreed with this. He'd known of men who'd gotten the shakes — the Irish jig, they called it — but he'd not known that drunks needed to be weaned off booze, like a baby needed weaning from the tit. He'd never heard of such a thing, but the Captain knew. Allingham had learned many things on the streets of Hell's Kitchen and he dutifully cared for all under his responsibility: the prisoners and the people of the town and his crew. He took care of them all.

Francis went back out after lunch and patrolled with the Captain on his mind. He reminded him a little of his old father who died in the war when Francis was not quite ten. In the little time he'd known his old man, he'd learned to love him. His father was a good man; a hardworking man, but he was not a fighter and that was the reason, Francis surmised, that he'd probably died.

His father hadn't been young when called

up. He'd had a family but the war had used up many men and his father was too poor to hire a substitute or pay the three hundred dollar commutation fee. So off to war he went and he never returned. It truly was the rich man's war and the poor man's fight, and Francis's father was dying proof of that.

He had been a conscientious man, quiet and gentle. He had been lined up shoulder to shoulder with a lot of other conscientious and quiet men and led into a hail of bullets and cut down at some inconsequential and unnecessary battle somewhere in Pennsylvania or Virginia. The government couldn't even tell them exactly where.

But in reality there was no reason in the world that Allingham should remind Francis of his father. His father was a nice, kind and warm-hearted gentleman. He talked and laughed and grinned all the time. It was where Francis got his happy-go-lucky attitude and Allingham wasn't anything like that. He was the opposite of it. But there was some strange connection for Francis and this amused him very much. He'd not thought of his old man for a long time.

All this musing brought him to the brothel and French Annie who'd by now softened a little toward Francis whom she found to be quite handsome, both inside and out.

Annie, despite her profession, and the hundreds of men she'd bedded, still liked men, still liked sex and Francis was one of the most handsome men she'd ever seen. It was his innocence and personality, really; that was the thing she liked most and found most attractive. She still hated Allingham, however, and never lost the opportunity to remind Francis of it.

He grinned as he wrote out her receipt.

"Look at what yer son of a bitch boss has done to me." Francis grinned wider and looked around. Only old women remained and this was poison to Annie's enterprise. Most of the old ones made her no money. They cooked and cleaned and watched the babies for the young ones who made all the money and now the young ones were gone. Francis laughed out loud. His boss was a genius.

"Well, you can't very well blame a whore for wantin' to be with her baby."

"No, I can't, Francis, but I can blame your boss for haulin' 'em all up to Flagstaff, calling them foundlings. That's bullshit! Pure bullshit." She smoked and spit her answers with smoky spittle at Francis who drew back, to pull himself from the line of fire.

He grinned again, putting her payment in a wallet. He tipped his hat and smiled pleasantly. "You have yourself a nice quiet day, Annie." He looked around at the empty bordello. "A nice quiet day."

Francis made his way next door to what was now French Annie's gaming house. It was busy there, but not nearly as busy as it was before Allingham arrived on the scene. He smiled and nodded at the manager behind the bar and began writing out a receipt. The manager paid him and offered Francis a beer — which he always did and which Francis always refused.

"Looks like some good commerce today, Frank." And it was. Frank didn't mind Allingham's brand of law. The ruffians never had much money anyway, and they were more trouble than they were worth. Allingham had increased the class of the clientele throughout the town and smart men like Frank Parks knew it. He, like everyone else, enjoyed Francis's company and was pleasant to him when he came in to collect the fees.

Francis took a coffee from Frank and began sauntering about the house, walking past tables, smiling and nodding at the men playing. Some he'd arrested, a few he'd clobbered and the ones who were especially annoying would not escape the deputy marshal's teasing.

He'd walk up behind them and laugh, "I'll be go to hell, you've got a winner there." And everyone at the table would fold. That was the most entertaining part of the job for Francis. He was no bully, but he loved to make mischief for the men who deserved it. He infuriated many of them.

He looked in the corner as one of the players called Francis a name, muttered quietly, but loudly enough to be understood by the men around him. They all had a good laugh and Francis, all the while smiling walked over to his table. "What's that?"

The man stared at his cards. "Nothin'."

"Oh, it was somethin'. What'd ya say?"

The man had only recently gotten released from jail after digging half a dozen privies in the Arizona sun. He hated Francis and the rest of the lawmen. "I said, never seen anyone smile so much who wasn't a damned woman or child or back washin' fairy in a Turkish bath."

Francis nodded and grinned wider. "So, you're really callin' me a Nancy, is that right?"

"Ain't callin' you nothin'. Just saying, a man who smiles all the time . . . don't know."

Francis walked up behind him, causing

the fellow to crane his neck to see what the lawman was up to.

"Well, ya are. I ain't no kid or woman, that's clear, only thing's left is a Nancy. So, I think ya are callin' me such."

"Take it as you will." The man spoke with progressively less enthusiasm. Privy digging was on his mind.

Francis grinned. "Trouble with you is, you don't smile enough. Maybe if you would, you'd not be such a miserable and hateful son of a bitch."

This did not elicit the proper response, as the man was a coward and did not want to fight with Francis or end up using the public works shovel again. He kept his mouth shut, but Francis could not let this insult go. He had a reputation to uphold, and there were many men who liked the idea of calling Francis a fairy. Francis probed a bit more, looking at the man's hand, which the dude held out, too conspicuously. "Like for instance, son, here you are, sittin' with a full house, aces high, and still you got a look on your face like there's a steel rod up yer backside."

That did it, as the man was losing big all morning. He was about to clean up and Francis had ruined it for him. He became furious, beet red in the face and he fairly

197

screamed at Francis, throwing the cards on the table in a huff. "I ought a put a ball in you, you idiot grinnin' fool."

At this Francis upended a beer over the man's head. "Dude, you're way too hot, and you need some coolin' off." He stood over the dripping man, his hand on the butt of his six shooter as he watched the wet and angry man. He went for his gun and Francis buffaloed him senseless with one stroke of his six shooter's handle.

He grinned at the rest of the players. "You boys tell him when he wakes up that he owes the jail a five-dollar fine."

He wandered out. No one would likely hurry to call Francis a Nancy again.

He finished collecting fees and had another two hours to kill until suppertime. They'd eat good tonight as Rosario had bought a nice young elk saddle from a market hunter. He was looking forward to that.

He had time to visit his sweetheart and was pleased to find she had finished her chores for the day. Francis discovered the young woman, who'd just turned nineteen and lived with her mother and father, immediately after becoming a deputy marshal. She was a beauty and he'd planned, from the first moment he'd seen her, to make her his wife. She thought this a good idea as well.

"Francis!" She looked about and, finding her parents otherwise occupied, gave Francis a long and passionate kiss on the mouth. They'd been kissing for two weeks now and thought their secret safe, though young Margaret's mother had known of the scandalous behavior from the very first day. "Ma, Pa, Francis is here."

They all came out to greet him. Everyone loved Francis. They thought him a kind and gentle man and, despite his lack of education, Margaret's father, a surveyor and engineer, did not object to him courting his only daughter. He shook the lad's hand and nodded kindly to the deputy.

Margaret's mother pressed his hand. "How are you, Francis?"

"Oh, fine as frog hair, ma'am. All good." He smiled and handed her some candy he'd confiscated from a prisoner he'd arrested recently. "All good."

Margaret's parents left them alone in the makeshift parlor — everything was makeshift in Canyon Diablo. Everything was thrown together and of a temporary nature in the hell hole of a settlement.

She looked in the direction her parents had gone, and when it was all clear she reached over and kissed him again, more passionately than before. "I missed you."

"Since yesterday?" He held her tightly and kissed her again.

"Uh huh." Her face was flushed and Francis loved it, loved the passion in her eyes. She kissed him again. It was driving him to distraction. It was too much for the circumstances and he pushed her away.

"Francis, let's go for a ride." He looked at her and thought hard about it. Her parents would never allow it; the girl did not ride a horse and they'd never be permitted to double up on his mount.

"How?"

"Pa." She reached over and kissed him again, steadying herself with a palm on his thigh, up high, higher than he'd ever been touched. He thought his heart would explode, had difficulty catching his breath. "Pa's got a carriage. Just arrived from the railroad company. For him to survey the tracks. We can go for a ride in it."

"Okay, Mags. Okay."

They had left the town behind, heading north and within half an hour were in a low washout, off the road where no one could see them. It was a magnificent evening, cool and clear. The sun would soon be down, the sky turning a wondrous purple and red.

Margaret had prepared well in advance and this tickled Francis to no end. The idea that she'd planned it made it that much more meaningful. He quickly forgot about the elk Rosario was preparing for dinner.

"Francis, I've got a basket and some wine, Pa's wine. It's good. Get makings for a fire."

He complied and when he returned she was waiting, the wine opened, blankets spread out on the desert floor the foodstuffs laid, ready for them to share an evening meal. Mags lay waiting as well, naked and vulnerable, she trembled though it was not particularly cold. She smiled as he stood, jaw agape. For the first time since she'd known him, Francis did not smile. For the first time in his life, it seemed, he was speechless. Never in his wildest dreams had he imagined such a thing.

"Mags!" He pulled himself together. She was stunning with her long raven-colored hair, eyes the blue of corn flowers in sunlight, and skin lily white, she brought to mind a fairy princess lying there on the rugged desert floor.

"I'll be go to hell."

She undressed him and kissed him more passionately than he'd ever known; every touch and caress jolting like an electric shock coursing through his body. Mags still trembled, but not as badly as before. She knew now, knew that it was all right and Francis's responses, caresses, attention, gave her more confidence. This would be the first and best time for them both, transcending any other emotion or experience either had yet known in their young lives.

"Marry me, Mags. Marry me."

They fell asleep and when they awoke it was full dark. They'd not gotten a fire made and could see nothing, as the moon was new and the night very dark. Francis moved his hands over her body, finding her face. He ran his hands over her eyes, nose and mouth, then back down the full length of her lovely form. He reached down, and, pulling her on top of him, made love to her again.

This time it was better. They took their time and slowly built the passion, found their rhythm. He felt her shudder and he moved just enough to keep her in her happy place.

"Mags, I, I have to say."

She could feel his lovely smile on her cheek. "Mags, that was the best thing that's ever happened in my life. That was better than, better than the best thing that's ever happened to me, I swear. That was better than once when I was out all night in the winter, and I finally made it back home and I got in bed, right under a big blanket and lyin' next to the fire and all the feelin' came back in my hands and feet. It was better'n that. It was better'n the one time when I was out on the range and I came upon a whole cowboy outfit some fellow'd left, for God knows why, but there was a nice saddle and six shooter and Winchester, and even three hundred dollars. It was better'n that. It was better than . . ."

"Francis?"

"Yes, Mags?"

"Shush."

"Yes, Mags."

CHAPTER X:
LUCK OF THE IRISH

The night in Canyon Diablo belonged to Paddy and Mike O'Shaughnessy. They'd had to kill no one in the time they'd been deputies. They were good coppers. Their old mother, a pious Catholic, worried over them as much as she bragged to anyone who'd listen about her boys, her two great and lovely boys. She said they were born to be policemen and she was right. They were the best coppers Allingham had ever known.

They'd taken to dressing alike and now no one could tell them apart. When they were asked which was which, they'd smile and twirl their nightsticks and speak in their calm lyrical brogue, "Ay, ye just don't trouble yourself over worrying about it. We're both Deputy O'Shaughnessy, and that's all ye need to know."

They could clear a room of ruffians quicker than any lawman in the land, usually by just holding up a hand, looking the deviants in the eye and ordering an end to the nonsense. They'd nod like a devoted father and speak softly and politely; they called every man sir. "Now, there, sir, just go on with ye. Go on home and sleep it off. It'll be better in the morning."

Early on, some of the stupider men decided to challenge them, and the O'Shaughnessy boys had only to break a few arms. They wielded their nightsticks as a knight from old would handle a broadsword. After that, few wanted to cross or disobey the big men.

They made little money for Allingham and he didn't much mind, as he knew they had the toughest job. Keeping the peace at night was a difficult task in Canyon Diablo, as this was when the animals were at their worst. They did not bother collecting fines, but did good service just ordering men to behave and this was fine with Allingham. They were the ones who were really responsible for decreasing the murder rate so significantly.

Their shift started at sunset and went on until sunrise and every evening, after a good meal with their newly adopted family, they'd stand up and stretch, finish their beer and kiss Rosario on the cheek.

"Good night, Mother," they'd say and

she'd pat them on their great broad shoulders.

"You be careful, mis pequeños. You be careful." She'd see them off to work.

This amused Francis, who'd been steadily learning the Spanish words, and he'd look on at Rosario. "Madre, those boys are as big as a barn."

"Ah, but they are my little ones, Francis, just like you, just like the Capitan. You are all my little ones."

This evening Mike was unusually quiet and Paddy, as always, sensed that something was on his brother's mind. He waited to hear what his partner and best friend had to say.

"Paddy, this place has become too civilized, too quiet. I fear we're doing too good a job."

Mike had the wanderlust about him and Paddy knew when it was time for them to move on. His brother had been dragging the both of them all over the US for as long as they'd been in the country.

His response was interrupted by gunfire down one of the alleys lined with shotgun houses. They moved toward it steadily, as the brothers never ran to investigate anything. They moved fearlessly, resolutely, and, not unlike Allingham, always at a walk.

The idiots were starting earlier than usual this night and, when the policemen arrived, they were greeted by two rail workers, big Negro men equal in size to the Irishmen. One was holding a ruffian, drunk and babbling, as the other handed a six shooter to Mike.

"This one was shootin' up the place, Cap'n."

Mike held up a hand. "You go on and deliver it to the jail tomorrow, lad, and collect your reward. Did this one," he pointed with his head to the scoundrel, "accost you fellows in any way?"

"No, Cap'n. He was just shootin'. Just drunk, I guess."

"Give me back my gun, nigger!" The man was small, but the drink had made him bold. Paddy moved his head solemnly from side to side.

"Now, none of that, sir. You need to apologize to the man." He took control of the ruffian and held him by the back of the neck, giving his shoulder a squeeze which the bad man understood to be a firm warning. Unfortunately, he was too dim to take heed.

"Apologize, my ass. You goddamned niggers and Irish, comin' in here, ruinin' everything. This place was good for a while, almost as good as the ol' south. Now it's ruined, ruined. You all can kiss my ass."

"Mikey, I'm sorry, but did you hear that? This gentleman wants you to kick him in the arse."

"Aye, Paddy, that's what I heard, that's what I heard, but me English, being just a lowly and dumb Irish scum, isn't as good as it could be. Maybe we understood him wrong."

The man was sobering up, but no less furious at his dilemma. "You stupid mick bastards, I said *kiss* my ass! Kiss, it, kiss it!" He pointed with a finger to his backside.

"Aye, there he said it again, Mikey, he wants you to kick his arse." And at that, Mike gave him a good boot, hurling him into the dusty street. The man landed face first, rolled about and Paddy towered over him, suddenly serious.

"Now, sir. You listen to me and listen good. You're going to apologize to these railroad men. Then you're going to go home, where e're that might be, and sleep it off."

The drunk looked up at them and then at the Negroes who were now having second thoughts about their own meddling into the affairs of the drunken man. They'd seen what men such as this could do when they got a mob behind them; they knew the law could do little when things got out of hand. They waited, not certain what to do.

"I'll never say I'm sorry to a stinkin' nigger, and I'll never do what a lousy papist bastard mackerel snappin' son of a bitch tells me. You and that asshole of a brother of yours can go to hell."

With that, Mike hauled him up with his great fists wrapped in his shirt and threw him against a wall. He handcuffed the drunk and pulled him along. A few days clearing horse manure from the streets would humble him sufficiently. He looked over his shoulder at the two railroad men.

"You bring that shooting iron in tomorrow, lads. The captain'll give you a reward."

As they walked, Paddy thought on it. It was one of Allingham's more brilliant plans. He never imposed laws against the citizenry taking action. To the contrary, he encouraged it. He never confiscated guns or imposed laws against carrying them. He rewarded the good people for helping in the peacekeeping endeavor.

Allingham knew from his years in Hell's Kitchen, knew from the stories of the West — like the debacle in Tombstone the year before — if you go around disarming the populace, you end up with unarmed good people and armed bad ones. Bad men cared nothing for the law; they certainly didn't mind breaking ordinances against carrying shooting irons and would simply move them from outside to inside their pants.

And besides, the lawmen were outnumbered. There were too many bad men, and they needed the numbers of the citizenry to offset the imbalance.

Paddy remembered back early on, smiling at young Francis's questioning. And then his brother, who always had a good anecdote, it seemed, for every situation, interjected. He said, "Aye, me boy, you don't pull the teeth of your good dogs before you put them in the fightin' pit." And with that, Francis understood.

The railroad workers would be rewarded well by Allingham the next day and the Irishmen would keep a watchful eye over them. They understood the plight of the Negro, knew what their own countrymen had done during the war in the great draft riots in New York and realized that it took only a half dozen bad men and plenty of liquor to form a lynch mob.

By midnight the town was at its worst. The gaming houses were packed full and the brothels were not doing badly, even if the madams could offer only the most mature of the lot to their clientele. Paddy overheard a young cowpoke speaking to his companion as he walked out, pushing his shirt back in his pants, "Any port in a storm."

The other one laughed, "Yeah, but next time, we're goin' to Holbrook. Whores are younger than a grandma there." He lit a smoke. "At least they got most of their teeth."

They backslapped and laughed and moved on. "Ever since Princess got it, this place has gone to the damned old toothless dogs."

Mike tipped his hat to One-Eyed Sal. "Ma'am."

"How are you gentlemen getting along this night?" Sal was pleasant to them always, even if she, like Annie, would have enjoyed sliding a blade into their boss's gut.

"Oh, quiet as a church, ma'am, quiet as a church."

With that, a loud scream erupted, then a cackle; one of the whores was having a good time.

Paddy shook his head from side to side. "Aye, you must be thinking of a church in Monto, me brother. Must be a church in Monto."

Mike looked at his watch and then across the way at French Annie's bordello and gaming house. He pointed with a nod of his head. "How's your friend, Miss Annie?"

Sal snorted. "She's not choked on her own vomit, I know that. Still alive and kicking."

"You have a nice evening, ma'am." They walked off to the other side of the street.

Annie was likewise glad to see them. She liked the big men. They were pleasant and incorruptible and this was a foreign concept to the madam, as she'd only ever known wretched and venal men.

She was sitting at the entrance to the gaming house, having a cigar and chatting with some of her whores. She nodded as the men passed, onto the gaming house next door.

Mike was the first one through the door when a smallish man approached him, too quickly, and socked the policeman with all his might on the jaw. Mike leaned back, slightly, as if a fly had landed on his chin.

Paddy quickly had the attacker in hand, holding him by the scruff of the neck, smiling at his brother.

He looked down at his attacker, all white and trembling.

"Goddamn, constable, I'm, I'm sorry." He threw up his hands to protect his face. "Don't kill me, please, don't kill me!"

Mike looked at Paddy and grinned as men gathered 'round, to see what would become of the little fellow.

One of the onlookers spoke up. "We dared him to hit the next man through the door, constable. Never thought he'd be takin' a poke at a mountain."

The men laughed louder as the Irishmen grinned. The story would add to the legend, as the little man, though he was diminutive, gave a pretty impressive swipe, and would have knocked a normal man to his knees.

Paddy reached over and petted the fellow on top of the head, as he would a scolded dog. "That'll cost you the labor of cleaning out three privies, me lad."

"Yes, sir. Yes, sir. Whatever you say." He was shaking but managed a grin. "Whatever you say, sir, whatever you say."

"And a couple of bottles of beer." He winked at his brother. "We don't drink on duty, lads, but this will go well with breakfast." He put the bottles, one in each big coat pocket.

He turned to leave and spoke to the crowd. "Ye remember this, lads, me brother's head is the last place you want to punch. It has no effect on him and it just might make him angry."

■ ■ ■ ■

They sat outside One-Eyed Sal's. It was coming on to four in the morning and the animals had finally burned themselves out. It was quiet now. Paddy looked at his brother, remembering his complaint about being bored in Canyon Diablo.

"What did ye have in mind, Mikey?"

"San Francisco."

"Why?"

"Want to see the other sea, Paddy." He stretched and lit a pipe and blew smoke at the street. "Want to try our hand at fishing."

"Fishing is it?" He sat and twisted a cigarette. Paddy did not like this idea. They had an uncle who was a fisherman back in Ireland, up north, and the man had drowned. Paddy did not like the water and had an unnatural fear of sharks. He was not fond of physical labor.

"Mikey, you get seasick looking at a horse trough. This is not a good plan. Anyway, we don't like heavy labor. If we wanted to break our backs, we could stay on here and go back to driving spikes for the railroad."

"Well, then, maybe not the sea. But California, I hear it's quite a land."

"When?"

"Oh, well, when this place is finished. There's no need for it to live after the bridge is done. It'll all go away and then we can move on."

He was pleased to hear this. Paddy liked the other policemen. He liked Allingham and Francis. He liked Rosario and Hobbs. He was having more fun than his brother was, but knew, just as well, that it was a temporary post. Mikey was right; in another year, Canyon Diablo would be no more.

He looked up and down the street. No one was stirring now. He looked at his watch. In another hour the merchants would be up, moving about, preparing for a day of commerce.

They were the good folks who made an honest living. They slept and while they did so, the Irishmen kept the peace so that they could rest and be refreshed to conduct their business another day; to live the lives of normal folks, making the place decent and livable. The Irishmen were good for Canyon Diablo.

Mikey dozed as Paddy kept watch. This was always the way. Mikey's mind wandered; was too active. Their old mother called him a restless baby, as from the very beginning he could never sit still. Paddy was the one to bear the burden of it, as Mikey's ideas and schemes were many and, more often than not, didn't pan out.

But Paddy kept his brother straight. They both promised their old mother and each other that they'd eventually make it back home, back to Ireland. Paddy was resolute in keeping this promise; he would see that they achieved the ultimate goal.

He took control of the finances, sending most of the money back home where Mother could live off a portion of it. The rest she squirreled away for when the lads returned. They would be Publicans one day and own the finest inn of their village. It was all worked out in Paddy's head.

He thought on it. By then, certainly, Mikey'd get the wandering out of his system. They could settle down, perhaps become landlords. They might even own some land and become gentlemen farmers. It was only a matter of time. It would all happen one day.

CHAPTER XI:
THE GUNFIGHTER

It was inevitable. The word traveled fast that a new lawman needed killing in Canyon Diablo. There'd been so many lawmen murdered in the settlement that it had become a special honor, a badge of courage, so to speak, for someone to kill a lawman there.

Most of these famous murderers were not themselves long for this world, and only two still lived to tell of their great triumph. Both of these men were cowards and back shooters and that is how they dispatched the lawmen. Now they wandered around the various dumps and dives in New Mexico so the real story of their exploits could be embellished with little risk of anyone adding any truth. They could be big men down there.

But Allingham was different, and this execution called for a specialist. And he arrived on a clear morning in the form of one

Norbert Sckogg who was peculiar from the other gunmen of the time, as he was not a southern survivor of the War Between the States. Rather, he was a man about thirty who hailed from a good and decent family in Wisconsin. There was no single reason for him to be a gunfighter or a murderer. He did it because he was evil to the very core of his being.

Evil was about the only way to describe him as he took a perverse pleasure in killing. He killed for entertainment and for profit, and one of his jobs early on was to kill Indians who were deemed squatters on lands owned by ranchers further up north. He also killed men accused of rustling, but none ever got so much as a trial. He was simply given names, locations where his victims could be found, and then he'd hunt them down, often killing them from a distance with a buffalo rifle.

He was well provisioned and finished for the season, as he'd killed many men and had been paid well for it. He heard about Allingham when he was bumming around down in Tombstone, associating with some of the cowboys who'd not been rubbed out by the Earps.

Allingham would be a free job. No one hired him, but Sckogg thought it would look good to kill a man like Allingham who'd already developed a reputation as a tough policeman. And, as Sckogg was new to Arizona and New Mexico, he wanted to seal his reputation in these parts. Killing Allingham would be a great advertisement of his special talent.

Sckogg was a big man, not unlike Allingham, yet he was handsome, unlike Allingham. He liked to dress well and wore city clothes, even out on the trail. He wore a fancy beaver hat and a sack suit with pinstripes, a high celluloid collar, like Allingham, and a gaudy gunbelt, black with red stitching, slung low on his hip. He had a silver six shooter with an ivory handle. He wore the buckle of his gun belt around back so that his cartridges, more than fifty, could be easily seen and grabbed from the front, when needed.

Francis thought him a regular Nancy and made fun of him a few times when collecting fees in the saloon where the murderer had set up headquarters. Despite the heckling, Sckogg didn't kill Francis as it did not fit into his plan, and something about the grinning deputy caused him to hesitate. Francis had something about him, a certain look to him that said, you might kill me, but it will cost you your life for doing so.

The gunfighter had a bigger prize on his mind.

One day, when Francis was leaving the saloon, Sckogg called out. "You there, deputy."

Francis stopped and grinned. "Yeah?"

"Tell your boss I've come looking for him."

"You tell him yourself. You've gotta big enough mouth." Francis turned and walked up to the man who was several inches taller. Looking up at the gunslinger, grin still in place, he said, "What's yer name, Mister?"

"Sckogg."

"Sckogg?" He laughed, "Sckogg, no shit. Well, I'll be go to hell." He looked over at the men standing about the bar drinking. They did not like the gunfighter as he was a bully and they were afraid of him. Francis turned back and looked at the assassin. "Yer shittin' me. Sckogg? Sounds like sumpin' you scrape off yer boot, don't it, boys?"

The men looked into their beers. No one wanted to laugh or offend Sckogg.

"Jesus Christ," Francis grinned again, "Just stepped in a pile a Sckogg outside." He laughed and continued. "Or somethin' that come outta yer ass once ya et something turned. Holy cow, looky there, I just shit a big Sckogg." He suddenly got serious. "Mr.

Sckogg, why don't you just go on outta here. Go find a rock to crawl under down in Mexico. Go kill someone down there to make you big. This place ain't for you, son. Let it go. Move on. Get the hell outta here."

Sckogg ignored his taunts and warnings. He was unnerved by the uppity Easterner. No one ever talked to him in such an impudent way and got away with it, but he still said nothing, made no move to pull a gun on Francis. He was surprised, himself, at his inaction.

Francis waited. He'd kill the bastard, himself, right now. But Sckogg wouldn't oblige. He shrugged and turned to walk out. "Don't any a you boys step in a pile a Sckogg on your way home." He could be heard laughing as he sauntered on down the street.

Allingham sat, stone-faced as Francis regaled them with the story of Sckogg. The Irishmen knew him. They had seen him strutting about like a cock of the walk. They ignored him and, he them. Now they looked at Allingham as their boss calculated and formed a plan in his mind.

"He's broken no laws."

Francis watched him. Allingham, he knew, was not yellow. He knew Allingham would not let it continue, but he'd use his brain and his police training from his time in New York to defeat Sckogg.

Allingham continued. "I'll make inquiries. It is likely his real name. He's probably wanted somewhere."

Francis laughed. "Goddamned, Captain, yer right about that. Who the hell'ed change their name to Sckogg?"

Rosario got up and topped off Francis's coffee. She reached over and absentmindedly patted the young man's curly head. "You be careful with this teasing, Francis. One day you will tease your way up to the hill." She pointed toward the new graveyard recently created by the captain.

"Ah, just funnin', Mamacita, just funnin'. Anyways, my ma, she always said, you got the bogeyman under yer bed, scarin' ya, just laugh at him, just laugh at him and he'll go away. Old Sckogg, he's nothin' but a big dumb-assed bogeyman."

Sckogg may have been a bogeyman, but he was no dumb-ass. He waited for Allingham who did not oblige. Sckogg decided to give the marshal a reason to visit him. This was no small task as everyone at the saloon gave the man a wide berth. Sckogg did not drink and did not gamble. He'd taken to sitting in a corner, sullenly glaring at everyone at the bar.

A Chinese served him stew and was immediately called back by the gunslinger as Sckogg pulled at a long black hair wrapped around the spoon. The lad grinned sheepishly and shrugged and for his impudence was grabbed by the neck, his face shoved brutally into the steaming bowl of food. The boy howled in pain and, grabbing Sckogg's arm, managed to free himself of the ruffian's grasp. He pushed the gunfighter against the wall, upending the remainder of his meal on the assassin's starched shirt front. Pulling his six shooter, Sckogg shot the lad through the head. He removed the empty shell case from his six shooter's cylinder, replacing it with a fresh cartridge. He spun the cylinder dramatically and reholstered his gun. The next bullet was for Allingham.

Francis chatted incessantly and loaded the ten gauge as he walked next to Allingham toward the end of town. Allingham was put out. He hadn't wanted the Chinese man to die, he felt responsible, even a bit indecisive. He should have run the son of a bitch out of town, killed him or faced him down.

This was all very different than in New

York. Back there, protocol had to be followed, and even the criminals seemed to have more sense. This man had murdered simply to draw Allingham out and it was confounding to him. Such a thing would not happen again and now Allingham understood fully what he was up against in this terrible and corrupt place. He would not make the same mistake twice.

He stopped Francis outside and ordered him to guard the door. He did this for two reasons. First, he did not want Francis shot and, secondly, he had to take this one down on his own. It would be good for the citizenry to see it and would go far in adding to Allingham's fame and legend, which he sought, not for his own self-aggrandizement, but to be more effective as a lawman.

Allingham did not consider letting this one kill him. It would go with his plan, but he didn't want Sckogg to get away. The gunman had to be stopped and Allingham would stop him. He would make certain the man was punished for the Chinaman's death and for all the other black-hearted things he'd done over the course of his miserable life.

"I ain't never bucked you, Captain, you know it, but there ain't no way you're goin' to stop me going in there with you."

Allingham looked Francis up and down. He was a good one and Allingham was proud of him. He moved quickly and decisively, knocking Francis to the ground with a powerful right hook.

He charged through the door and caught Sckogg unawares, sitting in his lair like a cornered rat, unable to get away. Allingham threw his body on him, pinning his six shooter to his side with his left hand, the marshal beat him in the face with his fist.

Blood poured freely from the gunman's nose and mouth, mixing with the stew stains on his shirt.

They were equally matched in weight and height and toughness and Sckogg, more quickly than one would expect from a big man who'd just been soundly pummeled, turned and pulled away. He got his arm free and came at Allingham, delivering a powerful blow to Allingham's bulbous nose.

The marshal reeled and fell back against the bar, the gunman on him, choking him through the policeman's stiff fancy collar. Allingham was losing consciousness as the bad man went for his six shooter. He was going to use that bullet to kill Allingham.

Desperately, the big copper reached for a weapon, anything to stop the attack, and found the fancy cigar lighter with the pretty red globe that had been delivered just that week, ordered from the Montgomery Ward catalog to add a little sophistication to the ramshackle saloon. He pushed it into Sckogg, igniting the celluloid collar into a flame encircling the man's head. It looked as if Satan himself had reached up from the bowels of hell and set a ring of fire around the miserable assassin's neck.

It was his turn to fall back and he screamed and grabbed for his gun. Changing his mind, he reached up and tore desperately at the flaming collar around his neck. But the fancy brass buttons held fast front and back as the assassin ran out past the recovering Francis who had the presence of mind to trip him with his army boot.

Sckogg tumbled, face forward, flopping about on the dusty street as men piled out of the bar, anxious to see what would happen next. Francis, slowly and methodically, found a bucket, checked it for holes and finding none, walked over to a watering trough, checking to see if it had sufficient water. He checked the temperature with his finger, then his elbow, just as he'd learned to do when bathing his little cousins. Only after he was satisfied did he dip the bucket in and upend it onto the burning man's head and neck, extinguishing the growing flame.

Francis turned and wandered past the onlookers into the bar. He looked his boss over and smiled. He almost ceremoniously, put a cigar in his mouth, walked over to the fancy lighter and, using it, puffed away. He regarded the barman, slack-jawed and speechless, trying to comprehend what Francis and his boss had just done to Sckogg.

One of the patrons nodded to Francis, and with shaking hands, handed the deputy his hat and shotgun, recovered from the boardwalk outside. Francis nodded a thank you and blew cigar smoke, pointing with his head to the street.

"Tried to get a light from old Sckogg, but he wouldn't stand still long enough, boys." He grinned, then laughed out loud, "I'll be go to hell. I swear, son of a bitch looked like a goddamned Roman candle dancin' around out there. I'll be go to hell."

No one laughed. The shaky man looked at Allingham staunching the blood from his nose and finally asked: "What do we do with him, Marshal?" He looked out the door at the assassin.

"Is he still alive?" Allingham was genuinely impressed.

"Yes, sir, just barely. But he's breathin'."

"Twenty dollars to the man who takes him down to the railroad hospital." He held up his handkerchief and examined it. He walked out.

Francis turned to follow. Slinging the shotgun over his shoulder, he looked at the barman and then at the fancy new cigar lighters on each end of the bar. "You boys be careful around them flames, wearin' fancy collars." He laughed. "Poof." He gestured with a tilt of his head. "Don't need no more Roman candles." He laughed and had a thought, "Don't none of you boys step in a pile of Sckogg when you come out."

By two in the morning, Sckogg was lying in the hospital bed at Winslow. They'd worked on him the best they could, and even the docs, who'd seen their fair share of steam injuries from the railroad, were at a loss for what to do for the man.

He reclined in the bed, covered in wet towels. He felt his face where he once had a nose, eyelids, eyes. He reached down; they'd taken his gun belt and six shooter. He felt some more, discovering that he was still wearing his trousers and vest. He found his pocket knife and slit his own throat. It was the most useful thing he'd yet done in his short, albeit miserable, life.

Next day Francis was gone up to Flagstaff to check on the retired whores and little Janie and to do some shopping. He was home for supper and Rosario quickly fixed him a plate. He dropped a half dozen new linen collars on Allingham's lap. "No more celluloid collars for you, Captain."

He sat down and ate and smiled his normal smile. They watched him, waiting for him to talk; to laugh and joke and entertain them as that is what Francis would do of an evening, and now supper was almost done.

When he had their attention he addressed Allingham. "Captain, all due respect, but if you ever knock me down again, make sure it's for good. Make sure you kill me, sir, because if you don't, you'll be sorry."

He turned back and regarded Rosario with a big smile. "Mamacita, that's some fine pork; some fine pork indeed." He finished his coffee and walked out.

Chapter XII:
The Foundling's Home

Allingham walked into the barracks and would have found more civilly had he poked his head into a hornet's nest. She was waiting for him, fuming and pacing; marching up and down.

"Good morning." Allingham was pleased to see her as she'd been away back East and had only just returned.

"Don't good morning me, Mr. Allingham."

"Marshal."

Francis grinned and spoke up at the same time, "Captain." He lost his grin when Rebecca Halsted glared at him. He did his best to try to make her smile. "Where's Mr. Sikh?"

"Singh!" This did not improve her mood as she was not certain if Francis was just ignorant or being downright discourteous.

He quickly corrected himself. "Er, eh, yes, beg your pardon, ma'am." He did not like to make the pretty woman angry. "That's what I meant; Singh, Mr. Singh. He's a Sikh, that's right, sorry ma'am. No offence intended."

Allingham watched the exchange as he poured a cup of coffee. He was waiting for her, expecting her to be angry and she did not disappoint him. It was the first drama he'd ever pulled off and he was not so certain now that he should have attempted it.

"What have you done?"

"How so?" Allingham was having a little fun now.

"You know right well how so. What have you done with the home, it's boarded up, no one around. What have you done, Mr. Allingham?"

Francis tried for peace again. "It's all in hand, ma'am, we . . ."

Allingham stopped him with a raised hand. "Come with me, Miss Halsted."

They rode in Rebecca Halsted's new carriage, just the two of them. Allingham sat motionless, showing no emotion but sneaking sideways glances at the pretty woman when he could. He was feeling good and had been feeling better every day. He really puzzled over why he felt so well and wondered at his out-of-character behavior. He was delighted to see Rebecca. She'd been gone for many weeks, visiting or something. Allingham didn't know what she had been doing and, initially, didn't care, but he had started missing her when she'd failed to show up at the expected time.

He knew she'd be angry at first. This was something out of character for Allingham, as he had no drama in his life. He never played tricks, instigated surprises, did anything for anyone that might appear to be a kindness or a pleasant intrigue. Allingham did not do such things. But he was doing this now and he liked it. It reminded him of when he was a child at Christmas and he'd buy a present for his mother. He remembered what it felt like to have the excited anticipation as he waited to give her his gift. This was how he was feeling now.

He also felt the sudden desire to compliment her, say something pleasant, which puzzled him, he just as quickly lost his nerve. His mind raced to come up with something, anything appropriate to say. He fumbled with his words, and finally blurted out:

"Mr. Singh, is he well?"

"He is. He had business at the railroad office. He'll ride back on the stagecoach later."

He was finally able to gaze at her. He could not contain himself any longer. "Miss Halsted, is, is Mr. Singh, is Mr. Singh . . ."

"Am I romantically involved?" She thought a lot of Allingham, but sometimes could not stand his bumbling monosyllabic attempts at conversation. She looked far down the road.

"When I was fourteen, I fell hopelessly in love with Mr. Singh. I intended to marry him and that lasted one month." She smiled and then looked Allingham in the eye which drove him nearly to distraction. "He and my father are business partners, Mr. Allingham. They both raised me from as long ago as I can remember. They are both the best of men, but no, Mr. Singh is more like my second father. There is nothing more than that."

"I see." Allingham's relief was nearly palpable.

She was calming down, not nearly so angry. She was impressed with Allingham's attempt at a personal question. The thought that he could imagine her with the Indian gave her hope, and was secretly pleased. It gave her confidence in the idea that he was taking her somewhere to show that he was not a complete fiend, that he had not dismantled her safe haven for the prostitutes without good reason.

She was certain Allingham had done something altruistic, even if he hadn't consulted her about it first. By now she felt that she knew the marshal well enough to surmise that he consulted no one on anything. Allingham ran things his way and of this, Rebecca could not complain. He was not a man to operate or be ruled by consensus or committees. He acted and did things on his own.

They rode on and he watched her handle the carriage. He liked that, too. She was thoroughly feminine, yet could handle horses, handle almost anything and this was nice to see. Already, by this time in New York, the lines between the sexes were more distinctly drawn. Men did manly things and women generally did not. Out West, it did not seem so much this way. Out West, if a woman was helpless or weak, it might not turn out so well. Everyone had to be self-reliant. There seemed to be few, if any, damsels in distress in this new land.

He directed her to a side street not far from the courthouse where he'd sat before the Safety Committee. They stopped outside a two-story house and Allingham escorted her inside. A nun greeted them at the door, as did the women Rebecca had hired back in Canyon Diablo to care for the safe house she'd put together there. Little Janie walked up to greet them. She handed Allingham a package.

"This is for Francis. See that he gets it, Captain. Please." Allingham nodded and placed it in his coat pocket. Janie smiled and wandered away. She looked over her shoulder at Rebecca Halsted. "Hi, lady." She smiled as she moved away.

Everything was in order: clean and decent. This was a real home, not a thrown together affair like back at the settlement. Several of the whores ran up to greet her. They held out their hands for Rebecca to take.

"Oh, thank you, ma'am. Thank you so much."

"For what?" Rebecca, confused, looked to Allingham for an explanation, finding that he'd somehow, in such a short time managed to disappear into another room. She looked the place over, jaw agape. She'd not expected anything like it.

"For this, ma'am." A beautiful young woman, holding a babe to her breast cast her hand across the room. "For this."

It was Allingham's work, but he'd not let them know it. He told a lie; an honorable one, but no less a lie, and had let everyone believe that Rebecca Halsted had arranged everything.

The enterprise served two purposes: he'd removed most of the workforce from the Canyon Diablo brothels, thereby crippling the industry there, and he'd created this safe haven for the girls. There was money enough to keep them off their backs, both from the fines and fees he'd collected and also from the enterprise he'd cooked up with the nuns. Now they could care for the babies without being molested, or under pressure to make money in the old way.

He contracted with a group of nuns and they now ran a decent laundry under his constantly watchful eye. He'd known even nuns could not always be trusted. His Irishmen had apprised him of that, as they'd known many a sad story of the Magdalene laundries back in their home on the Emerald Isle.

But these nuns were not Irish, they were German and not corrupt and not in the laundry trade. They were just nuns, recently arrived in Arizona and interested in helping anyone who needed it. They gave good service and treated the girls well. It was a winning hand all around, and Rebecca Halsted was the hero of the hour. The girls needed only to pledge not to engage in the trade, and they could stay as long as they liked. They would earn honest wages and plan for a future for both themselves and their babies.

They rode back in silence. She was deeply appreciative of what Allingham had accomplished and now held him in even higher regard. She wanted to keep him around a little longer. "Dine with me, Mr. Allingham."

Before he could protest, they were at the Bank Hotel, Rebecca leading the way and soon preparing to eat in the finest restaurant in town. She was chatty and Allingham found himself enjoying her light conversation. She talked about the hotel and its restaurant. She was pleased that the manager was varying the menu.

"The chef is French, you know." She didn't wait for Allingham to respond. "That is one thing I miss about England, Mr. Allingham. After a while, beef becomes rather boring. In London, you can find good food, not English food, but food from the continent, and it is all very nice as far as variety goes. Here, ah, out West, it seems the only variety is how the beef is cooked." She smiled and felt a little funny for talking so much. "I imagine you miss the variety in

New York."

Allingham looked on, forlornly, as this was exactly what he'd hoped to avoid. He stared at the menu but wasn't hungry. He tried his best to focus. The menu might as well have been written in a foreign tongue.

He was overwhelmed. He breathed deeply and wanted to cough, then suppressed it. He did not want to cough bloody phlegm into his handkerchief in front of the lady. She reminded him once again about how badly he did not want to die.

Rebecca could see that she was binding him up in knots. Maybe a little alcohol would sooth the monster of a man. "How about a bottle of wine, to celebrate, Mr. Allingham?"

He nodded. "As you wish."

She smiled at the waiter and ordered. Allingham nodded and matched her request. He was not certain what he'd selected.

As they waited, Rebecca told him all about her young life; what she'd done and how long she'd been in America. She told him about her father and Mr. Singh and what brought them to the country and to Arizona. She was intriguing and had the lovely lilting accent of an educated English woman, nothing like the coarse brogues he'd known in the poor places of New York. Rebecca Halsted was a refined English lady.

They sat in silence for a while. They had finished one bottle of wine and Rebecca stared Allingham down. She liked him. She liked the fact that he did not pursue her or try to impress her or banter with her. She liked what he'd done for the prostitutes and it wasn't all just a strategy to bring law and order to Canyon Diablo, she was certain of that.

No, he was acting on more than that. He was acting on compassion, on his own moral platform, on his feelings of repugnance toward the whole enterprise of prostitution. It was wrong and evil and she knew he was working on putting an end to it; she was convinced of that. He was a good and decent man and too much of a mystery for her to stand.

The more she stared the less engaged he'd become and soon he sat, like a marble sculpture, gazing at the plate before him. Now he was slightly drunk from the wine and the mesmerizing woman before him.

"You haven't touched your meal, Mr. Allingham. Do I put you off your food?" She smiled as she knew what effect she had on men. She smiled more broadly as his ears reddened. He was blushing and Rebecca was suddenly ashamed for making him so uncomfortable.

She changed her strategy and began asking him questions about his life.

"Tell me about yourself, Mr. Allingham."

"Oh, well, there is not much to tell. I have been a policeman since the war."

"You were in the war?"

"Yes."

"Which side?"

Allingham looked up at her. It seemed a silly question. He was a northerner. "The north."

"Oh." She grinned. "Don't tell my father. He was hoping the south would prevail. He hoped that England would get your country back."

He realized she was teasing him and he liked it. He felt his face flush again.

Eventually she tired of pulling answers from him and went on to other topics. She knew so much of the land and the people and he was impressed as he'd not known many educated and worldly women. The women he knew were mostly poor or at least working people and working women in New York City did not have much time on their hands to learn about worldly things: politics or culture or anything but working night and day and trying to get enough sleep and enough food to keep their families fed.

She talked more about herself and her time in Flagstaff. Everything about where she'd been and what she'd done. She told him about her family back in England and how her mother had died and how Mr. Singh had been in her life since she could remember and what a wonderful man he was. She talked and talked and he sat and finally could look her in the eye because she was wonderful and had the sweetest voice he'd ever heard. He felt as if he could sit there and listen to her talk on and on about herself for days. He thought that he could very well spend the rest of his life sitting there, in the sunny dining room of the Bank Hotel with his plate of French prepared food in Flagstaff, Arizona and listen to Rebecca Halsted until the day he died, however soon that might be.

But after two hours she stopped; it was time to move on. He hated that, but it had to be. She escorted him out and soon they were back in her carriage, which made no sense as he had no intention of letting her drive him all the way back to Canyon Diablo.

It would take too long and then she'd be stuck there and there were no accommodations remotely appropriate to serve Rebecca Halsted in the hellish place. But, as little sense as it all made, he dutifully sat beside her and watched her pretty hands once again deftly handle the reins and drive the horse.

She stopped the carriage in the middle of a side street and looked him in the eye.

"Why are you here?"

Allingham was struck dumb. He wanted to tell her; tell her he'd be dead by Christmas and that he didn't want to be dead. That he'd come to commit suicide by fighting bad men and now, everything he did was fulfilling and exciting and he was happy. Most especially, he wanted to tell her he was falling hopelessly and desperately in love with the beautiful creature beside him. He looked at her, then at his hands.

"That's my business."

"No, it's not."

The thought of her saying that amused him. It was his comment. It was what he said all the time to annoy people, not on purpose, but because he was compelled, always, to be right and let others know when they were wrong. She wouldn't let it go.

"It's not. It's not." She looked him in the eye and felt him move toward her; the great ugly monster of a man, with protruding ears that made him look like a living, ghastly, somehow poorly thrown toby jug, the great fat lips pursing and ready to meet hers.

They kissed and he suddenly blurted out. "You are the most beautiful creature I've ever known."

And just as quickly, he jumped from her carriage and fled from the scene. He could not stand to be with her a moment longer.

He wandered around Flagstaff and it was nearly dark before he remembered that he had no way of getting back to Canyon Diablo. He didn't care. He even thought about possibly walking back. He didn't want to talk to anyone now. He was thoroughly miserable and wanted only to be alone.

He thought about getting a room at the Bank Hotel. He'd stay there, in his room, and sulk and feel sorry for himself in the nice fancy bed with the crisp sheets. He would lie on his bed and listen to people moving about in the hotel; listen to people who were happy, living their lives, not knowing when they were going to die.

That was the crux of it. He, of course, accepted the fact that he'd someday die, but knowing more or less when was the worst thing imaginable. It was even worse for Allingham because he had no real faith. He did not believe in anything and everything always seemed so purposeless. The only way around despondency for him was constant work; constant and unrelenting work on project after project, solving one puzzle after the next. But now he knew more or less when he was going to die and he didn't want to know it.

He did not think that life was so miserable and purposeless now. It was not something to just pass through as quickly and painlessly as possible, and he did not want his to end so soon.

For all of his time on earth until now, he had moved through life automatically. He hadn't really thought about living before. Now, in the course of a few short weeks, since he had been told that his life was about to end, he had begun to enjoy himself and feel a sense of purpose. He had begun to feel as though his talent, what he was meant to do in life, was finally coming to fruition. He felt a sense of community with the people of Canyon Diablo, his crew of lawmen, Rosario, even the whores, as dysfunctional as they all were. And most especially, he felt a meaningful connection with Rebecca Halstead and her two fathers.

He didn't go to the hotel, but instead went to the livery stable where Rebecca Halsted had picked out his mount. He rented a good horse and rode in the dark, down the road to his town. His town.

When he'd first arrived in Canyon Diablo he had done his best to impose some sort of law and order. He heard the jeers, the same jeers he'd heard many times before back in New York. They amused him. The people doing the jeering thought they were being clever and mean and hurtful, but the insults had the opposite effect on Allingham. He felt that the jeers were a kind of barometer of his success. When the bad people called him names, it meant that he was doing a good job. The good ones would say nothing, but the bad ones always had a lot to say.

Now men and women called out to him; offered him a good morning. They were glad to have him. He'd changed their lives for the better. He'd had an impact and now he didn't want to commit suicide. He didn't want to die. He realized during that long ride home in the dark, he wanted to continue living in Canyon Diablo. He cried as he rode his rented horse through the dark night, as Allingham was passing through the dark night of his soul and wanted to continue into the light of love and life. He cried and rode through the dark where no one could hear or see him. He cried all the way home — to his home — in Canyon Diablo.

CHAPTER XIII:
MAGS

"Not so hard."

She pushed him away from her breasts and lay back in the hot sun. She loved him. But sometimes he was too rough. She was secretly delighted that she could arouse him to the point that he forgot himself and acted so aggressively. He'd learn soon enough what made her happy and what was going too far. They were both learning about love-making and what it meant to pleasure each other.

"Sorry, Mags." He grinned and lay back in the cool water washing over them. He smiled at his little beauty and kissed her again. He loved her more than he thought he'd ever love another person in the world. Now and again he'd just look at her and have difficulty believing that she was all his; his woman, soon to be his wife.

"I'm going to have a baby."

His heart raced. "Really, Mags? Really?"

He was pleased. He wanted a baby, thought a baby would seal the deal, make her his for the rest of their days.

"No, not really, not yet. But if we keep carrying on this way, we're sure to have a baby." She pulled him onto her body and for the third time that day, they made love.

They'd made it way south, Francis inventing a story about traveling to visit a family member and Mags about going to see a cousin in Tucson. They wanted to find the warmth of the mid-autumn Arizona sun. They wandered and camped in the beautiful red rocks, not far from Jerome, but far enough south to be pleasant and warm. They found a clear stream and a blue pool and stripped naked. They spent the day there, bathing in the water and the sun, reveling in their youth. They gloried in their passion for each other and Francis knew he would never be able to surpass this moment of ultimate happiness.

"When will you marry me, Mags?"

She rested, her cheek pressed to his. She felt him inside her and squeezed with all her might. "Soon. We've got to marry soon, Francis, or we're going to have troubles." She smiled at her own naughty thoughts. She never imagined she'd not be a virgin on her wedding day. Now, all she could think about was being this way with Francis. It was the most exciting thing that had ever happened in her life.

Getting up, Francis wrapped his love in a blanket. He built up a fire and they lay together. They ate and caressed and loved again. He was fairly exhausted by now and wanted to sleep but could not waste this time in slumber. He'd never had a woman in his life and now he had and she was the most perfect being he could imagine.

"Mags, when we get back, I'm going to ask your folks if we can be married. We'll marry and then we'll move up to Flagstaff. I'll get work. We'll have a proper home. I'll take you out of the camp towns and buy you a proper house, Mags. We'll have a decent life. You'll never have to live in a dump like Canyon Diablo again, I swear."

Margaret was awake before dawn and watched Francis sleep as he lay with his head in her lap. She ran her fingers through his curls and thought of him as her Samson. She loved him so much and every time she thought of him, of their lovemaking, she got a stirring down into the very core of her being. She loved the lovemaking and hoped, prayed, she was pregnant. She had done everything she had heard about to insure that it happened. She felt sure his seed had taken root and was even now growing. She wanted so badly to be pregnant with his baby that she could barely stand it.

She stretched and Francis didn't wake. She let him sleep and thought about what was happening to her. She became aware of the itching of her backside and realized that she had gotten a lot of exposure in places that were never supposed to know the feel of the sun's hot rays. It would be impossible to explain the tan she was acquiring to anyone but Francis.

Up to this point in her life, no one had been more important to her than her mother and father. She had a moment of panic as she realized just how significantly her life had changed since Francis had come into it. She was a woman now and realized it was time to leave the world of her childhood.

Francis was so much like her pa. He would make them a fine home. They would live in Flagstaff and have a good life. Francis, like her pa, would care for her and love her and she would do the same for him.

He awoke with a start as Margaret was crying. He looked about wildly, ready to fight, finding nothing but his love, sitting with her back to him, looking toward the little stream and pool below, her legs pulled up to her chest. She was sobbing.

"Mags," he sidled up beside her and threw a blanket over her shoulders. He smiled uneasily. "What's wrong, sweetheart, what's wrong?"

"I, I don't want to live in Flagstaff. I don't want to leave my Ma and Pa. I, I . . ." She began coughing and choking on her tears. She looked into Francis's eyes and cried all the harder. The love of his life, the young woman who'd shared everything intimate and private with him, looked like a little child.

"Okay." He smiled. "Okay."

Mags snorted and coughed again. She wiped her tears and nose with the back of her hand. "Really? Do you mean it?"

"Oh, sure, Mags. Oh, sure. But, you still want me, right?"

"More than anything in the world, Francis. More than anything in the world. I, I just don't want to leave them. I love them, Francis." She wiped her eyes again and looked up at him. "And my Pa, he knows I love you. He says he can find you work. I know you think it's not a good life, Francis, but it isn't so bad. It isn't really. The railroad people, they're good people — not the ones you have to fight with and arrest — the other ones, they're good hard-working people, and Pa makes good money. He and Ma, they know they don't, we don', live in a fancy house, and we don't have a life like most folks, but it's our life, and I don't want to leave them." She cried again as he comforted her.

He didn't much care where he lived as long as he was with his Mags. The thought of buying a house in Flagstaff actually terrified him, but he thought it would make her happy. He thought it was the grown up thing to do. He felt a little relieved. He reached over and kissed her forehead and pulled himself from under the blanket. He wrapped her snugly, then dressed and built another fire.

He made her coffee and breakfast and prepared for the journey back home. There'd be no secrets from now on. "Come on, Mags, let's go. We got a wedding to plan."

He glanced at her only to see she had thrown off the blanket. Lying back, opening her arms, she reached for the love of her life.

"Not just yet, darling, not just yet."

CHAPTER XIV:
PUBLIC WORKS

Francis patrolled and came upon Hobbs, some prisoners and his Chinese and Negro men. Every one of them looked as if they'd seen a ghost. They stood around an old well that had been dug many years ago, long before there was an idea of the new little settlement. Two of the prisoners stood, forlornly, with scarves over their noses and mouths. They sucked on peppermints, trying to keep their stomachs calm.

"You boys goin' to rob it or dig it out?" He grinned at the pale men.

The affair had been set up with a tripod and a great hook over the top on which hung a stout rope and a little seat, like what one would see on a trapeze in the circus.

Francis grinned and walked over to the well looking down into it, doubtfully.

"Jesus, boys, that smells worse than old Hobbsie's farts."

It was Allingham's idea to cap the well as

it stunk terribly. He knew what typhus could do, knew of the stories from Europe and England and even in the largest cities of the US. He wanted the thing capped but was told by some of the old timers that corpses had been dumped in it over the years. The remains would have to be cleaned out or it would continue to spoil the aquifer.

But no kind of threat or coercion could get the prisoners to go down into the well. So Hobbs found a young Chinese man who would do it — for enough wages, enough to set him up with a sandwich counter in Flagstaff. The man was being lowered, for the third time that day, to the bottom of the well.

He carried a bucket tied to a rope, and into this he deposited heads, arms, legs, feet, anything that was not attached to a corpse. These would then be hauled up to the gagging, pallid men. For the more intact remains, the young man made a loop, tied it off, and then was himself pulled back out to make room for the ghastly cargo. The stench was unbearable and by the end of the day, they had pulled eight full corpses, five heads, and bits and pieces from another half dozen poor souls from their last resting place.

"Jesus, Hobbsie." Francis lit a cigar to

mask the odor. He handed several to the men and they all smoked and tried their best to keep their lunches down. "I ain't never in all my days seen such a thing." He surveyed the collection of human remains, now piled respectfully on a buckboard. The heads were in varying stages of decay, and Francis looked each one in the eye or, for some, into the sockets where there once were eyes. "I'll be go to hell. These boys seen better days." It was all to be hauled off to the new graveyard at the end of town.

He looked at the young Chinese man, climbing back on his little perch, ready to be lowered again. He was remarkable as the task seemed to have no effect on him whatsoever. He didn't even cover his nose and mouth. "What's your name, mister?"

The Chinese man smiled as white men did not typically ask his name. "I am Lung Hay."

"Well, Mr. Lung Hay, I'd shake yer hand, but you stink to high heavens." Francis grinned. "Whatever they're payin' you, son, it ain't enough."

The young man nodded and grinned as he was lowered back into the well. He was a Christian and called back up, his voice echoing off the curved sides of the stone well. "Back to hell!"

Francis looked down into the well and could see to the bottom, as they'd put a lantern near the base. Mr. Lung Hay had it perched on one of the stones sticking out from the edge, just above the waterline. The well was nearly cleaned out now and did not stink so. Water flowed slowly under the remaining corpses and pieces of corpses, into the aquifer that they'd all been using for drinking. At the realization, Francis belched, took a deep breath and turned, running a distance away. He vomited until he had nothing more to give.

He wiped his mouth and gagged again at the thought of drinking water that had been steeped in the horrific unnatural tea of dead men.

"Jesus, Hobbsie, Mike and Paddy were right."

"How's that?" He smiled uneasily at Francis. Hobbs, himself, only just keeping his retching under control. Francis very nearly inspired him; "They said the water was bad and that's why they only drank beer." He belched again. "I'll be go to hell if they weren't right."

Lung Hay called up, "That's got a ring on it." Hobbsie looked into the bucket and sure enough, a gold ring could be seen on a swollen, nearly denuded hand. Francis looked on in curiosity.

Hobbs nodded. "He gets anything of value we pull out; part of the deal." He nodded at Mr. Lung Hay's treasure trove; a pile of jewelry, coins, a ruined watch, and three, rusted as all hell six shooters.

"I see." Francis smiled.

Lung Hay called up again. "We want cats?"

"Yes, anything that's not water, Lung Hay."

"Okay, rats, too, then." He filled the bucket and gave the line a tug.

Francis was feeling better now. He looked down and spoke to the top of the young man's head. "Hey, Mr. Lung Hay."

"What?"

"Looks like you've got some start-up meat for yer lunch counter."

The Chinese man laughed. Hobbs turned suddenly and pushed past Francis. "That's it." He ran away heaving as he went.

There were other public works projects, most not nearly so horrible or odiferous. Allingham set up a manure storage yard; again, downwind of the town and away from the clean water. He had the prisoners keep it filled. The streets were cleaner than the ones in New York and this resulted in fewer flies and less vermin. The contents of the yard full of manure were sold to the Indians nearby. The money would go to other improvements and, in this way, along with the fines and fees collected by the lawmen, the town was paying for its own upkeep.

Francis did his best to check on the prisoners as they did their duty of a day. He'd grin at the more annoying ones and point as he said something like, "Hey, son, you missed a turd." It was always in good fun and most of the time, taken in stride.

Francis was a joker, but he was fair, and not mean. He had many chances to bully and beat the men and give them a hard time, but that wasn't Francis's way. He would never do anything out of cruelty or to denigrate another man, no matter how low. But this did not stop him from teasing them.

And he was always, as were the Irishmen, quick to come to the defense of the colored of the settlement. Francis would not tolerate anyone harassing a Chinese or an Indian or a Negro; especially now that he knew and loved Rosario as a second mother. His ma had told him that his pa had died protecting all men. His ma had told him that every human being should be treated right and with respect and this was how Francis lived, every day of his life.

Boot Hill had been created, and from the first day of its establishment, the lawmen made good progress toward keeping it as empty as possible. Murders were down, but the graves were up, as Allingham had the prisoners retrieve any corpses that were discovered, hastily buried or hidden throughout the settlement. They'd all get a Christian burial or, if a different religion was known, to the custom of the man's faith. They were all put six feet under, no matter how rocky the terrain, or how high the heat of the day.

This, the public works project, was likely the best deterrent for the minor criminals. None of them wanted to sweat and dig holes for corpses or for the creation of privies. They didn't want to shovel manure or to move corpses from under the sidewalk or from shallow graves in the streets and, because of this, most of them learned to behave, more or less. Those who couldn't moved on.

CHAPTER XV:
NAVAJOS

Hosteen Redshirt sat ahorse outside the trading post while his sons conducted business inside. He was forty at the time of the great tribal roundup of 1864 and lost his entire family and all his worldly possessions then.

After the war he rebuilt, both his fortune and his family. He took another wife and had four fine sons and a daughter who was now deemed a princess. Three of his children were with him this day. He was a wealthy man as he had many sheep and horses and cattle. His family was famous for the blankets they wove and this, as well, added to their fortune.

Now he sat on a fine mount with a fancy tooled saddle and a finely woven blanket underneath. He wore an elaborate Mexican sombrero and spurs with huge rowels and silver inlays on the sides. Other than this, he was dressed as a prosperous Navajo with buckskin leggings and wrists adorned with massive silver ornaments. A crescent charm hung around his neck, displaying to all that he was a man of significant wealth and range. His reach extended far, from Mexico to the south on up to beyond the Grand Canyon, where his blankets were famous among prospectors, hunters, and adventurers alike.

He looked about the settlement and was impressed. He did not, just as all the other great business men of the region, like the shenanigans going on at Canyon Diablo. Now a decent trading post had been established. It was convenient as his ranch was close by and it saved him a trip all the way up to Flagstaff.

Neither he nor his sons drank or fooled about with gambling or whores. They were decent family men and more interested in conducting business and growing their wealth than to involve themselves with such decadence.

He checked his watch, as he eyed the men sauntering around. There were still plenty of miscreants about. He figured they'd never disappear completely. He'd gotten used to that since the white man had arrived many years ago. Now his people worried over the whites as much as they did the

Apaches to the south. He and his boys were tough men and could handle them, though.

If his boys were quick enough, they'd have time to visit Francis and the new lawman. He had heard many stories about the Yankee from New York and wanted to look him over. By the looks of the settlement, the stories were likely all true.

As the lads loaded the wagon, five men surrounded them. They were still drunk from the night before. They'd only recently gotten into town and Francis had locked up three of them over the course of the last several days. They'd made good use of the manure forks and shovels of the Canyon Diablo public works department, but this did not seem to stop them from being stupid and worthless and mean.

They began taunting the lads as the Indians worked to get things in order for their journey home. Redshirt's sons were good and were not provoked. They rarely even acknowledged men like these. In this way they avoided having to kill many loud-mouthed white men. They simply wanted to get on with the business at hand.

Redshirt moved quickly into action. He rode up on the most annoying man, putting himself and his mount between the tormentor and his youngest son.

"You must not do this." He looked at the man with a countenance that was neither angry nor mean. Redshirt was firm, but was never threatening.

In the span of less than a heartbeat firing erupted and four men lay dead. Redshirt's sons stood, smoking guns in hand, ready for any other trouble. They did not have to worry, the fifth man ran on urine soaked legs toward the jail. He did not want to fight them now that his pals were done for.

The patrón called to his boys to move the bodies into the shade, out of the way so that no one could trample them. Then they rode out.

Francis was in the middle of a yarn when the man, pale and shaking, barely able to speak, burst in on them. Allingham looked him over, noted the urine soaked trousers and ordered him to step back, out of the barracks; he could explain himself from the doorway.

"Marshal, Indians. They've come in and attacked the trading post."

Francis turned in his chair, "What Indians?"

"That old man, the one they call Redshirt, and his sons. Just came in and shot up four men."

"That's bullshit." Francis stood up and looked the man over. "You're a piss-soaked lying son of a bitch."

He ignored Francis and looked at Allingham who now stood up and prepared to investigate. "I ain't, Marshal, I ain't. I, I was there, just standing there, minding my own business when they come a thundering in, shooting an' whoopin' war cries and killing everyone in their paths. I, I'm lucky to be alive."

It was nonsense and everyone knew it, but the piss-soaked man was adamant. He signed an affidavit and Allingham had to follow up. He wrote up the warrant for the old man and his sons as Francis and his crew finished dinner.

"What are you plannin', Captain?"

He didn't wait for Allingham's answer but started in on one of his stories, as it was suppertime now, and he had the Irishmen and Hobbs and Rosario to entertain.

"You know, I'm big medicine with old Redshirt and his clan?" He again didn't wait for a reply.

"Back when I first came out here, I was scared shitless of Indians. Heard all the stories; heard about Custer. I thought, damn, I'm goin' to lose my scalp. And then, one day I was out, not far from here, on a big assed flat mesa and a lightning storm came up. Like you read about. Well, I wasn't worried about any Indians then, I was worried I was goin' to be electrocuted right on the spot. I started riding for all I was worth toward somethin'. Hell, I didn't even know what; a ditch or a swale, anything to get me down low, and then I saw him, away off in a distance: an Indian. He was, I swear, thinkin' the same damn thing and we rode, both at the same time for the same gully and wham, a big old bolt a lightning come down and knocked that old boy like he was no more'n a fly flicked off old Hobbsie's ass."

Rosario smiled at the thought of a fly resting on Hobbs's backside and looked at Francis. "What did you do, Francis?"

"Well, I can't tell you what I did first, Mamacita, but, if you'll recall that boy's pants, who was in here earlier, you'll get a good idea. But the second thing I did was walk up on that poor Indian fellar and looked him over and I swear, he was smokin' like a burned out mesquite branch lyin' on the ground. His horse got the worst of it; poor creature was dead and its feet were all smokin', and my God, the stench, like burned hair. Blood poured out of his ears and nose and mouth. He was shoed and those horseshoes must have been red-hot."

Mike spoke up between bites. He liked Francis's stories, but never believed most of them. "By Jasus and begorrah, this is no yarn. Tell us, Francis, this is no yarn."

Francis grinned. He was used to not being believed. He held up his hand in honor, "I swear, folks, may God send down another lightning bolt, just like that one, and strike me dead if I'm lyin'. It's all true, all true."

He sat back down and resumed his story. "Anyways, that old boy, well, he was really a young boy, he was dead as a church pew on payday, he was, and so I picked him up and hoisted him over my saddle. And you know what?"

"What?" They all leaned forward in their chairs. Francis had them now.

"I plopped that old boy down pretty hard, too hard I guess. It sort of made him start up again. Like kickin' a sleepin' pig it was. That old boy coughed and choked and hacked out a bunch a phlegm and he was fine as frog hair. So I pulled him back down and he sat and looked about. He had these silver bracelets on his wrists and you know, they burned hell out of his skin, and he lost a bit of hair, singed off like he got too close to a fire. But other than that, he was good.

So, I took him back to his home and I was a great hero and that was the son of old Redshirt, his oldest son Natani, and we're great friends now and," he turned to Allingham, "Captain, ain't no way in heaven or hell they did what that piss-soaked bastard said they did."

Allingham stood up. He had things to do. "I know it, Francis, but we've got four dead men to bury, and a man who claims he saw them murdered. We've got to follow it up. There's no way around it."

"So, what's the plan then, Captain?" Paddy spoke up. He did not like the idea of harassing anyone, even Navajos. If they killed in a fair fight, there was no harm done, and they'd just as likely saved the police force a future inconvenience.

"I'll go get them, take them up to the court in Flagstaff. I've got affidavits from the trading post people; all said the men are innocent of murder, all say the sons and Redshirt are in the clear."

This encouraged Francis and the men, but the young deputy suddenly had a thought. "No disrespect intended, Captain, but old Redshirt, he's not a big fan of the government, with the whole Kit Carson thing, and them wiping out his family and taking all his stock an' such."

Allingham stood, stone-faced. He hadn't thought about that. "Go on."

"Well, Captain," Francis scratched his chin. He could not think of a diplomatic way of saying it. "You, Captain, well, you could piss off the Pope in Rome. I mean, you could piss off Jesus Christ himself, just with a look."

Everyone laughed and then thought better of it and looked down at their plates as Francis continued. "Old Redshirt, he's a proud man, and a powerful man and, well, Captain, he might just as well cut your ears off and feed 'em to his hogs."

Allingham was amused but he wouldn't show it. "Are you going to get to the point, Francis? Or will we be here, listening to you blathering until midnight?"

"Yes, yes, Captain. Captain, I don't think you've got it in you to convince Redshirt to come in to court, get this thing cleared up. I don't think you're the man for the job." He looked around at the others. Everyone knew he was right. Allingham was good, in his own way, but he was no ambassador, no negotiator in any sense of the word. "Let me go. I'll talk to him. I'll get him to Flagstaff. We'll get it sorted, I swear, Captain, and I'll be back in no time at all, all good. What ya say, Captain?"

■ ■ ■ ■

Francis was up before sunrise and ready to ride. Rosario was there, holding the reins of his mount, sitting on Hobbs's favorite gelding. Francis looked at her with a wide grin.

"What's this, Mamacita?"

"I will go with you, Francis." She handed over his reins, turned and started riding out, forcing the young man to catch up. He did and rode up next to her. She looked extra pretty today and he wondered at that.

"What are you up to, ma'am? How the boys goin' to eat? They'll starve to death without you."

"No, they are fine. I made extra food and the boys are planning a stew, an Irish stew, God help them all, that sounds disgusting."

They rode and Francis thought on it and waited for her to tell him her big secret. He knew there must be a connection. Maybe she wasn't a Mexicana after all. Maybe she was some long-lost Navajo princess.

"I know Redshirt very well, Francis." She saw him grin and knew he didn't understand. She figured she'd just go ahead and get it over with. "He used to visit me when he was out this way doing business." She smiled and looked on at Francis who she

knew could be quite the bumpkin sometimes. He still did not understand. "In a
biblical way, Francis."

"Oh, oh!" He blushed and she smiled
again.

"He's a good one, Francis. He is a good
lover and he is a good man and good friend.
I am not going to give him any trouble. This
is our secret. Redshirt has a jealous wife.
You understand?"

"Sí, Mamacita, I understand. Mum's the
word." He put a finger to his lips. He rode
on and looked back at his companion. "You
are full of surprises, Mamacita, full of
surprises for sure."

"I know he trusts you, Francis, but he
trusts me, too. Between us we will get him
to go in, I am certain of this. We need to do
this. He's a good man, and he's had many
bad things from you gringos. Many bad
things have happened to the Navajos. Many
bad things."

Francis heard some of the stories. He was
not a good student of history, and most of
the newspaper accounts made it out that
the Indians were nothing more than sub-
human savages. They advocated that the
Indians needed rubbing out, declaring they
needed to be put on reservations where they
could be controlled. Most Easterners didn't

know how the Army had gotten them under control.

"Understood, Mamacita. All's I know is that Redshirt's a good fellar and he needs to be cleared of all this. Ain't no way I'm lettin' him be railroaded by a bunch of shitheads."

She smiled. "You are a good boy, Francis."

"And you're a good lady, Mamacita. You're a good lady, indeed."

They rode along together and Francis regarded his companion. She was the first Mexican he'd ever known and she fascinated him. She was a tough old gal, a long way from home, living in nothing much more than a little wood hut in the middle of the desert.

She caught him watching her and smiled. "Do you think me a bad woman, Francis, for carrying on like a whore?"

Francis looked pained by the suggestion that he harbored such ill thoughts. "Why would you call yourself that, Mamacita? I never thought any such thing. Why that's a terrible thing to say, ma'am."

She looked down the road on which they were riding. "I've been alone for a long time, Francis. I came to Arizona following my second husband. Then he died and I was alone." She looked at Francis again. "You know, men are not the only ones who get an itch, Francis. Men are not the only ones who like a warm body pressed against them on a cold night."

Francis blushed. He was not used to such free talk about relations, especially with a woman, and one who was old enough to be his mother. "I know, I know."

Redshirt's sons surrounded them on the road just outside the family ranch. It was not far from Canyon Diablo and the Indians expected visitors. Natani rode up to Francis and held out his hand. "Brother, it is good to see you again."

"And you, Natani." He nodded to Rosario. "You know Señora Rosario, I think." Natani removed his hat and bowed. He and his brothers escorted them to their home.

The ranch was impressive; it was expansive and well maintained. Redshirt was resourceful and varied his investments and stock. He loved the sheep, as they provided the wool so crucial to his weaving enterprise, but he also had goats, horses, and cattle. His sons were good horsemen and wranglers and captured many mustangs in the desert. These were properly broken and traded and bred. Everyone respected Redshirt's horses and they were sought out by cowboys as far away as Texas and New Mexico.

The main ranch house was built of adobe brick and parged with red mud. There were many outbuildings; they'd cropped up over the years, according to Redshirt's needs and cash flow. Francis was impressed, as much had changed for the better since his last visit.

He half regretted not taking the old man up on his offer, as the chief wanted to repay him for his kindness to his son. Francis had indeed saved the lad's life. It would have been a pretty easy life for Francis, as they liked him and he was entertaining, and the Indians liked to sit around of an evening and listen to stories. Francis always had good ones.

But Francis was more ambitious and had too much a wandering spirit; he had to move on. Once in a while, on especially cold or windy or wet nights, lying under nothing but his horse blanket, he often regretted his decision, and at least a dozen times vowed to get back to the Indian's ranch and take him up on his offer to cowboy for the old Navajo chief.

Redshirt was sitting by the fire and brightened when he saw them. He was waiting for the government men. He knew they would not leave this alone and was not certain what fate awaited him, but resigned to expect the worst. He hugged Francis and smiled warmly at Rosario, but not so warmly as to give their secret away. Rosario did not mind.

"You are an unlikely execution squad."

"We ain't here to do you harm, Chief." They sat down and the little children of the ranch gathered 'round as they loved Francis and wanted to hear some jokes. Francis greeted them all, letting them dig through his pockets for the hard candy he kept in good supply.

They dined and Francis joked and told stories. Finally, it was late and Redshirt looked him in the eye.

"So, Francis, you did not come to my home to tell jokes and stories and give out pieces of candy. What do we do now?"

"Well, Chief, you know I'm with the law now, down there in Canyon Diablo. We know you and your boys done nothing wrong. We know you were wronged and you had to kill them men. But one of the survivors, the yellow bastard who ran away when the killin' started, he wrote out a complaint, and there's four dead fellars. We got to have it cleared up. Got to get you to court in

Flagstaff. We got to get your version and your boys' version of what happened. We got depositions from the trading post. It's all going to be okay. I promise, Chief. We're askin' you, me and Miss Rosario, we're asking you to please come on with us tomorrow. I swear to you, no jail, no shackles, just us on a ride, up to court. One day, then back home."

Redshirt straightened. They could see the pain in his eyes. The scars of the roundup were deep and he remembered them too well. "Francis, you are a good man and I thank you. But the government men, the courts, the law, they have not been good to us. The whites, not all, but the bastards like the ones we killed yesterday, they never stop. Francis, they never stop, and we need to kill them all the time. They rustle our cattle and horses. They make trouble for my boys. They come because all the other lands in the US have pushed them out. It seems Arizona is a magnet for the bad ones. It is tiresome and the more that come, the more we have to fight. It seems like we never get any peace. We just want to be left alone."

He lit a cigarette and smoked and looked into the fire. "I am older than my years, Francis, and it is because of the white man. I am not so certain I want to spend my days

274

in a jail cell. I would rather they track me down, kill me and let me die in peace, than all that."

Francis felt a little desperate at the chief's words. He was not so good at convincing a man of something he himself thought a lot of nonsense. Redshirt was right, and he'd done right. Even going up to Flagstaff to make a statement, to Francis's mind, was too much to ask of him. It was too much of an imposition on the man, but it had to be. If it didn't happen, they'd send the National Guard or Army after him, and Francis knew, that very likely, that would very well end in disaster.

"Redshirt, my friend. I am not a selfish fellow, you know that. But a debt must be repaid."

Redshirt looked at Francis and then at his sons and on to Rosario. He was a little confused. Francis continued as he thought the drama added to his case.

"I saved Natani, and now he's my brother. You said that's your Indian way, and you said you are beholden to me. Remember that?"

"Of course." Redshirt now knew Francis's meaning.

"And I told you that I didn't want nothin', and that was true. But now I've changed my mind, Chief. I'm calling in the debt."

Redshirt grinned uneasily and shook his head. He fully understood what was on Francis's mind.

"Francis, you are a tricky fellow." He stroked his chin and thought on it. "What must we do to repay this debt, then?"

"Ride tomorrow, with me and Mamacita. We all ride in, armed. We talk to the sheriff of Flagstaff. We get the deposition outta the way and we come back here, to your home. Done!" He stood up and put out his hand for Redshirt to shake.

"And what if they, the government men up at Flagstaff, don't agree with this plan, Francis? What if they have other ideas?"

Francis became angry; not at the chief, he had only respect and admiration for the man. But the more he thought on the whole thing the more it angered him. "Jesus Christ, it's ridiculous to even think it. Indians on a murderous raiding rampage, stopping off at the trading post to do some shoppin'? Goddamned ridiculous."

He was getting angrier, outraged at the idea that the piss-soaked man would have the nerve to make such a claim and waste everyone's time. "See, Chief, this is the kinda idiots we gotta deal with every day in Canyon Diablo. It's enough to drive a fellar to drink. There is no way in hell any court is goin' to follow this through." He thought on it, "But if they do, then they can go to hell." He grinned. "And we'll all send 'em there."

Francis was tired and spent. He was in one of Redshirt's private rooms in the main house, a great honor as a man of Francis's stature would not normally rate anything more than a cot in the bunkhouse with the rest of the hands. He was alone and thinking of Mags when he heard a knock at the door.

He opened it, and standing there, as pretty as ever, was Redshirt's daughter. She smiled provocatively at Francis. It made him a bit uncomfortable.

"Hello, Francis." She slid past him, not waiting for an invitation to enter the room.

"Hello, Yanaba. How you doin'?" He looked down on the top of her head as Yanaba was a tiny young lady. His glance drifted down further to an ample bosom. He was pleased to see her, but felt a little nervous, as it was not appropriate for her to be in his bedroom. It was not so much that he was afraid of what Redshirt might think or do, Yanaba was a grown woman in the chief's eyes and her actions were her own.

But Francis had Mags on his mind. Mags would not like a beautiful Navajo princess in her fiancé's bedroom.

Yanaba was nearly eighteen and had been a widow for more than a year. She had two living children and she was the most beautiful woman Francis had known up until Mags. She liked Francis very much but was married when he had come into their lives. Now that her husband was dead, Yanaba thought it would be good to test the waters.

She reclined on his bed, her long raven-colored hair, freshly brushed, cascaded over her shoulders and down her back. She wore a sheer sleeping gown of silk covered by a brightly colored Chinese robe. It was flimsier yet and hung open, not by accident. She was barefoot and rested one leg on the bed, revealing her shapely brown legs to mid-thigh.

She could tell right off her expedition would not be fruitful.

"Who is she, Francis?"

"Who's who?" Francis was being a bumpkin again. He did not know how transparent his feelings were for Mags. The princess could tell, but Yanaba's actions and dress were also distracting him, he was finding it difficult to concentrate.

"The woman you love."

"Oh, oh." He blushed.

"Twist us a cigarette, Francis." She tossed her tobacco pouch at him. He did, and they smoked together in his room. Francis moved to the foot of the bed, sitting at Yanaba's pretty bare feet.

"She's a gal from the railroad. Her dad's a engineer."

"She is lucky, Francis."

"Thank you, Yanaba." He grinned. "I feel pretty darned lucky, too." He thought for a moment and felt the flutter. He was just getting the idea now. Yanaba was interested in him. This was vexing. But then again, girls always liked Francis, as he was handsome and kind and a little naïve. He was flattered and felt a little silly. Two beautiful women after him, but he could have only one.

He looked her over and could now see the hint of her desire in her pretty almond-shaped eyes. He could also clearly see through her flimsy outfit, the gifts given her by the Almighty, and this was confounding to him. He thought it a little wicked of her to do such a thing; he didn't realize fully that she was angling for him. She'd steal him if she could.

He could have her and they'd spend the night together and he'd have to tell Mags that the deal was off as he was now with

Yanaba, the Navajo princess, and he'd live out his days working on this ranch with Redshirt and his boys. He'd have an instant family, a boy and a girl and he and Yanaba would have more. They'd have lots of babies.

"Have you had her yet?" She regarded him through her cigarette smoke. She was overwhelmingly beautiful.

It brought Francis out of his trance. He looked at her. She was a child of seventeen, yet as grown-up, as mature as all the women of the ages. She had known love and birth and death in her short time on earth and this matured her beyond her limited years. She was a woman and he knew that she was smarter and worldlier than he would ever be. He blushed and his pulse pounded in his ears.

"I, I . . ." He looked at Yanaba, then away. "Yes."

She stood up. "Okay, Francis." She stubbed out her cigarette and kissed him on the cheek. He could smell her. She smelled of soap and good tobacco and a little perfume and the scent of Yanaba; she smelled like a very appealing woman. "Okay." She walked out.

He lay back on his bed and he could smell her again, on the bedclothes. His head pounded. If he'd a been a little drunk, he'd have asked her to stay, maybe. He thought on that. He wouldn't. He wouldn't, even though carrying on with Mags made the act the top item on his list of things he liked to do in the world. Being with a woman caused everything else to seem boring and mundane and commonplace and just not worth doing anymore. Being with a woman was the most fun he'd ever had in his life, and he could have had the same fun with Yanaba and no one would have been the wiser.

But that wasn't the right thing and Francis knew it. It would have been fun enough, but mechanical. There'd be no love in it. It would be no better than being with the whores. And perhaps he would have given Yanaba the wrong idea. She wasn't just looking to rut. She was looking to see if Francis might be interested in her. In all of her, not just her carnal offerings.

He sat up and began to undress, thought better of it and first walked over to bar the door. He wished he had a drink.

Francis got them to Flagstaff early and they tied up at the end of town, nearest to the courthouse and to the road back to Redshirt's ranch.

"Mamacita, need you to stay here with the horses. Be ready to make a break."

"Okay, Francis." She smiled and he gave her a wink.

"If it's all okay, I'll call for you, so you don't have to be here bored and alone. Okay, Mamacita?"

He looked at the Indians. "You boys, all put your guns inside your pants. They'll want you to give 'em up if they see you wearin' shootin' irons."

They complied and he was pleased with how they looked. The chief kept his gun tucked in a shoulder holster and a fighting knife tucked in the top of a boot. He pulled the legs of his pants out and let them fall over the boot tops. The knife was hidden. He, too, was ready.

"I'm goin' to carry a shotgun, so's we'll have plenty of firepower in the event we need it."

Redshirt looked on and nodded at Francis. He was proud of the young man; he knew he was a good lawman and took his duty seriously. He also knew that Francis would shoot his way out of the courthouse if events didn't happen the right way. The chief followed with his sons. He understood the sacrifice Francis was willing to make for him and his boys.

The judge arrived at nine, Allingham was

already there and waiting. He nodded to the chief and his sons. He looked at Francis, a little surprised at his choice of weaponry, and just as quickly figured out that Francis did not intend it to be used for guarding the prisoners. He, too, was proud of the young fellow.

The courtroom was fairly packed as Redshirt was a famous Indian in the territory. No one had any enmity for him. He was a respected member of society and they knew the terrible times he'd lived through. Most wanted to wish him well, stand as character witnesses, if necessary.

The judge eyed Francis standing next to the clan with his scattergun. "Is that a little much, deputy? Everyone knows the Redshirt clan. We don't believe you'll need that contraption."

"Yes, your honor," he nodded to the chief and walked out, almost running into Mr. Singh and Rebecca Halsted entering the courthouse. They, too, intended to support Redshirt and were ready to offer themselves as character witnesses on behalf of the Indian men.

Francis hollered down the street to Rosario, beckoning her forward. It was going to be all right. He handed her the shotgun and instructed her to come into court once she'd secured it on his mount.

It was Allingham's turn to perform. The judge liked Allingham, as the judge was a direct man. He did not like a lot of chatter and appreciated when folks attended his court properly attired. Allingham sat, arrow straight, waiting for his turn to be called.

"And Marshal Allingham, I will expect you to open these proceedings, as you took the affidavit."

"Yes, judge." Allingham never called judges your honor, he always called them judge. "I request these proceedings be cancelled and this deposition be dismissed."

"And why?" The judge was obliged to the Indians. He liked them, and botching this could spell further trouble for them later on. He wanted it closed properly.

"The person, this Smith, is no longer able to corroborate his testimony."

"Oh, and why is this, Marshal Allingham?"

"Because he is dead, judge."

The gavel came down. "Case dismissed. Chief Redshirt, please step forward."

Francis walked up next to the Indian as he still was not fully convinced or certain of the judge's intentions. He still had an idea he might have to rescue his friend. The judge now looked him in the eye. "You are a zealous deputy, young man, but Chief Redshirt here is not a fellow who needs guarding." He looked Francis over carefully. "How long have you been in Arizona, lad?"

"Two years, sir."

"Well, it might be worthwhile, if you are going to be any kind of lawman, to know who your friends are and who are your enemies. The chief here is a good man, a respected member of this community, and whatever happened to those men who ended up dead, well, it's no fault of the chief here. You'd do well to remember that, young man." He waved him off, as if shooing a fly from his dinner. "Go away."

Francis grinned sheepishly and then thought better of it. Grinning, to a severe judge, could be construed as a sign of contempt and Francis did not want to pay a fine. "Yes, your honor."

The judge escorted the Indian back to his chambers with a hand on Redshirt's shoulder, "My wife needs some new blankets, my friend."

Francis turned and left with the sons. They walked outside and he smiled at Rosario as he scratched his head. "I'll be go to hell."

CHAPTER XVI:
WORK

"This is a lotta bullshit and I aim to put an end to it." French Annie held court among the confederacy of misfits. Even One-Eyed Sal was in on it and both women were civil to each other for the first time, really, since they'd known each other. "That big-eared son of a bitch carpet bagger Yankee bastard."

The man who ran the gambling house was not as certain.

"Sure, Annie, he's run a lot of boys out. But that bunch, the worst of 'em, they never had any money, anyway. Hell, we used to serve a hundred men to make five hundred dollars, now we make the same amount serving less than half that."

She snorted, this was true for gaming houses and saloons, but her whorehouse wasn't faring so well and he knew it.

"I can't make any money like this. He's taken all the good girls. Bastard's probably boning half of them on the side." She spit and continued after wiping her mouth with the back of her hand. "And then the Princess getting killed, that was the limit. Now we can't make shit around here." She glared at Sal. "What the hell kinda lawman is he, anyway? The one who got Princess is still loose. Everyone knows The Ape didn't do it."

"Well, this's your fault. Not the Princess getting knocked off, no one would have ever thought The Ape would kill her, and he did, Annie, you know right well he did it. But, Jesus, you and Sal got some fertile girls. They can roll in a wet spot and get pregnant. What you need is a Madame Restell on your payroll."

"She cut her own throat, you know." The dim barman spoke up, pleased that he could offer something to the conversation.

"Not *the* Madame Restell, you fool, everyone knows she's dead. But these gals, it ain't a damned whorehouse, it's a goddamned rabbit farm. Couldn't swing a dead cat without hittin' a newborn babe or at least a whore with a swollen belly."

"There's nothin' wrong with lettin' the girls have babies. It was working out, we were doing fine until that jug-headed New York bastard came along. What we need," she lit a cigar, "is something like what they did down to those bastards in Tombstone. Carpet baggin' Yankee scum got theirs, at least some of 'em. That one, Wyatt Earp, he'll get his, soon enough. No doubt, he'll get his. Just a matter of time."

Sal looked serious through her good eye. "What are you suggesting?"

Annie stared through her smoke. "Get someone in here with a pair a balls to rub 'em out. All of 'em, that simple smilin' fool and those two micks, and the damned jug-eared bastard. Kill 'em all."

The gambling house man paled. This was a conspiracy to kill Federal Marshals, and he wasn't a violent, or even a criminally-minded, man. He just ran a saloon and a gambling house. He'd never really stepped outside the law. And besides, he had other scruples. He didn't like the brothels. He had a cousin who was a whore during the war in Washington and she ended up dying of syphilis. He was not a fan of brothels and pitied the whores.

He put up a cautionary hand. "Now, Annie, you've just got your blood up. Let's calm down, let's calm down. We don't know any assassins, and no one's yet been able to get at these men. No one's yet had the guts to take 'em on. Look what happened to that gunslinger."

The dim barman chimed in again. "He cut his own throat, too, you know?"

The manager ignored him and touched his trembling lips with his shaking fingers. "And besides, once the bridge is in, this place'll be no more. There'll be an end to it, an end to us; we'll all have to move on. There'll be plenty of end o' the line camps, and I doubt this marshal will be involved with any of them. He doesn't work for the railroad. Hell, in another six months, we'll have forgotten his name."

"Yeah, well, we've got some time left, maybe a year or more. The railroad's run outta money, I've heard. They're having trouble even payin' for the bridge, much less gettin' it down here. Anyway, *I've* got contacts. *I've* got some ideas. I'll show them, I'll show you. I'm not afraid to get a little blood on my hands." She looked more confident than she was and Sal knew it.

The one-eyed madam stood up. She looked on them dismissively and walked out. "You sound like a pair of children planning to steal marbles in the schoolyard." She was gone.

Allingham kept busy with work every day and tried not to think about dying. He avoided Rebecca Halsted and this was not difficult as she no longer had any need to visit Canyon Diablo since he'd taken the safe house away. He was embarrassed, really, to see her anyway with the way he'd behaved, jumping from her carriage like a frightened little schoolboy; but he knew of no other way around it.

It was preposterous to pursue her. He'd be dead soon. What could they do in a few months? He was nearly twice her age. He was hideous: malcontent, socially inept, unpleasant and a stone-hearted man. She was the opposite of everything he was, and she could have any of the finest gentlemen in Arizona. It was all completely absurd. He was convinced of this and believed that she was just so good, so decent that she'd briefly gotten caught up in the moment, letting him kiss her with his big ugly lips. She was reacting to the emotion of the foundling home. She was just grateful and surprised about what a fine and decent gesture it was. She had allowed the kiss as a sign of her gratitude.

He knew deep down that he was a good man. He was a very conscientious, good and decent man, and what he did for the whores was a reflection of that. Allingham did what was right and decent because it was the right thing to do. He worked quietly and thoroughly to uphold the law, not for recognition or accolades, but because it was moral and right. He was a good lawman because he possessed all the skills required for the job. He had nerve and intelligence and a sense of right and wrong and the work ethic to carry out his duties to the fullest of his abilities and talents.

Even when it came to the gunslinger, the big good-looking man, Sckogg. He could have let the bastard gun him down but he didn't. That was curious to him. Why didn't he? The Chinese fellow was the answer. He needed to make things right. He made a mistake, by his own reckoning, and it cost the poor Chinese cook his life. He couldn't let the bastard gunslinger get away with that. This was his problem with letting a bad man kill him. This was the fundamental flaw in his suicide plan. Because to let a man kill him meant that the man would go on to do more black-hearted mischief and Allingham could not let that happen. He had to make things right; to bring the bad men to justice, always.

All this pondering put him in a foul mood. He hated all this intellectual conflict, this self-examination of his, heretofore, unexamined life. He once again felt angry; cheated. He breathed deeply and tasted the metallic tang on his tongue, the acrid sting of death. He was furious. He otherwise felt fine. How could a dying man feel so physically well?

His thoughts were interrupted by an old woman. Upon closer examination, he realized she wasn't as old as he first thought. He took in her piercing blue eyes and silvery hair and noted that her fair skin fairly glowed in contrast to her black mourning dress. She stood in his way and he nearly walked into her as he had a lot on his mind and was in no mood for banter with miserable crones.

She was from Elyton, Alabama. Or at least was until it got gobbled up by Birmingham. It seemed that was the way of the woman's life; everything had been gobbled up. The Civil War had taken her sons and husband, reconstruction took her peaceful home and now a bad man had taken the only thing precious to her that she had left in the world. Her youngest son, conceived when she was forty years old, just before her husband had left to be killed in the war.

They hadn't wanted another child, not really. So he was a miracle baby. She raised him by herself and when he, as a young man, had announced he was going west to seek his fortune, she had begged and pleaded with him to stay home.

She had tried everything she could think of to get him to change his mind. But he wouldn't do it. He had heard about the riches found out west and had to go, seeking adventure and wealth.

He went, and got no farther than Canyon Diablo. And now she was here, in the hell hole, on Hell Street, to do something; visit his grave, bring him home, she really didn't know. She just needed to be near him one last time.

"Sir, are you the Marshal?"

"I am." He tried to keep walking, but couldn't. He stood impatiently before her.

She looked the Yankee up and down and pushed back her revulsion. She still could not bring herself to be kind to Yankees, after nearly twenty years.

She swallowed her pride and continued. "I would like to shake your hand." She held her hand out to him and he looked at her as if he didn't know what the custom meant. Reluctantly, he took her proffered hand and when he did she grabbed his big fist with both of her hands.

She turned and pointed north, just outside of town, as if Allingham had not heard of the cemetery and she was showing it to him for the first time. "You put my boy there and I thank you, Marshal. I thank you."

It was another of Allingham's good deeds, as not only was Hell Street initially lined with trash and waste, but many of its earlier victims, buried in shallow graves wherever they'd been cut down. These were the lucky ones. The unlucky ones were dumped in the back alleys or out in the desert to be torn apart and consumed as carrion.

Sometimes, when there was especially heavy horse buggy or freight wagon traffic, corpses would literally pop out of the ground, sit up in their decaying state, as if to look about themselves to see if anything had changed since they'd departed.

Allingham created Boot Hill. He had his prisoners dig up all the corpses from their inadequate resting places to give them a proper Christian burial, even going so far as marking the graves, and this poor woman was one of the victims who'd benefited from his act of decency and kindness, her son a victim of a senseless act of violence. He had been robbed of less than a dollar and left to rot where he fell.

Allingham looked her in the eye, could see her sadness and pain. It was just the kind of pain he did not want anyone to have for him, once he was gone. He didn't want the pretty lady, Rebecca Halsted, to feel anything for him and the epiphany gave him new resolve.

His back stiffened and he looked at her arrogantly, dismissively. "Well," he glared down his fat nose. "If you want to dig him up and take him home, you're welcome." He tipped his hat and moved around her, swiftly going on his way.

Rebecca Halsted looked on in horror. She and Mr. Singh witness to the lawman's callous act. Allingham marched away, leaving the old woman in the dusty street, dejected and dismayed. Mr. Singh went to her, took her gently by the arm and offered her the comfort that she had expected from the irascible Allingham. Rebecca charged after the marshal.

"Mr. Allingham!"

He was surprised to see her and hid his pleasure well.

"Yes?"

"I, I haven't seen you since, well, since we kissed." She smiled demurely and blushed.

"Yes, well. I'm sorry about that. That was inappropriate. That will not happen again." He began to move off and she stopped him.

"What is *wrong* with you?"

He looked her in the eye. "Nothing."

She became angry. "See, here, Mr. Allingham. I, I don't even know your first name."

She waited for him to tell her, realized that he would not and continued. "I, I don't *kiss* men, Mr. Allingham. I am not that sort. And, well, you, you . . ." she was becoming furious. She had another thought. "That poor woman, back there, that was terrible."

"I am sure she won't have trouble finding someone to transport the corpse back to her home."

"That's not what I mean and you know it, Mr. Allingham. Your actions and words are not the same. The woman just wanted a kind word. She wanted to thank you for treating her son's remains with dignity."

Rebecca was fairly shaking now; hardly able to contain her fury. "You spoke to her as if she wanted directions to the nearest saloon."

"Oh?" He looked in the direction of the jail. He started to leave and she stopped him again.

"You, you just stand there, Mr. Allingham." She pointed her finger at his face, demanding that he stay still. "I'm not finished with you. I'm not finished and you will not move!"

He stood still and waited. He felt himself sweating; she scared him a bit. Allingham never knew fear in the war or on the streets of New York, but he felt it now. She scared him.

"You do noble and kind things, then you, you stand there, like a stone wall; like you have no feelings at all. You make no sense, you . . ."

He cut her off. This all needed to end. "Miss Halsted, I am sorry." It was killing him to lie to her, to be the one to cause the pained expression in her eyes. "You have mistaken my actions for philanthropy." He reared back, spine straight and eyes cast down his fat nose. He stared into her eyes. "I have been hired to stop lawlessness in this town. Prostitution is not illegal, yet, regrettably, but I know how to put a brothel out of business, having done so on many occasions back home. I moved those children so that the desirable whores would follow, thereby crippling the commerce in this settlement. Nothing more."

He turned and pointed back at the old lady with Mr. Singh. "I don't care a hoot in hell for that old woman or her troubles. If she'd a raised her boy right, maybe he'd a not likely died in this horrible place. She is not my concern. If I had my way, they'd all live in filth in this dump with corpses popping out of the streets like dandelions, I don't care, madam. I simply don't care. I have a duty. I've taken money for a job and the job shall be done."

She stood, jaw agape. He *was* a monster inside and out. He pushed past her.

"Good day, madam. Good day."

He stormed into the barracks and found Francis and Rosario admiring a ring in a fancy box. Allingham fairly tripped over Hobbs's dog then screamed at it to get out. He was furious; they'd never seen the man in such a state.

"What's wrong, Captain?" Francis smiled his normal smile.

"Get that filthy animal out of here. No more." He pointed accusingly at the dog's bed. "No more." He poured a cup of water and drank it, looking at Francis holding the ring.

"It's for Mags, Captain. We're going to be married." He was proud and Rosario patted him on the shoulder. She was pleased to see the young fellow so happy.

"Then you'll not work for me anymore." He turned to storm out and Francis stood up.

"What do you mean, Captain?" Francis was shocked, the news striking him like a hammer blow.

Allingham turned, screamed and sprayed

spittle with his words. "I am *not* a captain! And you, you will not work for me when married. Married men do not fight, married men worry over their stupid wives and stupid children, and having a family and a stupid worthless life. You will not be married and work for me." He stormed out.

He rode into the desert as he could not work. He felt lower than he'd felt since he was told he had the cancer. He hated this. He hated being happy and he'd been happy. It wasn't an emotion he'd felt ever and he really didn't like it. He didn't like to be miserable, but he didn't like to be happy. He preferred to feel numb. He preferred to fill his thoughts and hours with work; only work, planning and outwitting bad men. That's what motivated him. That was what he was good at, that was what he did well.

He'd never permitted himself to receive accolades and the admiration or gratitude from the people he helped. He didn't like that, either. He owed them nothing and they owed him even less.

He stopped at the canyon; looked out and then down at the giant slash in the earth and thought that this was it, this was the thing that had changed his life. He looked at it and thought it must be some unholy or unnatural place. He'd heard stories of the people who'd died in the canyon: Indians had died in floods, cattlemen had died trying to get their herds across, Apaches had used it as a shooting gallery when anyone, Indian or white alike, tried to follow them after a raid. It was a place of death, as if the earth had opened up too deeply, too close to hell, and this place was the devil's own lair, the entrance to the underworld itself. Canyon Diablo had a most suitable name.

For the first time, he'd felt a real sense of belonging, out here in the wilds of Arizona. He had a family of sorts, the Irishmen and Francis and the Mexicana and Hobbs with his stinking dog. He had the good people who called out to him as he walked by on the dusty streets of the settlement. He had Rebecca Halsted and the Sikh. It was patently unfair. It was unfair because he had plodded contentedly, through life for almost forty years, and now this. Just when he was about to die, to know this; to know real living.

He rode until dark. He did not want to see or talk to anyone now.

Chapter XVII:
Assassins

The head assassin rode in front; he was only identifiable as such because of his lead position in the group. He was not an impressive man. He was fat, bald and certainly not handsome or manly in any way. He was not as smart as he thought he was, but he was ruthless and this is how he got men to follow him.

He'd found eight men for this job. Three of them were his regular gang, the others he'd picked up here and there. They were all low-life devils and all slower of wit than he. They were greedy and slothful, as well. He'd promised them a thousand dollars each, once the job was done.

This was preposterous, of course, as no one at Canyon Diablo had eight thousand dollars, and killing marshals was not nearly worth so much. This made the head assassin even more confident, as the men following him were thick and, thus, easily controlled. It was easy to lie to them because of their stupidity.

He was pleased to do this job as he hated anyone from the north and he hated the law. He was not much older than Francis, so too young for the war, but he'd grown up during the great reconstruction and felt the sting of the poverty that had run rampant through the south. He learned not only to feel sorry for himself, but to blame everyone and everything for his bad fortunes. He was not the kind of man who could or wanted to make his own way in the world. He wanted to live off the labor of others, and was a thoroughly worthless and despicable man.

He'd run with the cowboys down in Tombstone for a while until the Earps made it too hot. He was wise in this, as he never hung around any place that became too hot or dangerous. He was good at saving his own skin and this made him a dangerous individual.

He'd heard about Allingham and all the trouble he'd caused. He had learned that the man was fearless and this made him extra cautious. It is also why he'd recruited so many men.

Mr. Singh looked in on Rebecca at her writing desk. She'd been in a foul mood for more than a day, ever since her showdown with the marshal. He always gave her the same amount of time to brood, no more and no less; then he'd have a chat, mostly at the urging of Halsted, as Rebecca's father hated to see his daughter unhappy. Mr. Singh was much better equipped for dealing with such things.

The Sikh walked in with a tray on which sat a tea set, carefully, almost ceremoniously placing it on the corner of her writing desk. He was wearing his little oval glasses and Rebecca smiled up at him. He looked like an old grandfather when he wore the glasses and this was always more disarming. She knew they would talk now.

He never lectured her but, rather, served as her sounding board. She'd talk and he'd listen, then he'd have something kind and profound to say and everything would be all right, "What is wrong with this Allingham, Mr. Singh?"

He drank his tea and looked in his cup. He'd been thinking a lot about Allingham, as well. He was intrigued by the man, as he was by so many of the Americans. They were different from his people, different even than the Englishmen. Yet, not so different in their mores. Many of them were good men.

"Mr. Allingham is, I am afraid, a tortured soul, Rebecca." He looked into her eyes. He was not surprised or disappointed that she was attracted to the man. He was pleased with her ability to open her mind and her heart to such a man; someone so different from himself and her father.

He continued. "Perhaps he has not had a good or proper influence in his early life. He seems without faith, and I have known many men who are very upstanding and moral men without faith; they are often the least happy." He smiled as Rebecca regarded him, considering his words.

"God is great, Rebecca, and God looks upon the faithful well, because we know that to be good pleases God and makes us closer to Him. But, a man who has no faith but does have the same moral convictions of the faithful, well, he is a lost soul. He doesn't have the comfort of knowing God."

She smiled. She'd heard Mr. Singh's philosophy on life ever since she could remember. She had heard the same words and sentiments many times before, but Mr. Singh, like a great priest, had a way of making them relevant to the conversation at hand.

"I have been thinking the same thing, Bapu." She poured her tea and looked on.

"But there is something secretive about the man. He is too, eh, methodical to move to Arizona. He . . . , it is not in his character."

"I agree, Kaur." He thought again. "But, he is here, and he is a good man, and it is not our place to be too harsh with him. It is not our place to judge him, daughter." He smiled. "I believe Mr. Allingham will flourish with our love and support, and not with our stern words."

She got up and kissed Mr. Singh on the cheek. "I am the luckiest woman in the world." He smiled and she continued. "Most women are lucky to have one good father and I have two. Thank you, Bapu."

Francis wandered up on the town drunk and was disappointed to see the man lying near a pile of dung. He'd seen him recently and the man looked pretty good for a drunk. And Francis felt he'd had a hand in the improvement, that he had made a positive impact on the derelict. Now he had his doubts, as the poor devil'd evidently fallen off the wagon. He was a pitiable sight.

Francis nudged him awake and was a little surprised at the drunk's response. He hissed under the hat covering his eyes, "I ain't drunk, deputy."

Francis grinned and looked around; sure

he was the butt of some sort of practical joke. "Then why you lying so close to a pile a shit?"

"I, we can't be seen talkin'. Take me in to jail. I got something important to tell you, Francis."

With a flourish, he grabbed the man by his collar and marched him off to jail. Then, thinking better of it, as it was not empty of prisoners, took him on to the barracks. Only Hobbs and Rosario and Allingham were there, each absorbed in their own tasks.

The drunk came to life when he was safely inside.

"You been good to me, Francis, and I thank you. That's why I need to tell you something's up; something to get you all killed." He looked around the room through watery, bloodshot eyes. He nodded to Rosario. "Afternoon, Señora." She nodded back and smiled. She poured him a cup of coffee and handed it over with a plate of biscuits. He picked at them a little.

Allingham looked up from his work and then at Francis. He glared at the drunken man. "What is it?"

"The whore, French Annie. I heard her. She's hiring a bunch to come in an' rub you all out. She says you need to go the way of the Earps. She says she's tired of your nonsense." He grinned proudly. "I was takin' a snooze and they didn't know I was there." He nodded as Francis opened a bottle of beer and handed it to him, inspiring him to abandon Rosario's coffee. "Thank you." He drank deeply and belched as politely as he knew how.

"When is this assassination to happen?"

"Don't know, sir." The drunk always called Allingham sir. "Don't know, but I heard it the other day." He looked down at the floor self-consciously, ashamed. "I, I'm afraid I got in my cups and couldn't tell you sooner." He looked up at Francis. "Sorry, Francis."

Allingham looked at Hobbs. He began to speak then looked at the drunk. "Go away."

The man scurried out the door. He looked back quickly, before it was shut in his face by Allingham. "I'll leave the bottle by the door, Francis."

"Hobbs, get some of your Chinese men. Get two teams of mules or oxen, I don't care which, something you'd use to pull stumps from the ground. Bring them here." He stood up and walked out.

Walls creaked and gave way as a team of mules, one on each end of the building steadily pulled. Whores and cowboys in various stages of undress ran from the building, followed by a wild-eyed French Annie, pulling up her bloomers, interrupted, mid-stroke from the first job she'd had in a long time.

She ran up to Allingham who was calmly overseeing the job. "Have you lost your god-damned Yankee mind? You son of a bitch!" She turned to watch the place shudder, then shake, the roof finally collapsing. Allingham ignored her, looking past her to Hobbs.

"Drag it all into the desert. Burn every-thing: walls, roof, beds, furniture, floor. Burn it all."

"You bastard. You can't do this. You can't do this. You jug-eared son of a bitch bas-tard."

Allingham pulled his gun and grabbed her by the scrawny neck. Cocking his piece, he pressed it to her forehead. "I'm going to say this one time, bitch. You've got an hour to vacate this place, this whole place, the terri-tory of Arizona. You've got one hour, and if I see you after one hours' time, I'll kill you on the spot." He dropped her and walked away, remembered something and turned back to the whore sitting in the dusty street.

"How many did you hire and when are they supposed to be here?"

"I didn't, I didn't." She was crying now.

French Annie, the hardest madam in the county, was crying in the dusty street of Canyon Diablo. Allingham had finally broken her.

"It's true, sir."

Allingham glared at the gaming house manager. "What do you mean?"

"She, she lost her nerve, sir. I swear she did."

Allingham regarded the man cowering before him. "If that's not right, yours is next." He turned to walk away.

"Remember, Hobbs, all burned. I want nothing but an empty lot."

"Yes, sir."

He turned and looked at the growing crowd. He pointed to the wrecked building. "Anyone with an idea to hire assassins to kill me or my deputies will get worse." He wheeled and marched toward his jail.

Francis helped Annie up, handing his handkerchief to the distraught whore as he surveyed her ruined digs. "I'll be go to hell."

CHAPTER XVIII:
THE MEEHANS

John Meehan poured wine for everyone. He nodded and clicked his glass and drank to the news. His little girl was engaged. He'd known Francis for as long as the young man had been in the settlement. He had liked him immediately and even thought he'd make a good match for his only daughter. And now, as if he'd conjured up the whole idea himself, they were to be married.

John Meehan and Francis wandered out back as they awaited the call to dinner. He produced a six shooter and showed it to Francis. He loved novel and mechanical things.

"Just got it, lad. They call it a Schofield." He broke it at the hinge and showed Francis how it operated. The lad had only known of peacemakers. He was impressed.

John had an old dressmaker's dummy set up, a red cardboard cutout of a valentine heart placed over the mannequin's chest. At thirty paces, he fired and hit it cleanly through the center. He smiled and handed the six shooter to Francis who tried the new gun and matched his mark.

"You know the best place to shoot a man, Francis?"

"In the gourd, I guess." Francis smiled but was not certain what his future father-in-law was about. He didn't have to scare Francis; he loved the young man like a son and Francis felt likewise. The engineer read his mind.

"I don't look like I can handle a gun, do I, lad?"

He didn't but Francis lied. "I wouldn't say that, sir."

"I can. I was in the war, you know. An engineer. Was in three battles. Killed eight Yankees." He looked at Francis. He wasn't bragging. He'd never told anyone else about killing the men. He wasn't proud of it, but needed to tell Francis now.

"I know your Pop was a Yankee. I'm not proud of what I did, Francis. Not proud of that war or my part in it. It was a damnable thing, killing each other, killing a man because he was from the north."

He looked at the gun and opened the action. He picked the spent shell cases out, replacing them with fresh cartridges. "I was from Old Virginia, and I fought for my state. Damned foolish thing."

He once again offered the gun to Francis who refused it. "No, son, it's true. You'll kill a man quick shooting him in the head, but through the heart is the best shot." He pointed and put the next bullet in the same spot as his first. "And remember, it isn't over here," he pointed to his own chest on the left side. "It's closer to midline, closer to here." He pointed to the correct spot.

"Yes, sir."

They finished and Meehan put his arm around the young man's shoulder. It felt nice. It felt like it had when Francis was ten and his father was still alive. His father did such things a lot.

"Margaret says you'll stay with us, with the railroad."

"Yes, sir." He smiled. "Whatever Mags wants, Mags gets, sir."

"That's a good lad. I've spoiled both of them, ever since the day I met my Mary and ever since little Margaret was born. It's easy to spoil 'em when they're so good. And they are, my lad, they're good. They're spoiled but they aren't rotten." He smiled and Francis was glad, could see the love the old man had in his heart for both of them. "There's nothing wrong with spoiling the ladies you love, remember that, lad."

It was too early for supper and Meehan and Francis took a stroll to the northwestern corner of the settlement. It was strategically located; upwind of the settlement so the smoke and rotting odors would not assault them.

It was a place Francis knew well enough. He patrolled it every day and never needed to do anything more. This is where the hard working men of the railroad waited in their little tent city for the bridge to come back; waited to resume their lives.

Francis liked it as the folks there were always pleasant. They had their own little police force in the form of two ancient veterans: one a rebel, the other a Yankee. They were the best of friends and, despite their frail appearance, none of the animals down in the bowels of the town dared to tangle with them. The little tent city was left alone.

"These are the good ones, Francis." He held onto the young man's shoulder as he walked past the various camps, each a microcosm of the country. Francis could smell the different meals being prepared, each representative of the customs of the men living there. He was getting hungry.

The Chinese stayed in their section, the Negroes theirs, and the Irish theirs. Everyone got along, but preferred to remain in their various groupings, preferring the society they were familiar with and where they were most comfortable. The old tribalism was alive and well, and this was not necessarily a bad thing.

Francis was impressed with the respect John Meehan received from all of them, and Meehan was likewise pleased, as all along the way men called out to Francis, offering him a good evening. That was the way with Francis. Everyone, at least the decent folks, liked him and were pleased to see him. Meehan knew that Francis would be a good addition to their railroad family. He'd be a good guard for the enterprise.

Meehan was smart and decent and competent. He knew his job and did it well. He treated the workers well and Francis was a little surprised at this, as he'd been told for many years about the corrupt ways of the Southern man; the men who caused the terrible war, the men responsible for so much carnage, for the demise of his own father and many cousins, and uncles and old family friends.

John Meehan did not act like this. He was friendly to all of the men, regardless of their color or race, and it was evident, he wasn't putting on a show for Francis. They knew him and he them. Francis grinned and pointed, not really at anything in particular. "Them Chinamen and Negroes, they never give us any trouble, sir. Never once give us a hard time."

"Nope, nope, you won't see it in 'em." Meehan thought he'd have a little fun with Francis. He had a good idea what Francis was thinking about the men of the former rebel army. He suddenly blurted out. "It's the damned Irishmen you've got to watch." He looked out of the corner of his eye as Francis lost his smile. His feelings had been truly hurt.

Meehan went on. "Damned Irish. Nothing but trouble. Too damned smart for their own good is what it is. Always fighting, getting drunk. Half the time you can't get them to stop working, then the other half, especially after a good drunk, you won't see a lazier man on earth. Sons of bitches."

Francis could only think of *his* Irishmen. The O'Shaughnessy boys were his friends. They were really the only Irishmen he'd ever known and he didn't like to hear their race maligned. He didn't want to argue with his future father-in-law, but could not contain himself. He wasn't an argumentative man, but found himself, without really thinking, defending his friends. "I don't know, sir. My Ma, she said it was what was inside a man's heart and mind, not the color of his skin or the cut of his coat, made him any particular way. Don't think you can say all that about all the Irish. My partners, them Irish boys, the brothers, they're as reliable as a railroad watch. They're some good boys. Right as rain."

Meehan stopped and looked Francis in the eye. "That was a joke, son." He grinned. "I'm as Irish as your boys, Francis. Name's Meehan? Wouldn't do well to hate myself."

Francis grinned. He was being a bumpkin again.

Meehan continued as he walked along. "I know you think we all were big slave owners down south, Francis. I know the propaganda from the north; know you all needed good reasons to fight. I'm guessing you were told that we all had at least a half dozen slaves, if not more, and we didn't have time for anyone who wasn't as white as we were. But that wasn't the case. Truth is, hell, most of the boys who died in that damned war weren't even worth as much as a slave, let alone being able to own one. Lotta nonsense."

He twisted a cigarette and handed it over

to Francis, then twisted one for himself. They smoked and John Meehan continued. "No, Francis, I don't hate a man because of his color or because he's got slanty eyes or he's from Ireland or he's a Papist or a Jew. Don't really hate at all."

Francis grinned. He was confused now. It was all too black and white for him growing up. It was part of the coping process. The rebels had to be made out as monsters so the deaths of all the men from the North would not be in vain. He'd not met a southerner until Arizona, hadn't really met all that many Negroes and he'd never before met a Chinaman. "I'll be go to hell."

"I never did fight so those bastard rich-as-all-hell plantation owners could keep their slaves, Francis." He stopped; they were at the end of the line. He looked out at the desert and then slowly turned and headed back toward home. Supper would be ready soon. "To tell you the truth, my lad, now that I think on it, I don't even know now why I fought at all."

They dined and Mrs. Meehan was a sweet and gracious hostess. She was from Virginia as well and could trace her lineage back to President Washington. She laughed and said that the bloodline, but not the money, was passed down.

Francis smiled and thought about Meehan's comment at the tent city: The bastard rich-as-all-hell plantation owners. He wondered if the engineer thought of General Washington as such.

Mary Meehan had been living in the railroad settlements since the end of the war, when John Meehan married her. She never regretted it, never complained, and always made the ramshackle little huts into proper homes. She was resourceful and proud and could add a sense of style to the most humble abode.

"And, Francis, you know our homes aren't much to look at, but you'll have your own. Pa will make certain you and our little girl have your own."

"And Pa's got you a position, Francis. The railroad wants you to head security while the track is laid."

Francis was pleased and honored. It was a big job. Most men in such a position had run whole towns or worked for the Pinkertons or had some other significant law experience. He would not let the old man down. "And when do you suppose the bridge will be in, sir?"

"Ah, the bridge." John Meehan stroked his chin, feeling a little smug about the

318

bridge whenever it was brought up. "I told them, you know. I warned them. Told them the numbers were wrong. It wasn't the bridge builder's fault, my lad." He remembered the question. "But, if the money holds out, by Christmas I suppose."

They talked and laughed and enjoyed each other's company through the evening. By ten Ma looked at her watch and yawned. "Time to go to bed, Pa."

She stood up and kissed Francis on the cheek and looked down at the pretty ring on her girl's hand.

"I'll see you all later, folks. It's time I got back to the barracks, as well."

"No, my boy, it's too late for you to go a wandering in the dark. You stay."

The proposal was not lost on Francis. It was a silly notion, a feeble excuse to allow him to stay. Everyone knew Francis moved freely, night or day, in Canyon Diablo. He was being welcomed completely to their home. He looked about for a place to lie down. They grinned knowingly. And now Francis knew, too. It would be a good night.

She sat atop him and smiled the wonderful smile.

"Darling . . ."

"Shh."

He smiled. "I need to say something, Mags."

"Shh."

He waited for her to finish and drop down, onto his chest. She rested her head, cheek to cheek.

"Mags . . ."

"Shh."

CHAPTER XIX:
THE TRAP

The plan was to ride south to the nearest rail station, then on to Phoenix, the grandest town in the Arizona territory. Margaret was getting a wedding dress and her Pa declared that it would be the finest they could buy without going all the way to California or New York.

They were happy. Their little girl, the best gift they'd ever had, was going to marry the finest lad they could ever hope for. It had worried John Meehan since the child was born. He knew she was special and had never once given him a moment's grief. She was the perfect daughter and he used to worry over who'd she marry. Oh how he'd worried, wondered and hoped she would find a partner equal to her goodness and decency. It was something every man who loved his children worried over, particularly a man with a daughter.

She'd spend the rest of her life with this

person; this man who'd have to be good and decent and faithful. He'd have to be hardworking but balanced. He'd have to love his children and want to make their lives better. It was a tall order. There were so damned few good men around.

But his little Margaret had found one. She found one and he was pleased. He could not be more satisfied with her choice in Francis.

"Pa, what's Phoenix like? I was too young to remember it the last time we were there."

"Oh, well, I'll tell you, daughter. It's a place where we can find you a proper dress, I can say that." He winked at Ma who looked extra stunning today, despite the large dusters he had both of them wearing, protecting their dresses.

He wondered at that. He'd been dragging his wife from one rough place to the next and she never looked haggard or old or worn out. She was tough and knew how to take care of herself. She cared enough to keep herself well and pretty. He looked up the road as he was getting ideas about his wife and becoming distracted. He had to keep his mind on the task at hand.

It was all distracting: the knowledge of his daughter finally becoming a woman, babies would soon arrive, he'd be a grandfather and he suddenly felt happier than he'd ever been. He could not wait to be a grandfather. And Francis would be a good son, the son he'd not ever had. He'd be decent and faithful to his little girl and they'd be together for a long time, riding the rails, building the railroad. He could not have wished for better.

He saw the men a good distance away, but did not think much of it. They did not appear to be a threat. They appeared to be traveling and the road was a busy enough one. There was no reason to raise the alarm. The women were resting now, dozing as the road was good here, smooth and not pot-holed and the horses steadily trotted along.

But at a hundred yards, the riders picked up the pace and soon had surrounded them. John Meehan didn't like it. The leader moved in front of his team and raised his hand. John Meehan waited. He looked to his left and right and checked behind him. There were eight men and he had nothing more than his Schofield at hand, tucked in a holster under his left arm.

"Good day." They did not look so benign close up.

The leader looked at the appealing women. He tried to think of something clever and threatening to say, but he was too stupid. The words would not come. He grinned like an idiot.

John Meehan knew he had to act fast. "You there, give us the road. We have business to attend."

The rider did not move and Meehan urged the horses forward. They collided with the man's mount. A shot seared through John Meehan. One of the horses was down, anchoring the other. They were unable to move and had become sitting ducks.

He pulled his six shooter and one of the men shot him in the back. John Meehan tumbled onto the dusty road. His legs would not work and he lay, gazing skyward. He waited.

The outlaws worked quickly, pulling the women down. Their dusters were ripped away and their gowns soon followed. They were stripped of their clothing and stood, naked and shivering, in the pale sunlight with a chilly autumn breeze blowing over them. The men circled them, like a pack of wild dogs. One reached out and pulled at Margaret's breast. He looked at one of his companions, nodding. They were going to have fun with these two.

"Lookie there, her bottom's been in the

sun. Lookie there, boys, bet I know what she's been up to." They laughed as the women stood together, holding hands. Waiting.

The leader found his voice and looked down at Meehan as he lay dying on the dirt road. "We're all going to have our way with 'em, you know. Then we'll cut their throats. Maybe you'll be alive long enough to see it." The men cackled around him.

One looked down at John Meehan. He was grinning at the dying man until he saw the resolution in his eyes, the pistol in his hand. "Watch him!"

Mr. Singh was alone in Canyon Diablo conducting some lumber business with the railroad when the horse limped past him, into his stall at the livery stable. The Sikh recognized it as one of John Meehan's. He calmed the creature and, settling it down, walked the animal to the jail. He found Francis and Allingham there.

"Hey, there, Mr. Singh." Francis's smile faded at the realization of what the Sikh had brought him. He looked at Mr. Singh and called out to his boss. Allingham approached and surveyed the situation.

"Jesus, Captain, look at the state of him. The Meehans were going to catch the train and then go onto Phoenix. Jesus. Jesus Holy Christ."

"When did they go?" Allingham touched the animal's sides, felt the dryness of the blood there. The wound was fresh, not more than a few hours old. He didn't wait for an answer. "Hobbs?"

"Yes, Marshal?"

"We've got to follow this up. Tell the brothers they're on guard starting now." They prepared to move out.

Mr. Singh joined them and rode alongside Francis. They followed Allingham who rode alone up front. The lad was fairly beside himself. He could imagine that nothing benign could have caused the horse to be in such a terrible state. He worried over his new family, his Mags.

He smiled weakly at Mr. Singh who rode, arrow straight, in his usual dignified manner. Mr. Singh always looked dignified. Mr. Singh looked over at the young man and nodded gravely.

"This ain't good, is it, Mr. Singh?"

"No, Francis, it is not. Prepare yourself, Francis, because I do not think what we will find will be good." He looked past Allingham, down the road, to the horizon beyond.

"I'll be go to hell." He thought and regretted cursing around Mr. Singh. "I, I'm glad you said that, Mr. Singh." He felt like he was going to break down, lose it. His insides shook to the point of distraction, his teeth chattered and he was not certain he'd be able to face whatever was waiting for them. Somehow he had to get through whatever they were going to find and he was grateful the Sikh had prepared him. It would be easier expecting the worst.

"I thank you for your truthfulness, Mr. Singh." Mr. Singh did not respond.

They found them a few hours before dusk. The wagon had been burned, the dead horse still smoldering. The bodies lay where they had been cut down. Francis took it all in and said nothing.

Mr. Singh dismounted and quickly covered the ladies with the discarded dusters. He'd attend to them later but wanted simply to give them as much dignity as possible for now.

Allingham rode up next to John Meehan, the engineer lying on his back, the top of his head gone, the Schofield gone. He had a strange look on his face: satisfied, even a little smug.

"Francis?"

"Yes, Mr. Singh?" Francis answered too

calmly. He was not crying and this surprised both men.

"They were not defiled, Francis. They were not defiled."

"Thank you Mr. Singh." Suddenly Francis was down on the ground next to his love and the kindly woman he'd hoped to call Mother. He uncovered them and looked them over carefully. He got up and walked to John Meehan and looked him over, as well.

"He did this, gents." He pointed to Meehan. "He killed them. He shot 'em through the heart and then himself. He cheated the bastards. He did this to protect them. He did this. I'd swear to it, he did this to protect his girls."

Francis wandered off, appearing to be in a daze, he made it a good distance from the murder scene upwind, finally sitting on a small hill, obviously deep in thought. Old John Meehan was, he thought, the bravest man he'd ever known. He missed him already. He did not think of Mags. He couldn't. His mind wouldn't let him. He sat staring into the distance and thought about John Meehan, the bravest man he'd ever known.

Mr. Singh regarded Allingham, surveying

328

the scene with apparent indifference. Allingham looked at the body of John Meehan and envied him. The engineer had done it, gotten himself killed and now all his troubles were over. Why Allingham couldn't do this, he didn't understand. It looked easy enough to him now.

He breathed in again and felt the deep pain in his lung, the cancerous lung. He coughed, tasting the metallic tang of blood. He spit on the ground away from the dead man and his family. He looked at Mr. Singh with the lie in his eyes, as he'd never let the Sikh or Francis know of his plan. He pushed the feeling away and kept the stone countenance of the men of his craft, dismounted and began his investigation.

It was not that he did not care, but to show it might tip the Indian and the young deputy off. They'd see him being affected by this and perhaps misunderstand. He stiffened his back and went to work. He was sorry for Francis but emotion wouldn't help anyone.

Allingham's policing would, though. His many years of experience and his powers of observation would be helpful. It was the best he could offer his young friend.

This was no longer the death scene of Francis's new family, it was a puzzle to be reasoned out. It was the only way he would think about it now, as even Allingham's steady nerves could have been affected by the brutal scene. He'd not allow it, he'd get these black-hearted bastards for Francis.

He collected data and formulating a plan, and as he worked, he watched Mr. Singh who'd now found a bucket and a few canteens of water. The Sikh washed the women, using his kanga to comb their disheveled hair.

He found blankets and covered them. They looked to be only asleep now. He carried John Meehan over gently, cradling what was left of his head, not unlike the way one would carry a newborn babe. Mr. Singh was the gentlest warrior Allingham had ever known. The Indian laid the engineer next to his wife and cleaned him as well, placing John Meehan's hat on his head, hiding the horrific wound.

When he was finished, he approached Francis, touching him gently on the shoulder. "Come, Francis, see them. It's time to see them and let them go. It is time to say good bye."

Francis stood up, mechanically, stiffly. They walked together, Francis led by the hand, to see the three most important people in the young deputy's life.

"Ah, that is mighty fine, Mr. Singh." He smiled at the Sikh again. "That is mighty fine. I thank you."

Allingham joined them now. He looked at Francis who read his mind.

"I'm all right, Captain." He took a deep breath and the tears ran down his cheeks. He wiped them with the backs of his hands. "I'm all right."

"Are you sure?"

"Yeah, all right. Fine as frog hair."

"This was meant for us, Francis." He looked at Mr. Singh who nodded knowingly. "To draw us out." He pointed at the tracks. "Some went that way," he nodded toward a low mountain range to the north. "But," he walked a good distance away into the brush, "then most turned here, and went back to the settlement."

Francis nodded. "I see, Captain. What do you propose we do?"

Allingham thought about it. It would not be good to split up, but not following the ones going north might result in their escape.

"Mr. Allingham, may I suggest you and Francis get back to town. You will be needed there. You will need to help fight these men and your people will be outnumbered and taken unawares. I will bury these poor souls and then go after the ones who've ridden north."

"This isn't your business, Mr. Singh."

The Sikh regarded the corpses of the ladies lying nearby, then looked Allingham in the eye. "You know well enough that is not true, Mr. Allingham. This is all my business. To the very core of my being, this is my business." He turned slowly and pulled the charred shovel from Meehan's wagon, then reached out, giving Francis a fatherly squeeze on the shoulder "Fight well, Francis. Fight well."

CHAPTER XX:
VENGEANCE

They rode past Canyon Diablo to where the train tracks ended, rusting slowly in the dry desert air, symbolizing wasted time, wasted energy as the workers waited to span the gorge with the new bridge. Francis looked it over.

Indicating the disrupted railroad line with a tilt of his head, he called out to Allingham. "That's what's caused all this."

Allingham looked over at the gash in the earth, nodding.

"John Meehan told them the first bridge was too short, then he died. He should not have been around here. He should have been miles from here, layin' track. Instead he's lyin' in the desert with the top of his head gone."

He rode and thought some more. "And that canyon is what brought you here. Made this place so bad that a man like you had to come here and you, well, damn you, sir."

Allingham was jolted by the comment. He turned and looked at Francis who needed to say these things now.

"That's right. Damn you, sir, for bein' so goddamned good at what you do. Damn me for ever askin' for a job with you. Damn me and damn you and damn it all."

Allingham should have made a speech. He didn't, of course, but he should have told Francis he was wrong and that what he and Francis and the rest of them had done was good and noble and right, and that the villains, French Annie and all the corrupt devils they'd run out of the settlement were to blame. He should have told him that the bridge being too short was just bad luck and that John Meehan would say the same and that what happened to the Meehans was horrible and unfair and unjust, but it happened and the only ones to blame were the men who made John Meehan kill his family. But he didn't, he looked down the road and rode on, hopefully, to his death.

He was thinking of himself now and was resolved to get killed. He was ready, as John Meehan had inspired him. This had all gone on too long and he had to end it or risk wasting away in some hospital or sanatorium bed. He would not let that happen. He was ready to die.

Allingham was convinced that these were the assassins conjured up by French Annie; and there would be plenty of them. The others, the cowards in the town, would be emboldened and they'd certainly swell the numbers, they'd want to take a swipe at him as well. There'd be plenty to kill and he would do it, but he'd have to be careful. He wanted to kill as many of the bastards responsible for the horrible deed as possible before he, himself, was gunned down. That would be the tricky part, as he was good. He was good in a fight and fearless and he always won. Now he'd have to just partially win. He'd have to be almost good.

When they got to the barracks they discovered that the word had already gotten out. The bad men were in town and told what they had done to the Meehans. The Irishmen and Hobbs and Rosario knew, as well. They had Francis's drunkard to thank for this, as he'd come every hour or so, reporting on what was happening among the animals.

Allingham looked their preparations over, and was duly impressed. They'd only been at it a little over an hour, but all had pitched in. They were ready for the siege. The Irishmen rested on their cots; they'd been up for more than two days and needed the shut-eye in preparation for the impending battle.

Rosario was on young Francis at once. She cried and held him tightly and offered her condolences. She kissed him and worried over him until he held a hand gently to her cheek.

"It's all right, Mamacita. It's all right. Old John Meehan made it right and none of 'em suffered much and soon, I'll be with 'em." He gave his normal grin but it was not a happy one. Rosario did not like his ominous prediction.

The Mexicana went back to her tasks. She'd been preparing since she'd heard the news. She and Hobbs had cut shooting holes through the walls, down low. If they could keep the gang from burning them out, they should be able to survive and kill most of them. She made bandages and lots of food to keep them going. They'd stored water, as well, and enough firewood for a significant siege.

Hobbs and the Irishmen had loaded all the guns. There were Winchesters propped at each firing hole and Rosario emptied the contents of all the cartridge boxes, by caliber, into baskets reserved for foodstuffs so she could get to them more easily. She'd load as the men fired.

"Hobbsie," Francis nodded, then acknowledged the Irishmen, "Boys."

The men stirred from their slumber and Patrick gave a solemn nod. "We are sure sorry for your loss, Francis. Mike and I, we are sure sorry for your loss."

"I thank you, but it'll be all right. It'll be all right." He smiled again at Rosario and looked at the food she'd prepared, and grinned.

"Mamacita, I am sure glad there are no beans. Old Hobbsie would not do well in these tight quarters with beans." He laughed nervously, "And neither would we."

They laughed and he continued. "You, Hobbsie, I want to tell you somethin', somethin' John Meehan said." He nodded to Rosario. "He said it's okay to spoil your women. You do that, Hobbsie, for the rest of your days; spoil her. She's a good one and you spoil her. Make it so she never makes you beans again."

They all watched Francis move around. He was restless. He was moving in strange and unnatural ways and his eyes were wild. There was a kind of unsettling mania about him and they were all sad to see it, their favorite man in such a state. Francis had been broken and didn't even know it.

■ ■ ■ ■

He'd pass the night with Rosario. The animals were celebrating down in the worst part of town and, as the Irishmen were not on guard, the miscreants were raising hell this night. Shots were almost continuous, shouting and cursing and retching abounded. Rosario would keep watch while the men rested.

"Mamacita, you need some sleep, too." Francis looked out the little shooting hole next to the old woman lying on her belly. He put an arm over her, squeezing and patting her pudgy shoulder lovingly. She wanted to cry. Francis was not himself and his movements had become more erratic and unsettling as the night passed. Rosario knew what he was planning. He had no intention of living beyond morning and there was little, if anything, she could say or do to change his mind.

"We'll give 'em hell tomorrow, won't we, ma'am?"

"We will Francis. Now go, lie down, sleep a little."

"And you, what about you? We should take turns, Mamacita. We should take turns."

"I am an old woman, Francis, and no longer sleep." She smiled and watched him and waited. She hoped that he'd drift off to sleep. She could not stand to see the misery in his eyes; could not stand to see into his tortured soul.

He got up and poured more coffee, drinking cup after cup. He was so keyed up, now, that he had a tremor in his hands and voice. He returned to his spot next to the old woman, pressing his body against hers.

"Rosario?"

She was taken aback as it was the first time the lad had addressed her by her proper Christian name; Francis never did this. It was a habit of his to come up with nicknames or to call folks something besides their proper names.

"Yes, Francis?"

"Do you think there's ghosts?" He kept his eyes fixed, peering down the street, watching, waiting, hoping for someone to kill.

"I don't know, Francis, perhaps." She thought about it and decided to talk a little, hoping it might calm him down. "You know, in our country, we are Catholic. But there is the pagan celebration, el Día de los Muertos, the Day of the Dead."

Francis grinned. He liked to hear about

things of which he knew nothing. She continued. "Many people believe that the dead are among us all the time, and many even set a table for them, just as if they were alive."

"And you, do you do this, Mamacita?"

"No, Francis. I would have to have a table that was as long as the barracks to accommodate so many of my dead." She smiled and crossed herself.

"I had an old uncle, back in Pennsylvania. We used to think he was pretty addled. He used to tell us a story, all us kids, 'bout when his mother died." He stopped and squinted and pulled up his Winchester, then changed his mind. "Anyways, you know them black crepes they put on doors, on a person's house when they die?"

"Sí, Francis, I know this thing."

"Well, my old nutty uncle, he said, one time they had the crepe on the door, and his mother lying on a block of ice in the parlor. It was July and hotter than the hinges of hell. He was in bed sleepin' and he rolled over and felt something strange in his pillow. He got up and you know what?"

"What, Francis?" She liked the young man's stories, though no one ever believed even half were true. She smiled and regarded him as he spoke.

"That doggone crepe, it was stuffed in his pillowcase."

Rosario shivered and he felt it, looked at her and at the gooseflesh raised up on her chubby arm, then rubbed her shoulder briskly. "No kiddin'."

Rosario looked down the street, "No kiddin'."

"Rosario, I always thought that was just a lotta nonsense. But I gotta tell you this," he became serious and turned to look her in the eye. "When we was at the site, you know, where Mags and her family bought it. I saw her. I saw Mags." He cried and the tears ran down his cheeks. He didn't try to stop them. "She was out in the desert and," he looked at Rosario again, "you know we were together. You know, in that way, like you were with old Redshirt, and, and," he lowered his voice to a whisper and spoke into her ear, "with old Hobbsie."

"I see, Francis."

"Anyways, she was wearing the old Indian blanket we used when we did it out in the desert. It was wrapped around her and she was smiling. She was up on a high hill and she was dead. I know she was dead on account of she was so pale; but she smiled and nodded but didn't say anything. But she might as well had, she might as well had

341

just yelled it 'cause I knew. She told me, with a nod and a smile, she told me it was okay. She told me to hurry up."

Rosario pulled him closer, held him and kissed his cheek. "Don't pity or grieve for the dead, Francis. She is on to a better place now, a better place."

"Yes, ma'am. Yes ma'am."

She turned to see movement off in the distance, a group staggered down the dusty street toward them. They cursed Allingham and pulled their guns. They fired and the bullets hit against the stone wall of their little fortress. The shots had no effect.

Francis was up and out the door before Rosario could do or say anything. He fired into them, dropping three as a fourth limped away. He was back in the barracks and smiling before the Mexicana could fully comprehend.

"That'll give 'em somethin' to think about, Mama." He handed her the Winchester and she topped off the magazine. He smiled and had another coffee, drinking it down in one long gulp. "I think that one shoots a might to the right."

Allingham and the Irishmen stirred, Hobbs continued to snore. Francis smiled. "Got three and a half, Captain." He poured another cup of coffee. "Hit one in the ass."

They settled down again as Francis kept guard. He watched scavengers pour over the dead men. They were stripping the corpses. He thought for a moment about it all. The Irishmen were off duty one night and it was going back to the old ways. He shrugged and looked at Rosario, lying next to him. He sniffed the air.

"That dog's fartin' Mama. You've not been givin' him beans, I hope."

Rosario yawned and shook her head no.

"I like dogs. Even when they fart. Most of the time it don' smell near as bad as a man's farts anyway. My Ma, she always was fond of cats. We had half dozen cats over the years. You like cats?" He didn't wait for Rosario's answer. "I like cats all right. They're all right. Can't be trained. We once had a cat, female, bitch, I guess. No, that ain't right, a female dog's a bitch, don't know what you call a female cat. Anyways, she was good at catchin' things. Used to bring in snakes she'd captured. Little bitch used to shit in my shoes."

Rosario chuckled. "Francis, you tell funny stories." She loved him so. She now knew not to stop him from prattling on, at least he no longer spoke of the dead.

"Yep, my ma, she said, when a cat shits in yer shoes, means they especially like you.

Said it's good luck." He grabbed his coffee and watched the last corpse lose his pants, his naked backside glowing in the moonlight. "I don't know about that, but I tell you what, Mamacita. I'd rather that cat hate me."

She felt him trembling next to her. She put her arm around his shoulders, pulling him tightly to her, trying to make the shaking stop.

"Rosario?"

"Yes, Francis?"

"I sure am glad we met. I sure am glad I got to know you." He reached over and kissed her gently on the cheek.

"Me, too, Francis." She choked back the tears. "Me, too."

Just before sunrise Francis stood up and stretched as he watched the brothers quietly reciting their acts of contrition, interrupting them long enough to shake each man by the hand. He smiled at Rosario and gave her a loving pat on the cheek. "Nature calls, Mamacita." He picked up two Winchesters and checked them, propping them next to the door. He put on two more gun belts, arming himself with three six shooters and over a hundred rounds of ammunition.

She looked at him desperately. "Pee in the

chamberpot, Francis. Pee in the bucket."

He grinned and kissed her as if it was his very last kiss. "Ain't that sorta nature, Mamacita. Adios." He was gone.

Hira Singh rode on and knew where the trap would likely be laid. As he rode he considered the terrain, not unlike his home in India. He wondered about his home, as he'd not been there for more than twenty years.

The Arizona territory was not much different in many ways from India. He was an outsider there and was an outsider here. It was the way of the Sikhs everywhere, but he was happy in his new home in America.

He was particularly happy with his family, his old friend Robert Halsted, and his charge, his ward, Rebecca. They were good people. Halsted wasn't like the others. He'd gone native, as they say, and soon found himself more comfortable in the company of the Sikh officers than in the company of his own Englishmen. That was the way with Robert Halsted, and that was why his daughter had grown up to be an independent, free-thinking lady. She did not judge or hold people to a particular standard. Her yardstick was the universal truth of humility and respect, and she embraced everyone who reflected it, and more importantly, exhibited patience in those who didn't.

They fought together to help put down the mutiny, and, became inseparable friends. And when the battling was finished, after their military careers were at an end, they became lifelong business partners.

He felt ashamed of his countrymen, despite the fact that neither he, nor his Sikh brethren had engaged in the mutiny. It held no advantage for them to rebel or seek independence, and he'd always been loyal to his regiment. But the murder of Rebecca's mother weighed heavily on him, as much, even, as the murder of his own wife and children during the horrible conflagration.

So there was nothing, really, to hold him in India. After a few years in England, with he and Robert Halsted amassing a nice fortune there, they decided it was time to move on. They were both adventurers and the call west had a far reach. They were soon in the wilds of Arizona, seeking their destiny and adding to their wealth by timber hauling.

As he rode, he thought about Francis, not much older than Mr. Singh had been when he had lost the love of his life. At least Francis's new family had not been defiled and mutilated. Mr. Singh was relieved by that. There was some solace in the fact that John Meehan ended their lives quickly. And he was pleased that he was able to clean them up a bit, it was the best thing he could have done for young Francis.

His own poor family, as well as Rebecca's mother, were not so lucky. The visions haunted Mr. Singh nearly every night since that worst day of his life.

He considered the past weeks at Canyon Diablo, and could not help but be pleased with Allingham, despite the man's terse and standoffish demeanor. He'd done well, shedding little blood. He was effective. All the lawmen up to this point had been the opposite, as brutal as the brutes they were trying to contain. They were bloody and ineffective. But Allingham was different and this gave Mr. Singh further resolve, as he knew that once the conspiracy had been put down, like the great mutiny, there would be a chance at normalcy for the little town, however long it was to remain in existence.

He worried about Rebecca as well. From the time she was pulled from her dead nanny's arms, he worried over her.

These thoughts and memories were making him angry and he reflected on God and prayed and checked his temper. He did not want to be angry when the battle came. He would not be clear in his thinking and he did not want to kill the men out of rage. He would do his duty with humility and send the killers on to whatever fate God had planned for them.

He drank from his canteen and rode on and fixed his eye on the horizon. A rise up ahead was most likely where he'd find them. It was a bright night with many stars and he could easily make out the high spot in the desert.

He created the battle in his mind, as this is what he would do with all of the things that challenged him in life. From the time that he was a child, he remembered his father teaching him this method. He'd carry out the task in his mind, so that when the time for real action was upon him, it was not the first time he'd be carrying the act out. The method worked well for him, regardless of the situation.

So, as he rode, he pushed out the anger and thought about the impending battle. He imagined the day dawning and the light revealing the assassins. There were likely two, according to the tracks.

They would be waiting to ambush him. He'd have to receive their fire unless he could make them out before they spotted him. If he could, he'd flank them and kill them outright. He considered taking them prisoner and rejected it. He could not be slowed down by prisoners as he'd be needed in Canyon Diablo as soon as possible. He was already far away, at least ten miles, and it would be a difficult task to subdue the killers and then haul them along with him back to the fight. He'd need their horses, anyway, as his mount would be too tired for rigorous travel by then.

No, he'd kill them outright. They needed killing anyway. They'd been in on the conspiracy to murder the marshal and his men, and they had a hand in the death of the Meehans. These were capital offences and they'd have hung for them, anyway. Mr. Singh was used to fighting without quarter. He'd fought many battles in such a way.

Mr. Singh's horse dropped just as the sun shone clearly on him and his mount. A half second passed before the report of the shot could be heard.

The Sikh rolled away from the dying horse, pulling the Winchester from its scabbard. He looked in the direction of the sound. The assassins were up in the hills, too far away to see, too great for the Sikh's Winchester to reach.

Dirt and rock kicked up around him. He was in the open and the assassin was aiming for his saffron-colored turban, clearly illuminated by the morning sun.

He dashed forward, moving a bit closer, making it to a rise. The shooter could no longer see him and stopped firing. Mr. Singh sat listening, the man not more than a hundred yards away. He could hear him speaking loudly to another person and was certain he'd have two men to kill.

He checked his Winchester and six shooter. He did not need to check his kirpan, it was always with him, ready to give good service.

He listened to the men for a while, as the wind had changed and blew their words to him. As he'd suspected, there were only two of them. They joked and laughed and he could tell that they'd likely been drinking all night. They were going to shoot him and make sport of it.

He considered his terrain. They'd not sit around and wait much longer, and he thought about ambushing them when they came down. If they were on foot it would be easy, but they'd likely be mounted. This was taking too long. The men were lazy and bent on stretching out this execution. They were in no hurry to attack him.

He decided against waiting for them and moved east, along the gully created by the rise. He'd flank them. The sun would be at his back, he'd have yet another advantage.

In short order, he was above them. The man with the buffalo rifle declared he had hit him. The other had his doubts.

Mr. Singh looked at the sun, then his watch. He needed to get back to Canyon Diablo; he needed to help in the fight. He put the front sight of his Winchester on the man without the long distance rifle. He killed him where he sat.

The survivor turned awkwardly, the big rifle, bound by shooting sticks, as unwieldy as a ship's anchor. Mr. Singh was on him, deadly kirpan poised to do its work.

The assassin grinned broadly as he stood, finally free of the contraption. He liked a good knife fight, featured himself an expert and, instead of wrestling further with his big rifle or going for his six shooter, he pulled his own fighting knife.

"I heard you Arabs is handy with a knife. Come on, son, let's see what you got."

He stood like a boxer, wielding the Bowie, Mr. Singh impressed by the savagery in his eyes, suggesting that he'd done this before. He had been in knife fights and lived to fight again.

His movements were not so impressive, however as he was clumsy, a rank amateur. For his arrogance, he was rewarded with a quick slice across the forehead, just above the brow.

"Son of a bitch!" He stood back, blood flowing freely into his eyes. He blinked ineffectively. "Goddamn, that smarts!"

He looked about with difficulty, holding his free hand against the wound, trying unsuccessfully to staunch the blood. "Goddamned Arab, I'll get ya yet." He thrust again. This time Mr. Singh moved past him, deftly placing a swipe across the assassin's neck, finding and severing the jugular vein. The bad man sat down suddenly.

The Sikh watched the life leave the man's body, eyes dimming, color fading, he quickly approached death.

He looked up at Mr. Singh and said, with a half grin on his face. "Son of a bitch, yer fast for an old bastard."

In a final attempt at one last bad deed, he reached for his six shooter. If he couldn't knife the dark man, he'd shoot him. But Mr. Singh had other ideas, and, placing a foot on the man's gun hand, pinned the six shooter to his side. He felt the strength leave the ruffian's body through the sole of his boot. The man breathed out, uttering one final epithet. "Goddamned Arab."

Mr. Singh, in his soft voice responded, as he stared into the dying eyes, "I am no Arab, I am a Sikh."

The outlaws gathered after sunrise, as early rising was not a quality abiding in any of them. Only five of the original eight remained, as Mr. Singh had killed two and John Meehan had managed to drop one before taking his own life. The leader was not happy. Others from the settlement had joined his troop of miscreants, but he knew these men even less well than he had the ones he'd hired. Still, he now had more than twenty hoping for a chance to put a bullet or a blade into Allingham.

They rode up and dismounted close to the barracks. All except the leader who sat boldly ahorse. He waited for the men to prepare. Most fanned out, taking up shooting positions at every side of the building. The head bad man attempted a parlay.

"You there, Marshal."

"What?" Allingham spoke through a shooting hole.

"Come on out, we'll spare the rest. We just want you."

"No."

The leader was annoyed. He wanted to

353

string the Yankee up, make an example of him. He'd kill the rest later. Now he'd have to fight.

"You're goin' to let the pepper belly whore and old man and those two Irishmen and that simple-minded boy die for you?"

"No."

"Sounds like you are."

"You men are all under arrest. Come out from cover, hands high. We'll take you to the Federal court in Flagstaff for a fair trial."

The leader smirked. "You are in no position to arrest anyone, you Yankee carpet bagger bastard." He leaned forward on his horse and spit tobacco as two of his men laughed out loud.

He turned to address one as his head came apart, blood and brain spraying liberally on his companions. Now Francis fired into the rest of them. Four men lay dead as the leader's horse ran off. A cacophony of fire erupted, the barracks soon riddled with bullets, the noise deafening; dust kicked up making it difficult for the defenders to hit their marks.

Mr. Singh appeared next to Francis on the rooftop of the livery stable, the highest building in Canyon Diablo. They picked their targets carefully, dropping man after man.

"How you doin', Mr. Singh?" Francis smiled at the Sikh and saw the Indian had blood on his clothes. "How many'd ya get?"

"Two, Francis." He fired his Winchester and put a bullet through a bad man's eye. "Now three."

"I'll be go to hell. The captain warned us 'bout you, Mr. Singh. Said you could cut our throats before we cleared leather."

The Sikh gave a just discernible smile. He did not like to be proud, or bragged about, but could not help feeling a little pleased.

Men finally saw them and began returning fire. Francis ducked, then called to his companion. "Mr. Singh, you should not be wearin' a orange turban in a battle. My God, what a target!"

The Indian glanced at Francis as he loaded, the young fellow now lying in a substantial pool of blood. He'd been hit low, the bullet nicking his liver. Francis was as pale as washed rice.

"Francis, take care." He nodded toward the young man's wound.

Francis smiled. "It don't hurt none, Mr. Singh." He got up and waved the Sikh on. "You go on, Mr. Singh, finish 'em off down there. I gotta whore to visit." He was gone.

Mr. Singh now had fewer targets, as the Irishmen and Hobbs were finding their marks. One resourceful assassin ran with a torch, ready to throw when the Indian dropped him in his tracks. He burned and added to the smoke from the gunfire and dust kicked up by errant shots.

Inside, the Irishmen worked the Winchesters as Rosario loaded. No one had been hit as the bad men could place no good shots. She peered through a shooting hole as a young man, gut shot, not thirty yards away, cried for his mother. Rosario finished him off.

She looked at Hobbs and smiled. "He was a pathetic muchacho, my love."

Allingham decided it was time, and, opening the door to everyone's dismay, moved out among the survivors. They fired on him without effect. He walked up on them, cutting down man after man, and still no shots could find a mark to drop the ugly Yankee carpet bagger.

Mr. Singh watched in disbelief. It was as if the marshal wanted to die.

Finally, he moved up the street to the saloons and One-Eyed Sal's. Someone there needed killing. He hoped to find French Annie or at least someone who'd give him a fight.

He found Francis there, standing at the bar, bleeding and slowly dying as he waited for his boss.

"Captain." He grinned and looked over at the corner.

"It wasn't Annie, after all, Captain. It was that bitch there." He pointed at her with the muzzle of his gun.

"That's right." She held her arm, bleeding from Francis's shot. She steadied herself as her color faded.

Allingham looked her over. "You killed the Princess, too, didn't you?"

"That's right, you jug-eared bastard. I killed her and let that ape-faced sap take the blame for it. Has he hanged for it yet?"

"No."

She looked down at the life running from her body. "Damn, I was hoping to take more of you with me; more of you bastard men."

He pointed his pistol as One-Eyed Sal fired, dropping Francis, then turning to Allingham, hitting him low in the abdomen. Allingham put a ball through her breast.

Turning to Francis, Allingham propped the lad up to ease his breathing. Francis had taken five bullets and still smiled. "Captain, we gave 'em hell, din' we?"

"We did, Francis, we did."

Francis looked down at his own wounds, blood soaking his shirt and trousers, flowing with every beat of his heart. "I'll be go to hell, Captain. I think I'm gonna die." He grinned. "You don't look so good, yourself." He coughed and blood ran down his chin.

Allingham felt the searing pain. Perhaps this was it, he looked down, hopeful for a fatal wound. He was bleeding pretty well, but not nearly good enough, as Sal was not much of a shot. Mr. Singh arrived, looking on sadly, waiting for the young man to expire.

Francis looked at the Sikh and smiled. "You need to get rid of that damned orange turban, my friend. Regular doggone bull's eye, that." He grinned at both of them. "Don't look so glum, you two." He winced in pain and smiled. "I'm goin' on to my darlin', going on to my dear Mags." He took a deep breath and breathed out. "This life don't hold any interest for me anymore, gents. Don't want to be here anymore without my little darling, with my little Mags."

He reached up and touched Allingham, felt the tears on his cheeks, and looked into his boss's eyes. "We all had a bet goin', Captain. Said they'd be made a stone. Said you crapped marble and shed tears of stone." He grinned again and coughed.

Mr. Singh came forward and placed the ring that once belonged to Mags in Francis's hand. "We found this on one of the killers, Francis. It is safe now."

Francis handed it back, balling it up tightly in the Sikh's fist. "You give it to ol' Hobbsie. Tell him it's for Rosario. Tell him to spoil her, make her an honest woman, old Mamacita. Tell him to make it right." His color was gone. He was dead and did not yet know it. He smiled again. "Sure am glad I met you men. You boys be good." He remembered something. "Tell little Janie I said be good. Tell her, make sure, you boys, make sure she never goes back to bein' a whore." He suddenly smiled and looked beyond them, up high in the corner of the room, he grinned broadly. "Oh, there you are." Francis was dead.

One-Eyed Sal stirred as Allingham stood over her. He would shoot her but not before letting her have a go at him one last time. He hesitated just long enough.

She fired, hitting him low. Allingham went down.

CHAPTER XXI:
RESOLUTION

Allingham regarded the young doctor from his bed in the Winslow railroad hospital. The man sensed he was awake and smiled.

"Why am I not dead?"

"Oh, you were hit good, but not bad enough to be fatal. Bullets missed your liver by that much." The man held his fingers slightly apart. "But it was touch and go for a while. We thought we lost you a few times."

"No, I mean the cancer."

"Don't know of any cancer. What do you mean, Marshal?"

"I was told I had cancer of the lung. I was told I would be dead by now."

"Oh." The doctor sat down and offered Allingham a cigarette. He lit his own. "No, you've got no cancer. Consumption, likely, but they collapsed your lung. At least I assumed as much from the scar." He looked on as he smoked and was now a little confused. "You didn't know you had TB?"

"No." Allingham was annoyed. "I was told I had cancer of the lung, specifically *not* TB."

"I see. Well. I assumed you came to Arizona for your condition and they collapsed your lung to help."

"No. That was courtesy of an Italian. A Sicilian assassin we ran down."

"Ah, I see. A bad man?"

"Right. He was trying to do me and my men in."

"Well." The doctor stood up. "There's irony for you. He very well may have saved your life."

Allingham smiled for the first time in recent memory. He looked at the doctor, muttering under his breath. "I'll be go to hell."

Allingham arrived just before Christmas to the sound, not of gunfire or hooting or hollering or retching, but rather to that of hammers on rail spikes. It was the sound of a bridge being put into place; the sound of commerce and progress and of a railroad being put through Canyon Diablo.

He rode slowly, on the mount picked out by Rebecca Halsted, as he passed folks by. They nodded and greeted him. They called him Captain and Marshal and Sir. Some tipped their hats to the ugly eastern carpet bagger.

He headed for the jail and then changed his mind. He felt good. He felt like taking a ride and he needed to get up to Flagstaff.

He stood at the entrance to the laundry and breathed in the fresh odor of clean living; good work and clean living. Many of the young women approached him guardedly, as Allingham was still an imposing man, despite his recent infirmity. He'd killed One-Eyed Sal and many of the girls were overwhelmed by that. They still could not get over the idea of the matronly madam as a cutthroat and assassin.

One looked on nervously as the old madam turned the corner into the parlor, nearly colliding with him.

He recognized her at once and just as quickly caught himself. He stood with his hat in his hand and nodded a greeting to French Annie.

She was humble these days and looked him in the eye for a mere moment, much in the way a child looks when caught in some naughty or forbidden act. Casting her eyes to the floor, she spoke nervously. "Marshal, I know, I know you ran me out of Arizona, but . . ." She began to tremble, then cry, then do something none of the retired whores ever thought they would see French Annie do, not in all of their lifetimes.

She dropped to the floor, prostrating herself before Allingham as if he were the Pope in Rome. Bowing her head, she revealed a scrawny neck as if readying herself for the broad-axe or guillotine. "I, I beg you, Marshal, don't make me leave. Please, please don't make me leave. I got no place else to go."

Allingham looked about at the young women surrounding them, gawking at their former mistress cowering before him. He suddenly wanted to cry, his voice cracking as he called to her. He helped her to her feet.

He took a deep breath. "You, you may stay, Annie." He pulled her upright and looked her in the eye. "On one condition."

"Anything, anything."

"You stand before me, stand before us, right now. You renounce the whore's life. You tell me right here and now that whoring is wrong and immoral and that you will never engage in it or try to get these girls to act in such a way again. Not for as long as you tread this earth."

"I do, Marshal, I do. I, I was wrong. This was all wrong, and I am sorry. I've told the girls. I told them I ain't here to try any tricks. I want to live. I want to live out my days like this. I swear to you." She cried and wiped the tears with the backs of her hands. "I, I'm dying, Marshal. I'm dying and I ain't going to be around much longer. I just, just want to stay here and be as useful as I can. Please, you've got to believe me, please."

Allingham reached out, giving her a friendly pat on the shoulder. He half thought of telling her to get a second opinion, perhaps she wasn't really dying, same as him. But he didn't and instead stood by, speechless. He had no practice regarding compassionate gestures or kindnesses. He had a lot, yet, to learn.

One of the gals helped Annie to her room for a lie-down. She smiled at Allingham and it was not lost on him. She stopped short and nodded. "We're sure grateful for what you've done for us, Marshal." She cast her eyes about. "We're all glad you're better, glad to see you made a good recovery."

It was the first acknowledgement by any of them that he'd been instrumental in the creation of the safe house, the very thing that had improved their lives so profoundly. It was a nice feeling. He liked it when people smiled and were happy, liked to know that he'd affected such a change. He glanced around the place and looked each one over. They looked well, every one of them. He remembered the purpose of his visit.

"Where might I find Janie?"

"Oh, here, Marshal." He was led into another room.

He found her sitting and reading to some of the former whores' children. She looked up and smiled at Allingham with tears in her eyes as she'd been told of Francis's fate and knew the marshal was here to talk about him. She'd known for quite some time that Francis was dead but coped with it as best she could. She tried not to think of the young deputy dead. She pretended that he was just traveling, off on some adventure. "Hello, mister."

Allingham sat next to the little group of children and waited as Janie finished the lesson. She reminded him of a little woman, a miniature schoolmarm and Allingham thought that Francis would be pleased. He wanted to cry again.

Ever since nearly meeting his maker and learning that he wasn't about to die, he seemed to have these heightened emotions. It was a very queer experience indeed, as throughout his life, Allingham felt mostly numb. He never felt joy or sadness or exaltation; he just felt numb. Now he had difficulty not crying.

When the last child was gone, Allingham sat closer to the former prostitute. He had a difficult time believing it was the same young girl he'd run out of French Annie's bordello; the child with the beaten and damaged face. It all seemed an eternity ago.

"Janie, Francis wanted you to have this." He handed her a locket which opened to reveal pictures of Francis's mother and father.

"I see Francis in both of them." She closed the locket and held it tightly in her fist.

He took it back from her and opened another little door on the back. "Miss Rosario put some of Francis's hair in here for you, Janie."

She looked at it and then at Allingham. "He had nice curls, mister."

"He did indeed, Janie." He breathed in deeply and continued. "That locket was very special to him, and he wanted you to have it. To help you remember him."

"Don't need a locket for that, mister." She sniffed and smiled weakly. "No one who knew him could ever forget Francis."

He choked back the tears and cleared his

throat. He was not certain he'd get through this little drama without breaking down. It took all his courage and energy to continue. "You're right about that, Janie. You know, Francis was a good man, and I know you cared for him very much. I did, too. But, do you know what he said to me, Janie?"

She cried and looked at the locket and tried to remember Francis's face. "What?"

"He said he sure was glad he met all the good folks he'd worked with. And, Janie, that's the way I feel about Francis. That's the way we should both feel about him. Remember him as a good man, with that funny smile. Think about how lucky we were to know him, lucky just to have met him."

Janie smiled and looked up and sniffed hard as Allingham handed her his handkerchief. "He was always smiling, wasn't he, mister?"

"That he was, Janie. And he told me something about you."

"Me?" She brightened.

"Yes, you were very important to Francis. He said that you are a good sweet girl and that you just needed some love. He said to make sure you grow up to be a fine lady. Make sure you stay a good girl."

She cried harder and regarded the books, lying about in little piles at her feet. She knew her life would never be like it was back at Canyon Diablo. She knew things would be different, better from now on. "You can count on it, mister, you can count on it. I swear, I'll do Francis proud."

He rode back to Canyon Diablo with Francis on his mind. He was so sad now. He missed the young fellow with his funny grin and his constant joking. Francis was the kind of man Allingham could never be.

He wasn't angry or vengeful, just very sad. He didn't blame those men as much as he thought he would or should. He didn't blame One-Eyed Sal for hiring the assassins. He looked on it more as an overall kind of a universal degeneration. The place was a giant cesspool turned whirlpool that sucked all the badness of the land into it, until the vortex contained the giant soup of decadence and evil; contained the worst of human kind.

He'd known them well enough in his time, had good coppers who'd worked for him murdered by the bad ones. And he knew how to defeat them, at least to some extent. He'd chosen a zone, a bit of acreage and made it off limits to the bad ones. He'd never kill all the bad ones, never throw them all in jail, he knew that — he'd certainly never convert them.

He wondered at that. He'd converted French Annie, it seemed. And Francis had converted little Janie. He'd actually converted most of the whores. But then again, they weren't criminals. Little Janie wasn't a criminal. There was no malice in her actions or in the actions of the whores. They were more like sex slaves and not criminal in their intent. They were just trying to get by the best they knew how.

But he had done something in Canyon Diablo. He'd chosen his acreage, staked it out and told the bad ones, you shall not be here, and forced them to move on. That was the best he could ever hope to do as a law man. As long as he enforced the laws, as long as he protected and lived among human beings with their free will, the will to do what was right or what was wrong, it was the best he could hope to achieve.

It was inevitable that one or more of the men or women who helped him would die. He'd survived and Francis had not. But then again, he also knew that would have been too much to ask of Francis. Francis could not endure. No one who knew him could ask the young man to go on living after the loss he'd suffered. It was just not in him.

But his Irishmen and Rosario and Hobbs, and even Mr. Singh, had all survived. Was the tradeoff worth it? He did not know and this made him cry a bit more over the whole affair.

Francis was, indeed, the best of men. Was it worth it that he was the sacrificial lamb, offered up so that some people could live out a few days in a dusty settlement in the desert while a bridge was built up in Chicago? Was it worth it?

He'd given himself a headache at all this pondering. His wounds ached. He had to change his thoughts. He had to think of something else. Mercifully, his mind was soon filled by thoughts of Rebecca Halsted.

At the worst of his condition, when he was fevered and had lost so much blood and everyone thought he would die, she was there, in the God forsaken Winslow. The place was not worthy of her, but she was there, by his side the entire time. He remembered it. He remembered the doctors commenting about her, admiring her and even appearing a little jealous of Allingham as the pretty lady would not leave his side.

She even held his hand when she thought he was unconscious. But he wasn't. He was awake and felt that soft caress. He didn't dare move or twitch for fear of ruining the moment. And then, when he was recovering, lucid, he sent her away; sent her back home so that she wouldn't worry over him. He hated himself for that.

But he could see that she was uncomfortable and he wouldn't have that. He remembered Mr. Singh, sitting in a corner reading a book with his fine saffron turban. And all Allingham could think about was Francis telling him to change its color. He called it a damned bull's eye. Good old Mr. Singh.

Why were they so good to him? Mr. Singh was easiest to figure. He was a warrior-saint, it was in his nature to fight. Allingham knew that well enough, and Mr. Singh liked Allingham, he knew that as well. The Sikh understood Allingham, as a fellow warrior understands and appreciates one of his own.

And Allingham was a warrior, a soldier as all good lawmen were soldiers. They were soldiers in a war that never ended, a war against an enemy that would never be vanquished. It was an unending war, and Allingham was a soldier, but he was no saint, at least not yet.

Allingham knew well enough that he was certainly not up to Mr. Singh's standard. He was weak in the Sikh's eyes, not because of any notions on Mr. Singh's part of feeling any kind of superiority. But he was. Mr.

Singh was superior. He was a thoroughly good, kind, fearless and reverent man. Mr. Singh had a purpose, and that was to serve his God.

Allingham, too was a good man, but rudderless, even by his own reckoning. He wandered aimlessly; knew what was right, had a purpose so to speak, but he was not properly grounded, and this is what made him inferior to Mr. Singh. He lacked purpose and, more importantly, he lacked piety. He had not, up until now, understood the meaning of the word. But there was hope. He was learning. He rode on and felt the tears wetting his face. He tasted them; the result of a new emotion. They were a good and hopeful sign.

Rosario stood in the doorway of the barracks, wiping her hands on her apron. She smiled broadly. "Welcome home, Capitan, welcome home."

It struck him. He half thought of going back to New York and, now that didn't seem like home at all. It seemed like a previous life, another lifetime which he barely remembered. Rosario was right, he was home.

He stood up in his stirrups and tipped his hat. "Mamacita. Thank you. It's good to be home."

Hobbs smiled from behind his woman. "Captain, good to see you."

Allingham nodded, and with a grin to rival Francis's, called out. "And to see you, too, Hobbsie. Mighty good to see the both of you."

He turned to ride away as Hobbs stood, jaw agape. He looked Rosario in the eye. "What the hell?"

Rosario gave his hand a squeeze. "I don't know, darling, maybe he saw God down in Winslow." She smiled and looked back at her man, knowing that was unlikely. "Maybe he just got a little Francis in him. Maybe both; maybe Francis and God."

Hobbs laughed at the absurdity of Allingham as a man of God, then suddenly remembered something and hobbled out to meet him. "Marshal?" Allingham stopped and turned back, catching the dollar Hobbs tossed at him. "I owe you a buck."

Allingham put it in his pocket.

"Best bet I ever lost, Captain."

He tipped his hat. "Paid in full, Hobbsie. Paid in full."

He rode once more onto the canyon, the slash in the earth where Francis damned him. It did not look so large now, as the bridge spanning it made it smaller. The bridge that had started it all was now finished and track was being laid on the other side.

A new man rode up beside him; John Meehan's replacement. He nodded to Allingham and looked at the progress. "They finally got it right. Finally built it according to John's plan." He called out to some workers then addressed Allingham again.

"You're the marshal, aren't you?"

"I am."

"Well, you sure put this dump in order. Heard you had a time of it, though. Heard you gave the bad ones hell." He looked back at the town, now bustling. But despite its bustling, it was already being broken down. "Damn place'll be a ghost town soon and it hasn't even been alive two years."

Allingham looked back behind him, at his town, and then at the engineer.

"What will you do then, Marshal?"

Allingham sat, mind wandering. He thought about all the things he'd done, all the things his people had done. They were good things and they needed doing again. Not here, perhaps, but in other places. Arizona needed him. He looked the man in the eye.

"Mister, I'm going to live. That's exactly what I'm going to do. I'm going to live."

He turned and rode north, to Flagstaff. He had a lot to tell them up there. He had a lot to tell Rebecca Halsted.

The employees of Thorndike Press hope you have enjoyed this Large Print book. All our Thorndike, Wheeler, and Kennebec Large Print titles are designed for easy reading, and all our books are made to last. Other Thorndike Press Large Print books are available at your library, through selected bookstores, or directly from us.

For information about titles, please call:
  (800) 223-1244

or visit our Web site at:
  http://gale.cengage.com/thorndike

To share your comments, please write:
  Publisher
  Thorndike Press
  10 Water St., Suite 310
  Waterville, ME 04901